T0311019

BISON
BOOKS

BISON FRONTIERS OF IMAGINATION

PERFECT MURDERS

HORACE L. GOLD

INTRODUCTION TO THE
BISON BOOKS EDITION
BY E. J. GOLD

UNIVERSITY OF NEBRASKA PRESS
LINCOLN AND LONDON

Library of Congress Cataloging-in-Publication Data
Gold, H. L. (Horace Leonard), 1914–1996.
Perfect murders / Horace L. Gold.
p. cm. — (Bison frontiers of imagination series)
"Introduction to the Bison Books edition by E. J.
Gold."
Originally published by Gateways Books and
Tapes in 2002.
Summary: Collection of pulp and science-fiction
stories from legendary writer and editor Horace L.
Gold.
ISBN 978-0-8032-3359-1 (pbk. : alk. paper)
1. Science fiction, Canadian. I. Gold, E. J.
II. Title.
PR9199.3.G5975P47 2010
813'.54—dc22

2009052458

Contents

Introduction
E. J. Gold

My dad, Horace L. Gold, was born in Montreal in 1914. He grew up there until the family moved to Far Rockaway, where he met and married my mother, Evelyn Stein. He wrote his first science-fiction stories while living at home with his parents, and his folks were shocked to see a large check come in "for making black marks on a piece of paper." He spent some time as a freelance writer living in Greenwich Village and sold many of his sci-fi and fantasy stories to very successful magazines of the 1930s, including *Unknown Worlds*.

In 1944 he was drafted into World War II and served in the South Pacific. After the war, he returned to New York City, where we lived on 49th Street just across from where the United Nations was to be located. We moved to Stuyvesant Town in 1949 when the Russians decided to buy our building to use as their embassy (which they actually never did, as it turned out).

During this period, Horace was the highest paid comic-book writer in the world, writing Superman, Batman, Wonder Woman, and others, mostly for Action and DC under a variety of pseudonyms or no name at all (meaning that he wrote under the owner's name). He wrote the now famous "Origin of Superman" story, which explains Superman's superpowers as stemming from the high-density, higher-gravity planet of Krypton. He's bullet-proof because his body has a higher density than Earth objects, and gravity is less for him so he can jump higher than the tallest building. Nothing about aerodynamics or flight orientation and balance had been worked out, but for the comic audience, it didn't need to be.

During this same time, he wrote freelance for a number of magazines in a very large number of fields, from *True Romance* to *Dime Detective*. For the latter, he wrote several million words of printed material. He started to combine his detective thrillers with science-fiction and fantasy themes in about 1939 and continued to develop this fusion fiction until his last productive phase in the late 1980s.

He left a great legacy as editor of *Galaxy Science Fiction*, *If Science Fiction*, and *Beyond Fantasy Fiction* magazines. You can't really see his contributions unless you read *Galaxy, 30 Years of Innovative Science Fiction*, edited by Fred Pohl, Martin H. Greenberg, and Joseph D. Olander, in which you'll discover how much he influenced the sci-fi literature of his day.

He left an equally strong legacy in detective fiction, but other than by the few pseudonyms of which we are today aware, we cannot now trace his production from 1933 through 1955 in this field. However, there are a few dozen detective stories in *Dime Detective* that I've managed to trace to his very active Royal and Underwood typewriters. The very best of what he wrote in this genre were produced as sci-fi detective thrillers, and that's what I've included in this volume.

Although Horace is better known as an editor than as a writer, some of his short stories (such as "Trouble with Water" and "The Man with English"—retitled "The Man with Backspin" for the British market) are among the most often reprinted in the profession. One of his novels, *None But Lucifer*, which has about a 10 percent contribution by L. Sprague deCamp, is arguably considered one of the greatest fantasy novels ever written.

One day I recall with particular vividness. I had asked him how to write a novel. I was already writing short stories and felt quite comfortable at a production of 1,800 to 2,200 words, but I didn't have a clue how to get any further. "Write a bunch of short stories," he replied, "and then tack them together by having a common theme or a common character, which should be your protagonist."

I have already issued a collection of his best-known science-fiction short stories, along with notes on how he developed the stories. This present volume is a compendium of Horace's very best detective sci-fi tales. How I've connected them is exactly what he recommended for a novel—have the protagonist be the same throughout, with a common theme, which I've done with as little disruption to the story as I could manage. My notion was to keep his ideas and stories intact, to introduce as little invasion as possible—the exact opposite of his notorious editing practice of slashing a story to pieces and reassembling it as if it were his own. In his case, for *Galaxy*'s audience, it was a good idea and had a terrific, almost asteroidal impact on the sci-fi reading public of the 1950s, but it just won't wash today. I wouldn't and couldn't do that to his stories—they are tight, clean, and well developed just as they are.

I think you'll find that there's a wealth of ideas and material for further development in these stories, and if you are producing for the sci-fi, fantasy, and horror markets, you'll appreciate the sourdough starter kit in this sci-fi detective collection. Horace had enough ideas for thousands of stories, which is what made him a great editor. He knew how to develop a story and how to let go of the snapper at just the right time without telegraphing the ending to the reader too soon. What he didn't have was enough time to write all the stories he'd thought up, so he gave them away by the hundreds to other writers and spent the time and energy helping them bring the stories to market.

The stories he himself took the time to write were always crafted to the intended market and almost always written to a specified word count. He was so good at it that he wrote "The Biography Project" to fill an eight-hundred-word hole in one issue of *Galaxy*, and the word count is exactly eight hundred. In that short-short, which is the hardest type of story to write without telegraphing the ending or letting the snapper go too early or too late, he managed to produce what is now a classic short-short in the sci-fi genre.

He grew up around Ring Lardner's crowd of racetrack touts and was immersed in the detective-writing scene throughout the 1930s and 1940s. As had many of his author friends, Horace had made a fair living during the Depression years writing millions of words in the thriller genre. He loved to write detective thrillers, but by the time he was editing *Galaxy*, he had no market for straight detective and had already chosen sci-fi as his career path, thus making the sci-fi detective thriller his most natural form of artistic expression.

In 1964 Horace moved out to California, where I'd been living since I got out of the military. I had been making a fair income as a television scriptwriter, and Horace wanted and needed a collaborator to turn out some stories for market. He didn't have the energy to deliver words nor the necessary drive to get the jobs from editors, and his customary market, the sci-fi fantasy field, had all but dried up for the time being. I got a call from Harlan Ellison, who was working as story editor for *The Man from U.N.C.L.E.*, the most popular show on TV at the time. I tried to interest Horace in writing a script for the show, but by the time he got around to thinking about a potential story for *U.N.C.L.E.*, Harlan had left Arena Productions, not at all happy with how things were going.

I had been working for several months at *Tiger Beat/ Monkee Spectacular* as a feature writer and did some additional stories with Annie Moses. Of course this was far outside Horace's field, but, as he pointed out, so were true confessions and teen-girl love stories—he'd done those to make a living back in the late thirties. So we met for a story conference, came up with a slant on a story about how the Monkees met Jeannie of *I Dream of Jeannie*, wrote the thing at a quarter a word, and I delivered it the next day. Total time on the effort had been about two hours, with both of us slamming away at keyboards, he on his new Olivetti and me on my little Olivetti portable. Electric typewriters? Not for us—those things were strictly for sissies.

That was our first collaboration. Shortly after that, we got a chance to do a real story, sci-fi style, from Fred Pohl, who had taken over *Galaxy* when Horace had landed in the hospital due to a horrendous traffic accident—a moving van had collided with the taxicab he'd been riding in, leaving him an eighty-nine-pound wreck for a period of about two years. By the time he'd recovered and was ready to return to *Galaxy*, Fred had cemented his position and was now agent, writer under pseudonyms, and editor of *Galaxy* and refused to give the job back (which was why Horace ended up in Los Angeles in '64).

Fred sent us the cover artwork, a bunch of pointy-eared green men surrounding a bizarre, very unlikely, badly engineered, fancy battle-tank with Earthmen blazing away at the vicious little green men for some unspecified reason. Our job was to write a story around the cover illio, and we did. The green men and battle-tank were mentioned briefly as an image on a 3-D video screen, and we blasted into a real story about the president of an alien planet visiting Earth and landing in the middle of a detective mystery. "Villains from Vega IV" was the first of our real collaborations, and it didn't stop there.

Our next job was to turn out a script for *Star Trek*. Horace had received a call from his friend Gene Roddenberry:

"Horace? I've done all sorts of *Star Trek* stories, some from fantasy writers like Robert Bloch, but none from really hardcore, well-known sci-fi writers, and I'd like to see a script from you if you're interested."

"Science fiction, not sci-fi," Horace returned. He hated the term "sci-fi," which had been coined by his and my friend and agent Forrest J. Ackerman (aka Forry). "What kind of story do you want?"

"What comes to mind?" Gene answered. None came to mind, but I happened to be there when the call came in.

"How about 'Problem in Murder,' adapted to TV?" I prompted in a hoarse whisper.

"I have an idea that might work," Horace said into the phone. They concluded the conversation alone while I went into the kitchen to make some hot tea, which I poured over ice, the way Horace liked it. I drank a cold root beer and waited until he was ready to talk about it.

"Problem in Murder" was a story about a detective who gets changed into a dog. My first thought was that it should be Captain Kirk or Spock who gets morphed. Horace had no thoughts whatsoever on the subject. He hated space opera and especially hated space opera on pop television, so he was entirely unaware of the format or slant of *Star Trek*. (This spilled over to *Star Wars* as well. The only reason he accepted tickets for the premiere of *Star Wars* was to bring the grandkids to an event. He hated the movie and told George Lucas as much after the show.) I did my best to explain *Star Trek* to Horace, but he was disinterested. He wanted to concentrate on the characterization and to develop the tensions in the plot as a screenplay, so we went into writing mode and came up with a tentative script.

Horace never actually wrote scripts. He didn't have the training for it, but luckily I did. I put in the camera angles, long shots, close-ups, transitions, and some light directorial indications, knowing full well they'd end up in the round file (meaning wastebasket), but at that time you couldn't turn in a script without some camera work and some scene indications.

I still have the original script and three rewrites of that unmade *Star Trek* episode. It was returned by Gene with the comment that neither Bill Shatner nor Leonard Nimoy would surrender screen time for the part of the dog, nor would any of the other primary actors, so we went back to the drawing board. It couldn't be a minor character—using the usual yeoman fall-guy for the dog part would lack any sense of urgency, therefore the show would fall flat. Who cares if a yeoman gets turned into a dog and has to work out a way to communicate his plight to his fellow shipmates?

Later, "Spock's Brain" showed me how we might have handled it differently, in such a way that egos would not be bruised, but we didn't handle it differently. We had no chance to. By the time we worked out the problems in the script, *Star Trek* had been canceled. We didn't get a notification that this had happened. I got a phone call from Bjo Trimble, who was devastated by the event.

In the meantime, Horace and I churned out stories and articles for magazines, including one hilarious spoof on camera technique for *Photo Magazine* that offered such advice to pro photographers as: "Never have your nude model wait for a photo shoot in a basket-weave chair" and "Checking a camera for light leaks is easy—merely immerse it in a barrel of water and look for the bubbles." We made anywhere from a quarter a word to a walloping dollar a word, and we were both thankful for the extra income, but we really wanted to turn out a script, for a TV show if we couldn't break into theatrical releases.

Our next opportunity came when we sent the script in, rewritten, for *I Dream of Jeannie* ... Darrin gets the dog part. They seemed on the verge of accepting it, but the show got canceled. Same thing happened with several more hit shows. The script would be tentatively accepted then the show would be canceled within a matter of weeks. Our script became known as the "Kiss of Death" (as a matter of fact, I believe there was a *Star Trek* episode by that name, no relation to our script at all).

The final insult was when Screen Gems flatly refused to allow Davy Jones to get turned into a dog, and Chip Douglas recommended we try to sell the script to *Get Smart*. We'd already done that, and, true to form, the show was canceled. I called my friend Bob Crane and asked if he thought he'd like to get turned into a dog by some mad Nazi scientist. He laughed and said he'd already heard about the script from Forry, who'd told him the whole story.

So I still have the script here in my filing cabinet, in case there's a producer out there who is tired of the television game and needs to get a show canceled without taking the blame for it directly.

Horace got a number of offers to write stories, one from our friend Hugh Hefner. I couldn't help him with it because at the time I was totally immersed in making rock music at RCA with my friend Harry Nilsson. The story went out to Hef, who accepted it and wrote a check to Horace. Forry got the check and went out to Horace's house in La Canada to give it to him. By this time the aging process had taken its toll on Horace, and he refused the check, saying he didn't want his name to be associated with *Playboy*.

I tried several times to bail him out of writer's block, and we did succeed in writing a few more stories. We met at Disneyland several times for story conferences—I'm not entirely sure why he insisted on meeting there, but that's where he wanted to work out the stories. We came up with several corkers, including my favorite, "Shmuck-Slayer," about a genie who only slays shmucks, so if you are one, you can consider yourself as good as dead.

We were just on the verge of sending out a historical manuscript of "The Book of Irony," in which we explored a number of very strange events, and had reworked "The Old Die Rich" into a full-blown novel with time travel and all sorts of interesting items requiring me to investigate the lives of Mozart, Newton, and Ben Franklin and the oddities surrounding them, when Horace passed away quietly in his sleep on his living room couch. We had a great time collaborating, and everything I ever learned about writing, editing, and selling words I learned at his side. He was a hell of a writer and a hellion of an editor, and his legacy will surely live on for the benefit of readers and authors alike.

We talked many times about combining these stories into a single novelized format, but he didn't live to see its fruition. I offer the collection now as a tribute to his skill and ingenuity and his immeasurable and bountiful outpourings of fiction ideas.

I hope you enjoy these stories as much as I do and that they provide you with a larger glimpse into the expanded world of science fiction, fantasy, and horror, which knows no bounds, no limits, and is, by definition, "Out of the Box."

PERFECT MURDERS

At the Post

W hen Gilroy came into the Blue Ribbon, on Forty-ninth Street west of Broadway, he saw that nobody had told Doc Hawkins about his misfortune. Doc, a pub-crawling, nonpracticing general practitioner who wrote a daily medical column for a local tabloid, was celebrating his release from the alcoholic ward, but his guests at the rear table of the restaurant weren't in any mood for celebration.

"What's the matter with you—have you suddenly become immune to liquor?" Gilroy heard Doc ask irritably, while Gilroy was passing the gem merchants, who, because they needed natural daylight to do business, were traditionally accorded the tables nearest the windows. "I said the drinks were on me, didn't I?" Doc insisted. "Now let us have some bright laughter and sparkling wit, or must we wait until Gilroy shows up before there is levity in the house?"

Seeing the others glance toward the door, Doc turned

and looked at Gilroy. His mouth fell open silently, for the first time in Gilroy's memory.

"Good Lord!" he said after a moment. "Gilroy's become a *character*!"

Gilroy felt embarrassed. He still wasn't used to wearing a business suit of subdued gray, and black oxfords, instead of his usual brilliant sports jacket, slacks and two-tone suede shoes; a tie with timid little figures, whereas he had formerly been an authority on hand-painted cravats; and a plain wristwatch in place of his spectacular chronograph.

By all Broadway standards, he knew, Doc was correct—he'd become strange and eccentric, a character.

"It was Zelda's idea," Gilroy explained somberly, sitting down and shaking his head at the waiter who ambled over. "She wanted to make a gentleman out of me."

"*Wanted to?*" Doc reported, bewildered. "You two kids got married just before they took my snakes away. Don't tell me you phhtt already!"

Gilroy looked appealingly at the others. They became busy with drinks and paper napkins.

Naturally, Doc Hawkins knew the background: That Gilroy was a race handicapper—publisher, if you could call it that, of a tiny tip sheet—for Doc, in need of drinking money, had often consulted him professionally. Also that Gilroy had married Zelda, the noted Fifty-second Street striptease, who had social aspirations. What remained to be told had occurred during Doc's inevitably temporary cure.

4

"Isn't anybody going to tell me?" Doc demanded.

"It was right after you tried to take the warts off a fire hydrant and they came and got you," said Gilroy, "that Zelda started hearing voices. It got real bad."

"How bad?"

"She's at Glendale Center in an upholstered room. I just came back from visiting her."

Doc gulped his entire drink, a positive sign that he was upset, or happy, or not feeling anything in particular. Now, however, he was noticeably upset.

"Did the psychiatrists give you a diagnosis?" he asked.

"I got it memorized. Catatonia. Dementia praecox, what they used to call, one of the brain vets told me, and he said it's hopeless."

"Rough," said Doc. "Very rough. The outlook is never good in such cases."

"Maybe they can't help her," Gilroy said harshly, "but I will."

"People are not horses," Doc reminded him.

"I've noticed that," said Handy Sam, the armless wonder at the flea circus, drinking beer because he had an ingrown toenail and couldn't hold a shot glass. Now that Gilroy had told the grim story, he felt free to talk, which he did enthusiastically. "Gilroy's got a giant brain, Doc. Who was it said Warlock'd turn into a dog in his third year? Gilroy, the only dopester in the racket. And that's just one—"

"Zelda was my best flesh act," interrupted Arnold

Wilson Wyle, a ten-percenter whom video had saved from alimony jail. "A solid boffola in the bop basements. Nobody regrets her sad condition more than me, Gilroy, but it's a sure flop, what you got in mind. Think of your public. For instance, what's good at Hialeah? My bar bill is about to be foreclosed and I can use a long shot."

Gilroy bounced his fist on the moist table. "Those couch artists don't know what's wrong with Zelda. I do."

"You do?" Doc asked, startled.

"Well, almost. I'm so close, I can hear the finish-line camera clicking."

Buttonhole grasped Doc's lapel and hung on with characteristic avidity; he was perhaps Gilroy's most pious subscriber. "Doping races is a science. Gilroy maybe never doped the human race, but I got nine to five he can do it. Go on, tell him, Gilroy."

Doc Hawkins ran together the rings he had been making with the wet bottom of his tumbler. "I shall be most interested," he said with tabloid irony, clearly feeling that immediate disillusionment was the most humane thing for Gilroy. "Perhaps we can collaborate on an article for the psychiatric journals."

"All right, look." Gilroy pulled out charts resembling those he worked with when making turf selections. "Zelda's got catatonia, which is the last heat in the schizophrenia parlay. She used to be a hoofer before she started undressing for dough, and now she does time-steps all day."

Doc nodded into a fresh glass that the waiter had put before him. "Stereotyped movements are typical of catatonia. They derive from thwarted or repressed instinctual drive; in most instances, the residue of childhood frustrations."

"She dance all day, huh, Gilroy?" asked Oil Pocket, the Oklahoma Cherokee who, with the income of several wells, was famed for angeling bareback shows. He had a glass of tequila in one hand, the salted half of a lemon in the other. "She dance good?"

"That's just it," Gilroy said. "She does these time-steps, the first thing you learn in hoofing, over and over, ten-fifteen hours a day. And she keeps talking like she's giving lessons to some jerk kid who can't get it straight. And she was the babe with the hot routines, remember."

"The hottest," agreed Arnold Wilson Wyle. "Zelda doing time-steps is like Heifetz fiddling at weddings."

"I still like to put her in show," Oil Pocket grunted. "She stacked like brick tepee. Don't have to dance good."

"You'll have a long wait," observed Doc sympathetically, "in spite of what our young friend here says. Continue, young friend."

Gilroy spread his charts. He needed the whole table. The others removed their drinks, Handy Sam putting his on the floor so he could reach it more easily.

"This is what I got out of checking all the screwball factories I could reach personal and by mail," Gilroy said. "I went around and talked to the doctors and watched the patients in the places near here, and wrote to the places I couldn't get to. Then I broke everything down like it was a stud and track record."

Buttonhole tugged Doc's lapel. "That ain't scientific, I suppose," he challenged.

"Duplication of effort," Doc replied, patiently allowing Buttonhole to retain his grip. "It was all done in an organized fashion over a period of more than half a century. But let us hear the rest."

"First," said Gilroy, "there are more male bats than fillies."

"Females are inherently more stable, perhaps because they have a more balanced chromosome arrangement."

"There are more nuts in the brain rackets than labor chumps."

"Intellectual activity increases the area of conflict."

"There are less in the sticks than in the cities, and practically none among the savages. I mean real savages," Gilroy told Handy Sam, "not marks for con merchants."

"I was wondering," Handy Sam admitted.

"Complex civilization creates psychic insecurity," said Doc.

"When these catatonics pull out, they don't remember much or maybe nothing," Gilroy went on, referring to his charts.

Doc nodded his shaggy white head. "Protective amnesia."

"I seen hundreds of these mental gimps. They work harder and longer at what they're doing, even just laying down and doing nothing, than they ever did when they were regular citizens."

"Concentration of psychic energy, of course."

"And they don't get a damn cent for it."

Doc hesitated, put down his half-filled tumbler. "I beg your pardon?"

"I say they're getting stiffed," Gilroy stated. "Anybody who works that hard ought to get paid. I don't mean it's got to be money, although that's the only kind of pay Zelda'd work for. Right, Arnold?"

"Well, sure," said Arnold Wilson Wyle wonderingly. "I never thought of it like that. Zelda doing time-steps for nothing ten to fifteen hours a day—that ain't Zelda."

"If you ask me, she *likes* her job," Gilroy said. "Same with the other catatonics I seen. But for no pay?"

Doc surprisingly pushed his drink away, something that only a serious medical puzzle could ever accomplish. "I don't understand what you're getting at."

"I don't know these other cata-characters, but I do know Zelda," said Arnold Wilson Wyle. "She's got to get something out of all that work. Gilroy says it's the same with the others and I take his word. What are they knocking theirselves out for if it's for free?"

"They gain some obscure form of emotional release or repetitive gratification," Doc explained.

"Zelda?" exploded Gilroy. "You offer her a deal like that for a club date and she'd get ruptured laughing."

"I tell her top billing," Oil Pocket agreed, "plenty ads, plenty publicity, whole show built around her. Wampum, she says; save money on ads and publicity, give it to her. Zelda don't count coups."

Doc Hawkins called over the waiter, ordered five fingers instead of his customary three. "Let us not bicker," he told Gilroy. "Continue."

Gilroy looked at his charts again. "There ain't a line that ain't represented, even the heavy rackets and short grifts. It's a regular human steeplechase. And these sour apples do mostly whatever they did for a living—draw pictures, sell shoes, do lab experiments, sew clothes, Zelda with her time-steps. By the hour! In the air!"

"In the air?" Handy Sam repeated. "Flying?"

"Imaginary functioning," Doc elaborated for him. "They have nothing in their hands. Pure hallucination. Systematic delusion."

"Sign language?" Oil Pocket suggested.

"That," said Gilroy, before Doc Hawkins could reject the notion, "is on the schnoz, Injun. Buttonhole says I'm like doping races. He's right. I'm working out what some numbers-runner tells me is probabilities. I got it all here," he rapped the charts, "and it's the same thing all these flop-ears got in common. Not their age, not their jobs, not their—you should pardon the expression—sex. They're teaching."

Buttonhole looked baffled. He almost let go of Doc's lapel.

Handy Sam scratched the back of his neck thoughtfully with a big toe. "Teaching, Gilroy? Who? You said they're kept in solitary."

"They are. I don't know who. I'm working on that now."

Doc shoved the charts aside belligerently to make room for his beefy elbows. He leaned forward and glowered at Gilroy. "Your theory belongs in the Sunday supplement of the alleged newspaper I write for. Not all catatonics work, as you call it. What about those who stand rigid and those who lie in bed all the time?"

"I guess you think that's easy," Gilroy retorted. "You try it sometime. I did. It's work, I tell you." He folded his charts and put them back into the inside pocket of his conservative jacket. He looked sick with longing and loneliness. "Damn, I miss that mouse. I got to save her, Doc! Don't you get that?"

Doc Hawkins put a chunky hand gently on Gilroy's arm. "Of course, boy. But how can you succeed when trained men can't?"

"Well, take Zelda. She did time-steps when she was maybe five and going to dancing school—"

"Time-steps have some symbolic significance to her," Doc said with more than his usual tact. "My theory is that she was compelled to go against her will, and this is a form of unconscious rebellion."

"They don't have no significance to her," Gilroy argued doggedly. "She can do time-steps blindfolded and on her knees with both ankles tied behind her back." He pried Buttonhole's hand off Doc's lapel, and took hold of both of them himself. "I tell you she's teaching, explaining, breaking in some dummy who can't get the hang of it!"

"But who?" Doc objected. "Psychiatrists? Nurses? You? Admit it, Gilroy—she goes on doing time-steps whether she's alone or not. In fact, she never knows if anybody is with her. Isn't that so?"

"Yeah," Gilroy said grudgingly. "That's what has me boxed."

Oil Pocket grunted tentatively, "White men not believe in spirits. Injuns do. Maybe Zelda talk to spirits."

"I been thinking of that," confessed Gilroy, looking at the red angel unhappily. "Spirits is all I can figure. Ghosts. Spooks. But if Zelda and these other catatonics are teaching ghosts, these ghosts are the dumbest jerks anywhere. They make her and the rest go through time-steps or sewing or selling shoes again and again. If they had half a brain, they'd get it in no time."

"Maybe spirits not hear good," Oil Pocket offered, encouraged by Gilroy's willingness to consider the hypothesis.

"Could be," Gilroy said with partial conviction. "If we can't see them, it may be just as hard for them to see or hear us."

Oil Pocket anxiously hitched his chair closer. "Old squaw name Dry Ground Never Rainy Season—what you call old maid—hear spirits all the time. She keep telling us what they say. Nobody listen."

"How come?" asked Gilroy interestedly.

"She deaf, blind. Not hear thunder. Walk into cactus,

yell like hell. She hardly see us, not hear us at all, how come she see and hear spirits? Just talk, talk, talk all the time."

Gilroy frowned, thinking. "These catatonics don't see or hear us, but they sure as Citation hear and see something."

Doc Hawkins stood up with dignity, hardly weaving, and handed a bill to the waiter. "I was hoping to get a private racing tip from you, Gilroy. Freshly sprung from the alcoholic ward, I can use some money. But I see that your objectivity is impaired by emotional considerations. I wouldn't risk a dime on your advice even after a race is run."

"I didn't expect you to believe me," said Gilroy despairingly. "None of you pill-pushers ever do."

"I can't say about your psycho-doping," declared Arnold Wilson Wyle, also rising. "But I got faith in your handicapping. I'd still like a long shot at Hialeah if you happen to have one."

"I been too busy trying to help Zelda," Gilroy said in apology.

They left, Doc Hawkins pausing at the bar to pick up a credit bottle to see him through his overdue medical column.

Handy Sam slipped on his shoes to go. "Stick with it, Gilroy. I said you was a scientist—"

"I said it," contradicted Buttonhole, lifting himself out of the chair on Handy Sam's lapels. "If anybody can lick this caper, Gilroy can."

Oil Pocket glumly watched them leave. "Doctors not think spirits real," he said. "I get sick, go to Reservation doctor. He give me medicine. I get sicker. Medicine man see evil spirits make me sick. Shakes rattle. Dances. Evil spirits go. I get better."

"I don't know what in hell to think," confided Gilroy, miserable and confused. "If it would help Zelda, I'd cut my throat from head to foot so I could become a spirit and get the others to lay off her."

"Then you spirit, she alive. Making love not very practical."

"Then what do I do—hire a medium?"

"Get medicine man from Reservation. He drive out evil spirits."

Gilroy pushed away from the table. "So help me, I'll do it if I can't come up with something cheaper than paying freight from Oklahoma."

"Get Zelda out, I pay and put her in show."

"Then if I haul the guy here and it don't work, I'm in hock to you. Thanks, Oil Pocket, but I'll try my way first."

Back in his hotel room, waiting for the next day so he could visit Zelda, Gilroy was like an addict at the track with every cent on a hunch. After weeks of neglecting his tip sheet to study catatonia, he felt close to the payoff.

He spent most of the night smoking and walking around the room, trying not to look at the jars and hairbrushes on the bureau. He missed the bobby pins on the floor, the nylons drying across the shower rack, the toothpaste tubes squeezed from the top. He'd put her perfumes in a drawer, but the smell was so pervasively haunting that it was like having her stand invisibly behind him.

As soon as the sun came up, he hurried out and took a cab. He'd have to wait until visiting hours, but he couldn't stand the slowness of the train. Just being in the same building with her would—almost—be enough.

When he finally was allowed into Zelda's room, he spent all his time watching her silently, taking in every intently mumbled word and movement. Her movements, in spite of their gratingly basic monotony, were particularly something to watch, for Zelda had blue-black hair down to her shapely shoulders, wide-apart blue eyes, sulky mouth, and an astonishing body. She used all her physical equipment with unconscious provocativeness, except her eyes, which were blankly distant.

Gilroy stood it as long as he could and then burst out, "Damn it, Zelda, how long can they take to learn a time-step?"

She didn't answer. She didn't see him, hear him, or feel him. Even when he kissed her on the back of the neck, her special place, she did not twist her shoulder up with the sudden thrill.

He took out the portable phonograph he'd had permission to bring in, and hopefully played three of her old numbers—a ballet tap, a soft shoe, and, most potent of all, her favorite slinky strip tune. Ordinarily, the beat would have thrown her off, but not anymore.

"Dead to this world," muttered Gilroy dejectedly.

He shook Zelda. Even when she was off-balance, her feet tapped out the elementary routine.

"Look, kid," he said, his voice tense and angry, "I don't know who these squares are that you're working for, but tell them if they got you, they got to take me, too."

Whatever he expected—ghostly figures to materialize or a chill wind from nowhere—nothing happened. She went on tapping.

He sat down on her bed. *They* picked people the way he picked horses, except he picked to win and they picked to show. To show? Of course. Zelda was showing them how to dance and also, probably, teaching them about the entertainment business. The others had obviously been selected for what they knew, which they went about doing as single-mindedly as she did.

He had a scheme that he hadn't told Doc because he knew it was crazy. At any rate, he hoped it was. The weeks without her had been a hell of loneliness—for him, not for her; she wasn't even aware of the awful loss. He'd settle for that, but even better would be freeing her somehow. The only way he could do it would be to find out who controlled her and what they were after. Even with that information, he couldn't be sure of succeeding, and there was a good chance that he might also be caught, but that didn't matter.

The idea was to interest *them* in what he knew so *they*

would want to have him explain all he knew about racing. After that—well, he'd make his plans when he knew the setup.

Gilroy came close to the automatic time-step machine that had been his wife. He began talking to her, very loudly, about the detailed knowledge needed to select winners, based on stud records, past performances of mounts and jockeys, condition of track and the influence of the weather—always, however, leaving out the data that would make sense of the whole complicated industry. It was like roping a patsy and holding back the buzzer until the dough was down. He knew he risked being cold-decked, but it was worth the gamble. His only worry was that hoarseness would stop him before he hooked *their* interest.

An orderly, passing in the corridor, heard his voice, opened the door and asked with ponderous humor, "What you doing, Gilroy—trying to take out a membership card in this country club?"

Gilroy leaped slightly. "Uh, working on a private theory," he said, collected his things with a little more haste than he would have liked to show, kissed Zelda without getting any response whatever, and left for the day.

But he kept coming back every morning. He was about to give up when the first feelings of unreality dazed and dazzled him. He carefully suppressed his excitement and talked more loudly about racing. The world seemed to be slipping away from him. He could have hung onto it if he had wanted. He didn't. He let the voices come, vague and far away, distorted, not quite meaningless, but not adding up to much, either.

And then, one day, he didn't notice the orderly come in to tell him that visiting hours were over. Gilroy was explaining the fundamentals of horse racing... meticulously, with immense patience, over and over and over ... and didn't hear him.

It had been so easy that Gilroy was disappointed. The first voices had argued gently and reasonably over him, each claiming priority for one reason or another, until one either was assigned or pulled rank. That was the voice that Gilroy eventually kept hearing—a quiet, calm voice that constantly faded and grew stronger, as if it came from a great distance and had trouble with static. Gilroy remembered the crystal set his father had bought when radio was still a toy. It was like that.

Then the unreality vanished and was replaced by a dramatic new reality. He was somewhere far away. He knew it wasn't on Earth, for this was like nothing except, perhaps, a World's Fair.

The buildings were low and attractively designed, impressive in spite of their softly blended spectrum of pastel colors. He was in a huge square that was grass-covered and tree-shaded and decorated with classical sculpture. Hundreds of people stood with him, and they all looked shaken and scared. Gilroy felt nothing but elation; he'd arrived. It made no difference that he didn't know where he was or anything about the setup. He was where Zelda was.

"How did I get here?" asked a little man with bifocals and a vest that had pins and threaded needles stuck in it. "I can't take time for pleasure trips. Mrs. Jacobs is coming in for her fitting tomorrow and she'll positively murder me if her dress ain't ready."

"She can't," Gilroy said. "Not anymore."

"You mean we're dead?" someone else asked, awed. It was a softly pudgy woman with excessively blonde hair, a greasily red-lipped smile and a flowered housecoat. She looked around with great approval. "Hey, this ain't bad! Like I always said, either I'm no worse than anybody else or they're no better'n me. How about that, dearie?"

"Don't ask me," Gilroy evaded. "I think somebody's going to get an earful, but you ain't dead. That much I can tell you."

The woman looked disappointed.

Some people in the crowd were complaining that they had families to take care of while others were worried about leaving their businesses. They all grew silent, however, when a man climbed up on a sort of marble rostrum in front of them. He was very tall and dignified and wore formal clothes and had a white beard parted in the center.

"Please feel at ease," he said in a big, deep, soothing voice, like a radio announcer for a symphony broadcast. "You are not in any danger. No harm will come to you."

"You *sure* we ain't dead, sweetie?" the woman in the flowered housecoat asked Gilroy. "Isn't that—"

"No," said Gilroy. "He'd have a halo, wouldn't he?"

"Yeah, I guess so," she agreed doubtfully.

The white-bearded man went on, "If you will listen carefully to this orientation lecture, you will know where you are and why. May I introduce Gerald W. Harding? Dr. Harding is in charge of this reception center. Ladies and gentlemen, Dr. Harding."

A number of people applauded out of habit...probably lecture fans or semi-pro TV studio audiences. The rest, including Gilroy, waited as an aging man in a white lab smock, heavy-rimmed eyeglasses and smooth pink cheeks, looking like a benevolent doctor in a mouthwash ad, stood up and faced the crowd. He put his hands behind his back, rocked on his toes a few times, and smiled benevolently.

"Thank you, Mr. Calhoun," he said to the bearded man who was seating himself on a marble bench. "Friends— and I trust you will soon regard us *as* your friends—I know you are puzzled at all this." He waved a white hand at the buildings around them. "Let me explain. You have been chosen—yes, carefully screened and selected—to help see that you are asking yourselves *why* you were selected and what this cause is. I shall describe it briefly. You'll learn more about it as we work together in this vast and noble experiment."

The woman in the flowered housecoat looked enormously flattered. The little tailor was nodding to show he understood the points covered thus far. Glancing at the rest of the crowd, Crocker realized that he was the only one who had this speech pegged. It was a pitch. These men were out for something.

He wished Doc Hawkins and Oil Pocket were there. Doc doubtless would have searched his unconscious for symbols of childhood traumas to explain the whole thing; he would never have accepted it as some kind of reality. Oil Pocket, on the other hand, would somehow have tried to equate the substantial Mr. Calhoun and Dr. Harding with tribal spirits. Of the two, Gilroy felt that Oil Pocket would have been closer.

Or maybe he was in his own corner of psychosis, while Oil Pocket would have been in another, more suited to Indians. Spirits or figments? Whatever they were, they looked as real as anybody he'd ever known, but perhaps that was the naturalness of the supernatural or the logic of insanity.

Gilroy shivered, aware that he had to wait for the answer. The one thing he did know, as an authority on cons, was that this had the smell of one, supernatural or otherwise. He watched and listened like a detective shadowing an escape artist.

"This may be something of a shock," Dr. Harding continued with a humorous, sympathetic smile. "I hope it will not be for long. Let me state it in its simplest terms. You know that there are billions of stars in the Universe, and that stars have planets as naturally as cats have kittens. A good many of these planets are inhabited. Some life-forms are intelligent, very much so, while others are not. In almost all instances, the dominant form of life is quite different from—yours."

Unable to see the direction of the con, Gilroy felt irritated.

"Why do I say *yours*, not *ours*?" asked Dr. Harding. "Because, dear friends, Mr. Calhoun and I are not of your planet or solar system. No commotion, please!" he urged, raising his hands as the crowd stirred bewilderedly. "Our names are not Calhoun and Harding; we adopted those because our own are so alien that you would be unable to pronounce them. We are not formed as you see us, but this is how we *might* look if we were human beings, which, of course, we are not. Our true appearance seems to be—ah—rather confusing to human eyes."

Nuts, Gilroy thought irreverently. Get to the point.

"I don't think this is the time for detailed explanations," Dr. Harding hurried on before there were any questions. "We are friendly, even altruistic inhabitants of a planet ten thousand light-years from Earth. Quite a distance, you are thinking; how did we get here? The truth is that we are not 'here' and neither are you. 'Here' is a projection of thought, a hypothetical point in space, a place that exists only by mental force. Our physical appearances and yours are telepathic representations. Actually, our bodies are on our own respective planets."

"Very confusing," complained a man who looked like a banker. "Do you have any idea of what he's trying to tell us?"

"Not yet," Gilroy replied with patient cynicism. "He'll give us the convincer after the buildup."

The man who looked like a banker stared sharply at Gilroy and moved away. Gilroy shrugged. He was more concerned with why he didn't feel tired or bored just standing there and listening. There was not even an overpowering sense of urgency and annoyance, although he wanted to find Zelda and this lecture was keeping him from looking for her. It was as if his emotions were somehow being reduced in intensity. They existed, but lacked the strength they should have had.

So he stood almost patiently and listened to Dr. Harding say, "Our civilization is considerably older than yours. For many of your centuries, we have explored the Universe, both physically and telepathically. During this exploration, we discovered your planet. We tried to establish communication, but there were grave difficulties. It was the time of your Dark Ages, and I'm sorry to report that those people we made contact with were generally burned at the stake." He shook his head regretfully. "Although your civilization has made many advances in some ways, communication is still hampered—as much by false knowledge as by real ignorance. You'll see in a moment why it is very unfortunate."

"Here it comes," Gilroy said to those around him. "He's getting ready finally to slip us the sting."

The woman in the housecoat looked indignant. "The nerve of a crumb like you making a crack about such a fine, decent gentleman!"

"A blind man could see he's sincere," argued the tailor. "Just think of it—me, in a big experiment! Will Molly be surprised when she finds out!"

"She won't find out and I'll bet she's surprised right now," Gilroy assured him.

"The human body is an unbelievably complicated organism," Dr. Harding was saying. The statement halted the private discussion and seemed to please his listeners for some reason. "We learned that when we tried to assume control of individuals for the purpose of communication. Billions of neural relays, thousands of unvolitional functions—it is no exaggeration to compare our efforts with those of a monkey in a power plant. At our direction, for example, several writers produced books that were fearfully garbled. Our attempts with artists were no more successful. The static of interstellar space was partly responsible, but mostly it was the fact that we simply couldn't work our way through the maze that is the human mind and body."

The crowd was sympathetic. Gilroy was neither weary nor bored, merely longing for Zelda and, as a student of grifts, dimly irritated. Why hold back when the chumps were set up?

"I don't want to make a long story of our problems," smiled Dr. Harding. "If we could visit your planet in person, there would be no difficulty. But ten thousand light-years is an impossible barrier to all except thought waves, which, of course, travel at infinite speed. And this, as I said before, is very unfortunate, because the human race is doomed."

The tailor stiffened. "Doomed? Molly? My kids? All my customers?"

"*Your* customers?" yelped the woman in the housecoat. "How about mine? What's gonna happen, the world should be doomed?"

Gilroy found admiration for Dr. Harding's approach. It was a line tried habitually by politicians, but they didn't have the same kind of captive audience, the control, the contrived background. A cosmic pitch like this could bring a galactic payoff, whatever it might be. But it didn't take his mind off Zelda.

"I see you are somewhat aghast," Dr. Harding observed. "But is my statement *really* so unexpected? You know the history of your own race—a record of incessant war, each more devastating than the last. Now, finally, Man has achieved the power of worldwide destruction. The next war, or the one after that, will unquestionably be the end not only of civilization, but of humanity—perhaps even your entire planet. Our peaceful, altruistic civilization might help avert catastrophe, but that would require our physical landing on Earth, which is not possible. Even if it were, there is not enough time. Armageddon draws near.

"Then why have we brought you here?" asked Dr. Harding. "Because Man, in spite of his suicidal blunders, is a magnificent race. He must not vanish without leaving a *complete record* of his achievements."

The crowd nodded soberly. Gilroy wished he had a cigarette and his wife. In her right mind, Zelda was unswervingly practical and she would have had some noteworthy comments to make.

"This is the task we must work together on," said Dr. Harding forcefully. "Each of you has a skill, a talent, a special knowledge we need for the immense record we are compiling. Every area of human society must be covered. We need you—urgently! Your data will become part of an imperishable social document that shall exist untold eons after mankind has perished."

Visibly, the woman in the housecoat was stunned. "They want to put down what I can tell them?"

"And tailoring?" asked the little man with the pincushion vest. "How to make buttonholes and press clothes?"

The man who looked like a banker had his chin up and a pleased expression on his pudgy face.

"I always knew I'd be appreciated some day," he stated smugly. "I can tell them things about finance that those idiots in the main office can't even guess at."

Mr. Calhoun stood up beside Dr. Harding on the rostrum. He seemed infinitely benign as he raised his hands and his deep voice.

"Friends, we need *your* help, *your* knowledge. I *know* you don't want the human race to vanish without a *trace*, as though it had never existed. I'm *sure* it thrills you to realize that some researcher, *far* in the *future*, will one day use the very knowledge that *you* gave. Think what it means to leave *your* personal imprint indelibly on cosmic history!" He paused and leaned forward. "Will you help us?"

The faces glowed, the hands went up, the voices cried that they would.

Dazzled by the success of the sell, Gilroy watched the people happily and flatteredly follow their frock-coated guides toward the various buildings, which appeared to have been laid out according to very broad categories of human occupation.

He found himself impelled along with the chattering, excited woman in the housecoat toward a cerise structure marked *Sports and Rackets*. It seemed that she had been angry at not having been interviewed for a recent epic survey, and this was her chance to decant the experiences of twenty years.

Gilroy stopped listening to her gabble and looked for the building that Zelda would probably be in. He saw *Arts and Entertainment*, but when he tried to go there, he felt some compulsion keep him heading toward his own destination.

Looking back helplessly, he went inside.

He found that he was in a cubicle with a fatherly kind of man who had thin gray hair, kindly eyes, and a firm jaw, and who introduced himself as Eric Barnes. He took Gilroy's name, age, specific trade, and gave him a serial number which, he explained, would go on file at the central archives on his home planet, cross-indexed in multiple ways for instant reference.

"Now," said Barnes, "here is our problem, Mr. Gilroy. We are making two kinds of perpetual records. One is written; more precisely, microscribed. The other is a wonderfully exact duplicate of your cerebral pattern—in more durable material than brain matter, of course."

"Of course," Gilroy said, nodding like an obedient patsy.

"The verbal record is difficult enough, since much of the data you give us must be, by its nature, foreign to us. The duplication of your cerebral pattern, however, is even more troublesome. Besides the inevitable distortion caused by a distance of ten thousand light-years and the fields of gravitation and radiation of all types intervening, the substance we use in place of brain cells absorbs memory quite slowly." Barnes smiled reassuringly. "But you'll be happy to know that the impression, once made, can never be lost or erased!"

"Delighted," Gilroy said flatly. "Tickled to pieces."

"I knew you would be. Well, let us proceed. First, a basic description of horse racing."

Gilroy began to give it. Barnes held him down to a single sentence—"To check reception and retention," he said.

The communication box on the desk lit up when Gilroy repeated the sentence a few times, and a voice from the box said, "Increase output. Initial impression weak. Also wave distortion. Correct and continue."

Barnes carefully adjusted the dials and Gilroy went on repeating the sentence, slowing down to the speed

Barnes requested. He did it automatically after a while, which gave him a chance to think.

He had no plan to get Zelda out of here; he was improvising and he didn't like it. The setup still had him puzzled. He knew he wasn't dreaming all this, for there were details his imagination could never have supplied, and the notion of spirits with scientific devices would baffle even Oil Pocket.

Everybody else appeared to accept these men as the aliens they claimed to be, but Gilroy, fearing a con he couldn't understand, refused to. He had no other explanation, though, no evidence of any kind except deep suspicion of any noble-sounding enterprise. In his harsh experience, they always had a profit angle hidden somewhere.

Until he knew more, he had to go along with the routine, hoping he would eventually find a way out for Zelda and himself. While he was repeating his monotonous sentence, he wondered what his body was doing back on Earth. Lying in a bed, probably, since he wasn't being asked to perform any physical jobs like Zelda's endless time-step.

That reminded him of Doc Hawkins and the psychiatrists. There must be some here; he wished vengefully that he could meet them and see what they thought of their theories now.

Then came the end of what was apparently the work day. "We're making splendid progress," Barnes told him. "I know how tiresome it is to keep saying the same thing over and over, but the distance is *such* a great obstacle. I think it's amazing that we can even *bridge* it, don't you? Just imagine—the light that's reaching Earth at this very minute left our star when mammoths were roaming your western states and mankind lived in caves! And yet, with our thought-wave boosters, we are in instantaneous communication!"

The soap, Gilroy thought, to make him feel he was doing something important.

"Well, you are doing something important," Barnes said, as though Gilroy had spoken.

Gilroy would have turned red if he had been able to. As it was, he felt dismay and embarrassment.

"Do you realize the size and value of this project?" Barnes went on. "We have a more detailed record of human society than Man himself ever had! There will be not even the most insignificant corner of your civilization left unrecorded! Your life, my life—the life of this Zelda whom you came here to rescue—all are trivial, for we must die eventually, but the project will last eternally!"

Gilroy stood up, his eyes hard and worried. "You're telling me you know what I'm here for?"

"To secure the return of your wife. I would naturally be aware that you had submitted yourself to our control voluntarily. It was in your file, which was sent to me by Admissions."

"Then why did you let me in?"

"Because, my dear friend—"

"Leave out the 'friend' pitch. I'm here on business."

Barnes shrugged. "As you wish. We let you in, as you express it, because you have knowledge that we should include in our archives. We hoped you would recognize the merit and scope of our undertaking. Most people do, once they are told."

"Zelda, too?"

"Oh, yes," Barnes said emphatically. "I had that checked by Statistics. She is extremely cooperative, quite convinced—"

"Don't hand me that!"

Barnes rose. Straightening the papers on his desk, he said, "You want to speak to her and see for yourself? Fair enough."

He led Gilroy out of the building. They crossed the great square to a vast, low structure that Barnes referred to as the Education and Recreation Center.

"Unless there are special problems," Barnes said, "our human associates work twelve or fourteen of your hours, and the rest of the time is their own. Sleep isn't necessary to the psychic projection, of course, though it is to the body on Earth. And what, Mr. Gilroy, would you imagine they choose as their main amusements?"

"Pinball machines?" Gilroy suggested ironically. "Crap games?"

"Lectures," said Barnes with pride. "They are eager to learn everything possible about our project. We've actually had the director himself address them! Oh, it was inspiring. Mr. Gilroy—color films in three dimensions, showing the great extent of our archives, the many millions of synthetic brains, each with indestructible memories of skills and crafts and professions and experiences that soon will be no more—"

"Save it. Find Zelda for me and then blow. I want to talk to her alone."

Barnes checked with the equivalent of a box office at the Center, where, he told Gilroy, members of the audience and staff were required to report before entering, in case of emergency.

"Like what?" Gilroy asked.

"You have a suspicious mind," said Barnes patiently. "Faulty neuron circuit in a synthetic duplicate brain, for example, Photon storms interfering with reception. Things of that sort."

"So where's the emergency?"

"We have so little time. We ask the human associate in question to record again whatever was not received. The percentage of refusal is actually zero! Isn't that splendid?"

"Best third degree I ever heard of," Gilroy admitted through clamped teeth. "The cops on Earth would sell out every guy they get graft from to buy a thing like this."

They found Zelda in a small lecture hall, where a matronly woman from the other planet was urging her listeners to conceal nothing, however intimate, while recording—"Because," she said, "this must be a psychological as well as a cultural and sociological history."

Seeing Zelda, Gilroy rushed to her chair, hauled her upright, kissed her, squeezed her.

"Baby!" he said, more choked up than he thought his control would allow. "Let's get out of here!"

She looked at him without surprise. "Oh, hello, Gilroy. Later, I want to hear the rest of this lecture."

"Ain't you glad to see me?" he asked, hurt. "I spend months and shoot every dime I got just to find you—"

"Sure I'm glad to see you, hon," she said, trying to look past him at the speaker. "But this is so important—"

Barnes came up, bowed politely. "If you don't mind, Miss Zelda, I think you ought to talk to your husband."

"But what about the lecture?" asked Zelda anxiously.

"I can get a transcription for you to study later."

"Well, all right," she agreed reluctantly.

Barnes left them on a strangely warm stone bench in the great square, after asking them to report back to work at the usual time. Zelda, instead of looking at Gilroy, watched Barnes walk away. Her eyes were bright; she almost radiated.

"Isn't he wonderful, Gilroy?" she said. "Aren't they all wonderful? Regular scientists, every one of them, devoting their whole life to this terrific cause!"

"What's so wonderful about that?" he all but snarled.

She turned and gazed at him in mild astonishment. "They could let the Earth go boom. It wouldn't mean a thing to them. Everybody wiped out just like there never were any people. Not even as much record of us as the dinosaurs! Wouldn't that make you feel simply awful?"

"I wouldn't feel a thing." He took her unresponsive hand. "All I'm worried about is us, baby. Who cares about the rest of the world doing a disappearing act?"

"I do. And so do they. They aren't selfish like some people I could mention."

"Selfish? You're damned right I am!"

He pulled her to him, kissed her neck in her favorite place. It got a reaction—restrained annoyance.

"I'm selfish," he said, "because I got a wife I'm nuts about and I want her back. They got you wrapped, baby. Can't you see that? You belong with me in some fancy apartment, the minute I can afford it, like one I saw over on Riverside Drive—seven big rooms, three baths, one of them with a stall shower like you always wanted, the Hudson River and Jersey for our front lawn—"

"That's all in the past, hon," she said with quiet dignity. "I have to help out on this project. It's the least I can do for history."

"The hell with history! What did history ever do for us?" He put his mouth near her ear, breathing gently in the way that once used to make her squirm in his arms like a tickled doe. "Go turn in your time card, baby. Tell them you got a date with me back on Earth."

She pulled away and jumped up. "No! This is my job as much as theirs. More, even. They don't keep anybody here against their will. I'm staying because I want to, Gilroy."

Furious, he snatched her off her feet. "I say you're coming back with me! If you don't want to, I'll drag you, see?"

"How?" she asked calmly.

He put her down again slowly, frustratedly. "Ask them to let you go, baby. Oil Pocket said he'd put you in a musical. You always did want to hit the big time—"

"Not anymore." She smoothed down her dress and patted up her hair. "Well, I want to catch the rest of that lecture, hon. See you around if you decide to stay."

He sat down morosely and watched her snake-hip toward the Center, realizing that her seductive walk was no more than professional conditioning. She had grown in some mysterious way, become more serene—at peace.

He had wondered what catatonics got for their work. He knew now—the slickest job of hypnotic flattery ever invented. That was *their* pay.

But what did the pitchmen get in return?

Gilroy put in a call for Barnes at the box office of the Center. Barnes left a lecture for researchers from his planet and joined Gilroy with no more than polite curiosity on his paternal face. Gilroy told him briefly and bitterly about his talk with Zelda, and asked bluntly what was in it for the aliens.

"I think you can answer that," said Barnes. "You're a scientist of a sort. You determine the probable performance of a group of horses by their heredity, previous races, and other factors. A very laborious computation, calling for considerable aptitude and skill. With that same expenditure of energy, couldn't you earn more in other fields?"

"I guess so," Gilroy said. "But I like the track."

"Well, there you are. The only human form of gain we share is desire for knowledge. You devote your skill to predicting a race that is about to be run; we devote ours to recording a race that is about to destroy itself."

Gilroy grabbed the alien's coat, pushed his face grimly close. "There, that's the hook! Take away the doom push and this racket folds."

Barnes looked bewildered. "I don't comprehend—"

"Listen, suppose everything's square. Let's say you guys really are leveling, these marks aren't being roped, you're knocking yourself out because your guess is that we're going to commit suicide."

"Oh." Barnes nodded somberly. "Is there any doubt of it? Do you honestly believe the holocaust can be averted?"

"I think it can be stopped, yeah. But you birds act like you don't want it to be. You're just laying back, letting us bunch up, collecting the insurance before the spill happens."

"What else can we do? We're scientists, not politicians. Besides, we've tried repeatedly to spread the warning and never once succeeded in transmitting it.

Gilroy released his grip on the front of Barnes's jacket. "You take me to the president or commissioner or whoever runs this club. Maybe we can work something out."

"We have a board of directors," Barnes said doubtfully. "But I can't see—"

"Don't rupture yourself trying. Just take me there and let me do the talking."

Barnes moved his shoulders resignedly. He led Gilroy to the Administration Building and inside to a large room with paneled walls, a long, solid table and heavy, carved chairs. The men who sat around the table appeared as solid and respectable as the furniture. Gilroy's guess was that they had been chosen deliberately, along with the decorations, to inspire confidence in the customer. He had been in rigged horse parlors and bond stores and he knew the approach.

Mr. Calhoun, the character with the white beard, was chairman of the board. He looked unhappily at Gilroy.

"I was afraid there would be trouble," he said. "I voted against accepting you, you know. My colleagues, however, thought that you, as our first voluntary associate, might indicate new methods, but I fear my judgment has been vindicated."

"Still, if he knows how extinction can be prevented—" began Dr. Harding, the one who had given the orientation lecture.

"He knows no such thing," a man with several chins said in an emphatic basso voice. "Man is the most destructive dominant race we have ever encountered. He despoiled his own planet, exterminated lower species that were important to his own existence, oppressed, suppressed, brutalized, corrupted—it's the saddest chronicle in the Universe."

"Therefore his achievements," said Dr. Harding, "deserve all the more recognition!"

Gilroy broke in: "If you'll lay off the gab, I'd like to get my bet down."

"Sorry," said Mr. Calhoun. "Please proceed, Mr. Gilroy."

Gilroy rested his knuckles on the table and leaned over them. "I have to take your word you ain't human, but you don't have to take mine. I never worried about anybody but Zelda and myself; that makes me human. All I want is to get along and not hurt anybody if I can help it; that makes me what some people call the common man. Some of my best friends are common men. Come to think of it, they all are. They wouldn't want to get extinct. If we do, it won't be our fault."

Several of the men nodded sympathetic agreement.

"I don't read much except the sport sheets, but I got an idea what's coming up," Gilroy continued, "and it's a long shot that any country can finish in the money. We'd like to stop war for good, all of us. Little guys who do the fighting and the dying. Yeah, and lots of big guys, too. But we can't do it alone."

"That's precisely our point," said Calhoun.

"I mean us back on Earth. People are afraid, but they just don't know for sure that we can knock ourselves off. Between these catatonics and me, we could tell them what it's all about. I notice you got people from all over the world here, all getting along fine because they have a job to do and no time to hate each other. Well, it could be like that on Earth. You let us go back and you'll see a selling job on making it like up here like you never saw before."

Mr. Calhoun and Dr. Harding looked at each other and around the table. Nobody seemed willing to answer.

Mr. Calhoun finally sighed and got out of this big chair. "Mr. Gilroy, besides striving for international understanding, we have experimented in the manner you suggest. We released many of our human associates to tell what our science predicts on the basis of probability. A human psychological mechanism defeated us."

"Yeah?" Gilroy asked warily. "What was that?"

"Protective amnesia. They completely and absolutely forgot everything they had learned here."

Gilroy slumped a bit. "I know. I talked to some of these 'cured' catatonics—people you probably sprung because you got all you wanted from them. They didn't remember anything." He braced again. "Look, there has to be a way out. Maybe if you snatch these politicians in all the countries, yank them up here, they couldn't stumble us into a war."

"Examine your history," said Dr. Harding sadly, "and you will find that we have done this experimentally. It doesn't work. There are always others, often more unthinking, ignorant, stupid or vicious, ready to take their places."

Gilroy looked challengingly at every member of the

board of directors before demanding, "What are the odds on me remembering?"

"You are our first volunteer," said a little man at the side of the table. "Any answer we give would be a guess."

"All right, guess."

"We have a theory that your psychic censor might not operate. Of course, you realize that's only a theory—"

"That ain't all I don't realize. What's it mean?"

"Our control, regrettably, is a wrench to the mind. Lifting it results in amnesia, which is a psychological defense against disturbing memories."

"I walked into this, don't forget," Gilroy reminded him. "I didn't know what I was getting into, but I was ready to take anything."

"That," said the little man, "is the unknown factor. Yes, you did submit voluntarily and you were ready to take anything—but were you psychologically prepared for this? We don't know. We *think* there may be no characteristic wrench—"

"Meaning I won't have amnesia?"

"Meaning that you *may* not. We cannot be certain until a test has been made."

"Then," said Gilroy, "I want a deal. It's Zelda I want; you know that, at any rate. You say you're after a record of us in case we bump ourselves off, but you also say you'd like us not to. I'll buy that. I don't want us to, either, and there's a chance that we can stop it together."

"An extremely remote one," Mr. Calhoun stated.

"Maybe, but a chance. Now if you let me out and I'm

the first case that don't get amnesia, I can tell the world about all this. I might be able to steer other guys, scientists and decent politicians, into coming here to get the dope straighter than I could. Maybe that'd give Earth a chance to cop a pardon on getting extinct. Even if it don't work, it's better than hanging around the radio waiting for the results."

Dr. Harding hissed on his glasses and wiped them thoughtfully, an adopted mannerism, obviously, because he seemed to see as well without them. "You have a point, Mr. Gilroy, but it would mean losing your contribution to our archives."

"Well, which is more important?" Gilroy argued. "Would you rather have any record than have us save ourselves?"

"Both," said Mr. Calhoun. "We see very little hope of your success, while we regard your knowledge as having important sociological significance. A very desirable contribution."

The others agreed.

"Look, I'll come back if I lame out," Gilroy desperately offered. "You can pick me up any time you want. But if I make headway, you got to let Zelda go, too."

"A reasonable proposition," said Dr. Harding. "I call for a vote."

They took one. The best Gilroy could get was a compromise.

"We will lift our control," Mr. Calhoun said, "for a suitable time. If you can arouse a measurable opposition to racial suicide—measurable, mind you; we're not requiring that you reverse the lemming march alone—we agree to release your wife and revise our policy completely. If, on the other hand, as seems more likely—"

"I come back here and go on giving you the inside on racing," Gilroy finished for him. "How much time do I get?"

Dr. Harding turned his hands palm up on the table. "We do not wish to be arbitrary. We earnestly hope you gain your objective and we shall give you every opportunity to do so. If you fail, you will know it. So shall we."

"You're pretty sure I'll get scratched, aren't you?" Gilroy asked angrily. "It's like me telling a jockey he don't stand a chance—he's whammied before he even gets to the paddock. Anybody'd think do-gooders like you claim you are would wish me luck."

"But we do!" exclaimed Mr. Calhoun. He shook Gilroy's hand warmly and sincerely. "Haven't we consented to release you? Doesn't this prove our honest concern? If releasing all our human associates would save humanity, we would do so instantly. But we have tried again and again. And so, to use your own professional terminology, we are hedging our bets by continuing to make our anthropological record until you demonstrate another method . . . if you do."

"Good enough," approved Gilroy. "Thanks for the kind word."

The other board members followed and shook Gilroy's hand and wished him well.

42

Barnes, being last, did the same and added, "You may see your wife, if you care to, before you leave."

"If I care to?" Gilroy repeated. "What in hell do you think I came here for in the first place?"

Zelda was brought to him and they were left alone in a pleasant reading room. Soft music came from the walls, which glowed with enough light to read by. Zelda's lovely face was warm with emotion when she sat down beside him and put her hands in his.

"They tell me you're leaving, hon," she said.

"I made a deal, baby. If it works—well, it'll be like it was before, only better."

"I hate to see you leave. Not just for me," she added as he lit up hopefully. "I still love you, hon, but it's different now. I used to want you near me every minute. Now it's loving you without starving for you. You know what I mean?"

"That's just the control they got on you. It's like that with me, too, only I know what it is and you don't."

"But the big thing is the project. Why, we're footnotes in history! Stay here, hon. I'd feel so much better knowing you were here, making your contribution like they say."

He kissed her lips. They were soft and warm and clinging, and so were her arms around his neck. This was more like the Zelda he had been missing.

"They gave you a hypo, sweetheart," he told her. "You're hooked; I'm not. Maybe being a footnote is more important than doing something to save our skin, but I don't think so. If I can do anything about it, I want to do it."

"Like what?"

"I don't know," he admitted. "I'm hoping I get an idea when I'm paroled."

She nuzzled under his chin. "Hon, I want you and me to be footnotes. I want it awful bad."

"That's not what really counts, baby. Don't you see that? It's having you and stopping us humans from being just a bunch of old footnotes. Once we do that, we can always come back here and make the record, if it means that much to you."

"Oh, it does!"

He stood and drew her up so he could hold her more tightly. "You do want to go on being my wife, don't you, baby?"

"Of course! Only I was hoping it could be here."

"Well, it can't. But that's all I wanted to know. The rest is just details."

He kissed her again, including the side of her neck, which produced a subdued wriggle of pleasure, and then he went back to the Administration Building for his release.

Awakening was no more complicated than opening his eyes, except for a bit of fogginess and fatigue that wore off quickly, and Gilroy saw he was in a white room with a doctor, a nurse and an orderly around his bed.

"Reflexes normal," the doctor said. He told Gilroy, "You see and hear us. You know what I'm saying."

"Sure," Gilroy replied. "Why shouldn't I?"

"That's right," the doctor evaded. "How do you feel?"

Gilroy thought about it. He was a little thirsty and the idea of a steak interested him, but otherwise he felt no pain or confusion. He remembered that he had not been hungry or thirsty for a long time, and that made him recall going over the border after Zelda.

There were no gaps in his recollection.

He didn't have protective amnesia.

"You know what it's like there?" he asked the doctor eagerly. "A big place where everybody from all over the world tell these aliens about their job or racket." He frowned. "I just remembered something funny. Wonder why I didn't notice it at the time. Everybody talks the same language. Maybe that's because there's only one language for thinking." He shrugged off the problem. "The guys who run the shop take it all down as a record for whoever wants to know about us a zillion years from now. That's on account of us humans are about to close down the track and go home."

The doctor bent close intently. "Is that what you believe *now* or—while you were—disturbed?"

Gilroy's impulse to blurt the whole story was stopped at the gate. The doctor was staring too studiously at him. He didn't have his story set yet; he needed time to think, and that meant getting out of this hospital and talking it over with himself.

"You kidding?" he asked, using the same grin that he met complainers with when his turf predictions went sour. "While my head was out of the stirrups, of course."

The doctor, the nurse and the orderly relaxed.

"I ought to write a book," Gilroy went on, being doggedly humorous. "What screwball ideas I got! How'd I act?"

"Not bad," said the orderly. "When I found you yakking in your wife's room, I thought maybe it was catching and I'd better go find another job. But Doc here told me I was too stable to go psychotic."

"I wasn't any trouble?"

"Nah. All you did was talk about how to handicap races. I got quite a few pointers. Hell, you went over them often enough for anybody to get them straight!"

"I'm glad somebody made a profit," said Gilroy. He asked the doctor, "When do I get out of here?"

"We'll have to give you a few tests first."

"Bring them on," Gilroy said confidently.

They were clever tests, designed to trip him into revealing whether he still believed in his delusions. But once he realized that, he meticulously joked about them.

"Well?" he asked when the tests were finished.

"You're all right," said the doctor. "Just try not to worry about your wife, avoid overworking, get plenty of rest—"

46

Before Gilroy left, he went to see Zelda. She had evidently recorded the time-step satisfactorily, because she was on a soft-shoe routine that she must have had down pat by the time she'd been ten.

He kissed her unresponsive mouth, knowing that she was far away in space and could not feel, see, or hear him. But that didn't matter. He felt his own good, honest, genuine longing for her, unchecked by the aliens' control of emotions.

"I'll spring you yet, baby," he said. "And what I told you about that big apartment on Riverside Drive still goes. We'll have a time together that ought to be a footnote in history all by itself. I'll see you . . . after I get the real job done."

He heard the soft-shoe rhythm all the way down the corridor, out of the hospital, and clear back to the city.

Gilroy's bank balance was sick, the circulation of his tip sheet gone. But he didn't worry about it; there were bigger problems.

He studied the newspapers before even giving himself time to think. The news was as bad as usual. He could feel the heat of fission, close his eyes and see all the cities and farms in the world going up in a blinding cloud. As far as he was concerned, Barnes and Harding and the rest weren't working fast enough; he could see doom sprinting in half a field ahead of the completion of the record.

The first thing he could have done was recapture the circulation of the tip sheet. The first thing he actually did do was write the story of his experience just as it had happened, and send it to a magazine.

When he finally went to work on his sheet, it was to cut down the racing data to a few columns and fill the rest of it with warnings.

"This is what you want?" the typesetter asked, staring at the copy Gilroy turned in. "You sure this is what you want?"

"Sure I'm sure. Set it and let's get the edition out early. I'm doubling the print order."

"Doubling?"

"You heard me."

When the issue was out, Gilroy waited around the main newsstands on Broadway. He watched the customers buy, study unbelievingly, and wander off looking as if all the tracks in the country had burned down simultaneously.

Doc Hawkins found him there.

"Gilroy, my boy! You have no idea how anxious we were about you. But you're looking fit, I'm glad to say."

"Thanks," Gilroy said abstractedly. "I wish I could say the same about you and the rest of the world."

Doc laughed. "No need to worry about us. We'll muddle along somehow."

"You think so, huh?"

"Well, if the end is approaching, let us greet it at the Blue Ribbon. I believe we can still find the lads there."

They were, and they greeted Gilroy with gladness and drinks. Diplomatically, they made only the most delicate

48

references to the revamping job Gilroy had done on his tip sheet.

"It's just like opening night, that's all," comforted Arnold Wilson Wyle. "You'll get back into your routine pretty soon."

"I don't want to," said Gilroy pugnaciously. "Handicapping is only a way to get people to read what I *really* want to tell them."

"Took me many minutes to find horses," Oil Pocket put in. "See one I want to bet on, but rest of paper make me too worried to bother betting. Okay with Injun, though—horse lost. And soon you get happy again, stick to handicapping, let others worry about world."

Buttonhole tightened his grip on Gilroy's lapel. "Sure, boy. As long as the bobtails run, who cares what happens to anything else?"

"Maybe I went too easy," said Gilroy tensely. "I didn't print the whole thing, just a little part of it. Here's the rest."

They were silent while he talked, seeming stunned with the terrible significance of his story.

"Did you explain all this to the doctors?" Doc Hawkins asked.

"You think I'm crazy?" Gilroy retorted. "They'd have kept me packed away and I'd never get a crack at telling anybody."

"Don't let it trouble you," said Doc. "Some vestiges of delusion can be expected to persist for a while, but you'll get rid of them. I have faith in your ability to distinguish between the real and unreal."

"But it all happened! If you guys don't believe me, who will? And you've got to so I can get Zelda back!"

"Of course, of course," said Doc hastily. "We'll discuss it further some other time. Right now I really must start putting my medical column together for the paper."

"What about you, Handy Sam?" Gilroy challenged.

Handy Sam, with one foot up on the table and a pencil between his toes, was doodling self-consciously on a paper napkin. "We all get these ideas, Gilroy. I used to dream about having arms and I'd wake up still thinking so, till I didn't know if I did or didn't. But like Doc says, then you figure out what's real and it don't mix you up any more."

"All right," Gilroy said belligerently to Oil Pocket. "You think my story's batty, too?"

"Can savvy evil spirits, good spirits," Oil Pocket replied with stolid tact. "Injun spirits, though, not white ones."

"But I keep telling you they ain't spirits. They ain't even human. They're from some world way across the Universe—"

Oil Pocket shook his head. "Can savvy Injun spirits, Gilroy. No spirits, no savvy."

"Look, you see the ones we're all in, don't you?" Gilroy appealed to the whole group. "Do you mean to tell me you can't feel we're getting set to blow the joint? Wouldn't you want to stop it?"

"If we could, my boy, gladly," Doc said. "However, there's not much that any individual or group of individuals can do."

"But how in hell does anything get started? With one guy, two guys—before you know it, you got a crowd, a political party, a country—"

"What about the other countries, though?" asked Buttonhole. "So we're sold on your story in America, let's say. What do we do—let the rest of the world walk in and take us over?"

"We educate them," Gilroy explained despairingly. "We start it here and it spreads to there. It doesn't have to be everybody. Mr. Calhoun said I just have to convince a few people and that'll show them it can be done and then I get Zelda back."

Doc stood up and glanced around the table. "I believe I speak for all of us, Gilroy, when I state that we shall do all within our power to aid you."

"Like telling other people?" Gilroy asked eagerly.

"Well, that's going pretty—"

"Forget it, then. Go write your column. I'll see you chumps around—around ten miles up, shaped like a mushroom."

He stamped out, so angry that he untypically let the others settle his bill.

Gilroy's experiment with the newspaper failed so badly that it was not worth the expense of putting it out; people refused to buy. Gilroy had three-sheets printed and hired sandwich men to parade them through the city. He made violent speeches in Columbus Circle, where he lost his audience to revivalist orators; Union Square, where he was told heatedly to bring his message to Wall Street; and Times Square, where the police made him move along so he wouldn't block traffic. He obeyed, shouting his message as he walked, until he remembered how amusedly he used to listen to those who cried that Doomsday was near. He wondered if they were catatonics under imperfect control. It didn't matter; nobody paid serious attention to his or their warnings.

The next step, logically, was a barrage of letters to the heads of nations, to the UN, to editors of newspapers. Only a few of his letters were printed. The ones in Doc's tabloid did best, drawing such comments as:

"Who does this jerk think he is, telling us everybody's going to get killed off? Maybe they will, but not in Brooklyn!"

"When I was a young girl, some fifty years ago, I had a similar experience to Mr. Gilroy's. But my explanation is quite simple. The persons I saw proved to be my ancestors. Mr. Gilroy's new-found friends will, I am sure, prove to be the same. The World Beyond knows all and tells all, and my Control, with whom I am in daily communication Over There, assures me that mankind is in no danger whatever, except from the evil effects of tobacco and alcohol and the disrespect of youth for their elders."

"The guy's nuts! He ought to go back to Russia. He's

nothing but a nut or a Communist and in my book that's the same thing."

"He isn't telling us anything new. We all know who the enemy is. The only way to protect ourselves is to build TWO GUNS FOR ONE!"

"Is this Gilroy character selling us the idea that we all ought to go batty to save the world?"

Saddened and defeated, Gilroy went through his accumulated mail. There were politely noncommittal acknowledgments from embassies and the UN. There was also a check for his article from the magazine he'd sent it to; the amount was astonishingly large.

He used part of it to buy radio time, the balance for ads in rural newspapers and magazines. City people, he figured, were hardened by publicity gags, and he might stir up the less suspicious and sophisticated hinterland. The replies he received, though, advised him to buy some farmland and let the metropolises be destroyed, which, he was assured, would be a mighty good thing all around.

The magazine came out the same day he tried to get into the UN to shout a speech from the balcony. He was quietly surrounded by a uniformed guard and moved, rather than forced, outside.

He went dejectedly to his hotel. He stayed there for several days, dialing numbers he selected randomly from the telephone book, and getting the brush-off from business offices, housewives, and maids. They were all very busy or the boss wasn't in or they expected important calls.

That was when he was warmly invited by letter to see the editor of the magazine that had bought his article.

Elated for actually the first time since his discharge from the hospital, Gilroy took a cab to a handsome building, showed his invitation to a pretty and courteous receptionist, and was escorted into an elaborate office where a smiling man came around a wide bleached-mahogany desk and shook hands with him.

"Mr. Gilroy," said the editor, "I'm happy to tell you that we've had a wonderful response to your story."

"Article," Gilroy corrected.

The editor smiled. "Do you produce so much that you can't remember what you sold us? It was about—"

"I know," Gilroy cut in. "But it wasn't a story. It was an article. It really—"

"Now, now. The first thing a writer must learn is not to take his ideas too seriously. Very dangerous, especially in a piece of fiction like yours."

"But the whole thing is true!"

"Certainly—while you were writing it." The editor shoved a pile of mail across the desk toward him. "Here are some of the comments that have come in. I think you'll enjoy seeing the reaction."

Gilroy went through them, hoping anxiously for no more than a single note that would show his message had come through to somebody. He finished and looked up blankly.

"You see?" the editor asked proudly. "You're a find."

"The new Mark Twain or Jonathan Swift. A comic."

"A satirist," the editor amended. He leaned across the desk on his crossed forearms. "A mail response like this indicates a talent worth developing. We would like to discuss a series of stories—"

"Articles."

"Whatever you choose to call them. We're prepared to—"

"You ever been off your rocket?" Gilroy asked abruptly.

The editor sat back, smiling with polite puzzlement. "Why, no."

"You ought to try it some time." Gilroy lifted himself out of the chair and went to the door. "That's what I want, what I was trying to sell in my article. We all ought to go to hospitals and get ourselves let in and have these aliens take over and show us where we're going."

"You think that would be an improvement?"

"What wouldn't?" asked Gilroy, opening the door.

"But about the series—"

"I've got your name and address. I'll let you know if anything turns up."

Gilroy closed the door behind him, went out of the handsome building, and called a taxi. All through the long ride, he stared at the thinning out of the city, the huddled suburban communities, the stretches of grass and well-behaved woods that were permitted to survive.

He climbed out at Glendale Center Hospital, paid the hackie, and went to the admitting desk. The nurse gave him a smile.

"We were wondering when you'd come visit your wife," she said. "Been away?"

"Sort of," he answered, with as little emotion as he had felt while he was being controlled. "I'll be seeing plenty of her from now on. I want my old room back."

"But you're perfectly normal!"

"That depends on how you look at it. Give me ten minutes alone and any brain vet will be glad to give me a cushioned stall."

Hands in his pockets, Gilroy went into the elevator, walked down the corridor to his old room without pausing to visit Zelda. It was the live Zelda he wanted to see, not the tapping automaton.

He went in and shut the door.

"Okay, you were right and I was wrong," Gilroy told the board of directors. "Turn me over to Barnes and I'll give him the rest of the dope on racing. Just let me see Zelda once in a while and you won't have any trouble with me."

"Then you are convinced that you have failed," said Mr. Calhoun.

"I'm no dummy. I know when I'm licked. I also pay anything I owe."

Mr. Calhoun leaned back. "And so do we, Mr. Gilroy. Naturally, you have no way of detecting the effect you've had. We do. The result is that, because of your experiment, we are gladly revising our policy."

"Huh?" Gilroy looked around at the comfortable aliens

in their comfortable chairs. Solid and respectable, every one of them. "Is this a rib?"

"Visits to catatonics have increased considerably," explained Dr. Harding. "When the visitors are alone with our human associates, they tentatively follow the directions you gave in your article. Not all do, to be sure; only those who feel as strongly about being with their loved ones as you do about your wife."

"We have accepted four voluntary applicants," said Mr. Calhoun.

Gilroy's mouth seemed to be filled with cracker crumbs that wouldn't go down and allow him to speak.

"And now," Dr. Harding went on, "we are setting up an Information Section to teach the applicants what you have learned and make the same arrangement we made with you. We are certain that we shall, before long, have to increase our staff as the number of voluntary applicants increases geometrically, after we release the first few to continue the work you have so admirably begun."

"You mean I *made* it?" Gilroy croaked unbelievingly.

"Perhaps this will prove it to you," said Mr. Calhoun.

He motioned and the door opened and Zelda came in.

"Hello, hon," she said. "I'm glad you're back. I missed you."

"Not like I missed you, baby! There wasn't anybody controlling my feelings."

Mr. Calhoun put his hands on their shoulders. "Whenever you care to, Mr. Gilroy, you and your wife are free to leave."

Gilroy held Zelda's hands and her calmly fond gaze. "We owe these guys plenty, baby," he said to her. "We'll help make the record before we take off. Ain't that what you want?"

"Oh, it is, hon! And then I want you."

"Then let's get started," he said. "The quicker we do, the quicker we get back."

I Know Suicide

I was out of the hotel and into the street almost before the scream ended in a stomach-turning splash on the sidewalk outside. Standing near a pillar in the Blake's lobby, I'd heard the scream, starting thin and high, getting louder—like a falling bomb in the movies.

Only it wasn't a bomb.

It was a woman.

From the force she'd landed on her back with, she must have gone out one of the top stories of the hotel.

Cars stopped and people ran up for a fast look. They wished they hadn't. I'd put in my time as a city detective, where I saw plenty of ledge hoppers, and every one of them made me remember my breakfast.

Carlton, the hotel manager, came puffing out. His prim, maidenly face was whiter than usual. He squeezed his hands and looked as if he'd have a good cry.

"This is terrible, Gilroy," he moaned. "Terrible! Mr.

Blake will have a fit when it hits the papers. Why didn't you stop her?"

"I didn't have my catcher's mitt," I said.

"Who is she?"

I lifted my shoulders and let them fall. "I didn't see her when she checked in—if she ever did."

"You mean she might not be a guest?" Carlton glared angrily at the smashed body. "The nerve! Jumping out of my hotel when she's not even registered!"

"I didn't say she wasn't," I told him. "She checked in when I wasn't around, probably. The Blake's a big hotel for just one dick," I added. "Especially on the salary I get."

Carlton stopped glaring at the woman and turned his air-conditioned eye on me. "This is a fine time to be crabbing about pay. Make sure this gets as little publicity as possible or you may not even have a job."

"Now I'm a press agent," I grumbled.

He went back in as Reilly, the beat cop, took over. The Homicide heap rolled up in a little while, the boys went to work and pretty soon there was nothing but a puddle of blood and a lot of press photographers for the crowd to gawk at. Then one of the porters came out with a mop and a bucket of hot black coffee, and not even the blood was left. The photographers followed the squad into the hotel, so the mob broke into twos and threes and melted away.

It didn't take long to identify the corpse. A chesty young blonde named Mrs. Horne came tearing out of the elevator, took a glom, and hit the deck. When she sat up, she had hysterics. Finally she calmed down to mere convulsions and sobbed out her pitch.

"It's Lucille," she said. "My maid. I hired her in Sioux Falls. Fred and I—my husband, Mr. Horne—we came from Salt Lake City. We—we're going to South America. We registered here late—late last night—and Lucille has committed suicide already and—and we aren't even unpacked! Oh, why did she do it? Why? Why?"

"Maybe you can tell us, Mrs. Horne," said Lieutenant Steckel, as hard a guy as Homicide ever had in its history of human ironsides. "What reason would she have for killing herself?"

"I can't imagine," blubbered Mrs. Horne. "I've only known her a few days. We hired her because I needed a maid and she seemed nice and she wanted to travel."

A homicide boy scratched his nose. "Maybe she took this job to ditch a bum love deal," he offered Steckel.

"Or maybe she was pushed out the window," Steckel said. "Let's go up and take a look around your rooms, Mrs. Horne."

I tagged along, keeping my big fat mouth shut except when I had to answer questions, which weren't many once the looie saw there wasn't much I could answer. The blood-and-clues detail know their jobs and they don't like free advice. Maybe I saw a few things they didn't see, but they weren't asking and I wasn't giving. My orders were to get this cooling as little publicity as possible, one way or another, and what I'd noticed would have given the hotel a circus press.

Fred Horne was dressing when we walked in. he'd been taking a shower, he said, when his wife heard the commotion, noticed the maid missing and the open window, and grabbed the down elevator to find she was employer to a stiff.

It was pretty routine. The police checkup showed a Lucille Benson had left Sioux Falls for New York, and that the Hornes, known as a very respectable couple in Salt Lake City, had lived there several years. No dope on why Lucille took a permanent lam, but that didn't mean, of course, there wasn't a reason.

The fingerprint man said, "Who'd want to dump off a maid?" and that was the way it looked to Lieutenant Steckel. He had the body sent down for the required p-m and wrote it off as suicide. He told the Hornes to stay in town in case the autopsy showed something, but it was just cop talk—the case had really been buttoned up.

Carlton, the manager, grew a bad-fitting smile when I brought the afternoon papers to his office. He didn't wear a smile very often and he looked it. But he was plenty happy.

"A stick of type buried in the back of each rag," he gloated. "Swell, Gilroy! By tomorrow it'll be forgotten. Mr. Blake will be delighted."

"Maybe," I said. "But I won't."

His grin went sour and he swung his bifocals on me like a third-degree spotlight. "What's bothering you?"

"That Benson dame didn't stroll out the window," I informed him. "She was pushed or tossed."

"Oh?" Carlton squeaked back in his swivel chair and gave me his other smile, the one that says he's hotel manager and you're just something that staggered in off the street. "You were fired off the force for drunkenness and inefficiency, and you know more than the Homicide Bureau?"

I kept the red out of my eyes. "It happens. And I haven't had a drink on duty since I started keyhole sleuthing here. Also, one more reference to my past, Mr. Carlton, and our hitherto unpleasant association will be terminated by a sock in the kisser. From me to you, that is."

"I'm going to report this—this insubordination to Mr. Blake!" he yelled, hopping out of his chair. "The Blake Hotel has an enviable reputation for morality. Wives aren't afraid to have their husbands register here; they know it's not a hotel where you ring a bell at four in the morning and everybody goes back to their own rooms. That's how we intend to keep it, too. If you're unhappy about the pay and the work, remember you're not on contract."

I sighed tiredly and sat down without being asked to. That always made Carlton mad, which is why I did it. Then I lit a dinched snipe that I'd had to put out when the desk called me half an hour ago, and tossed the match in his wastebasket. I knew he'd look to make sure the match was out, and he did.

"Getting back to the Lucille Benson babe," I said, "she didn't commit suicide. She was murdered."

"The cops say suicide," he snapped. "That's good enough for me. And it better be good enough for you, Gilroy."

I flicked my ash in his wastebasket and got him to take another fast involuntary look. I said, "Jobs aren't as important as murder, Mr. Carlton," and we sat and stared at each other in grim silence for a few minutes.

"How do you figure murder?" he finally asked. "Not that I want you to do anything about it, understand. I'm just curious."

"Lucille Benson hit the sidewalk a little after eleven a.m. Her hair was still in a net; her upper lip had lipstick on, but not her lower lip. In other words, she wasn't fully dressed yet."

"From which you deduce what, Holmes?" I skipped the sarcasm. "She'd just gotten up, probably because they checked in so late last night—about 2:30. She was just putting on makeup. Now I've seen a lot of suicides and you can take my word for it—suicides don't check out right in the middle of dressing. Especially women. Babes like to look their best when they take off. They'll do it every time."

"So?"

"So she was helped out the window. And that, my dear old stiff-collared chum, is murder."

His nasty smile got nastier. "And who do you think did the job?"

"The Hornes, of course. Nobody else was in the suite."

"And why would they want to kill their maid—with help as hard to get as it is?"

I stood up and mashed out my cigarette. "That's what I aim to find out."

He jumped to his feet and started waving his skinny finger at me. "You let this case alone, Gilroy! Suicide is bad enough. Murder will mean endless publicity. If you go to the cops, you'll be collecting unemployment insurance tomorrow."

"Don't wilt your collar; I'm not going to the cops," I said and walked out leaving his door open, because I knew it annoyed him as much as using his wastebasket for an ashtray.

I didn't like chaperoning at the Blake, but I didn't like the idea of a pink slip either. Not until I had some evidence, at lease, instead of just a suspicion. I wasn't kidding myself that breaking the case would get me back on the force. Proving the PD is a gang of chumps is no way to get back on. But it might give me enough of a name to draw an offer from one of the big private agencies.

More than a better job, though, I don't feel happy when I think somebody is getting away with murder. Think of the cases you've read about—999 out of 1,000, the victim is a pretty good character who had the tough luck to walk in front of some heel. We need all the decent citizens we've got. But let the heels beat the rap and they'll think they have a foolproof patent. Then what happens to our decent citizens?

I guess you'd say my philosophy of murder is: I don't

see anything funny about a handmade corpse and I want the killer to get my point of view.

But putting a zipper on the case was another deal. The Hornes had hired Lucille in Sioux Falls, all right, and there was nothing to show they ever knew her before that. It couldn't be money; the Hornes had dough and looked it, and a babe doesn't become a maid if she has a wad worth killing for. Neither could I figure Mrs. Horne being jealous of her. From what was left of Lucille, she'd been small, not built much and close to thirty; Mrs. Horne was twenty-five and stacked like a brick shipyard.

And that left what for a motive after the way all the facts about their backgrounds checked? Nothing.

But I stuck to the couple closer than a mustard plaster. It wasn't easy. Every so often I had to be near the desk so Carlton would think I was watching the traffic between rooms and stopping bottles from being smuggled in. As long as the Hornes stayed in their suite, I could keep an eye on the elevators. It was when they went out that I had to race to the delivery entrance, scoot around front and play tag on my arches or in a cab, then beat them back in before Carlton missed me.

My wallet, calluses, and nerves all took a beating. My murder theory got nowhere at all.

In a couple of days, I tailed them to the Oat Exchange Bank, some South American consulates, department stores, the movies, shoe and lingerie shoppes, ladies accessories joints, soda fountains, cigar stores. All glad frills for the madame and smokes for the boss. Fred Horne himself seemed well stocked from skimmers to feetboats.

Oh, yeah. And a swap shop.

The swap shop they went into put a line between my eyebrows till next morning, when a little guy visited the Horne suite and came out with a package almost as big as himself. He was grinning from scalp to chest as if he'd just bagged enough dough to retire on.

He showed a slip at the desk and got a nod from the clerk to take the load on out. Before the little guy could get it up on his shoulder, I trudged over and stopped him.

"What's the matter?" he argued. "I got a clearance slip from Mr. Horne. See?"

"Just routine," I said. "We always make sure there's no hotel property in the bundle. You'd be surprised what crooks some people are."

"I don't think I would be," he answered and followed me into the switchboard room.

Sally Fletcher, the operator, was taking her relief. You ought to see that jane. Black hair and blue eyes that turn me soft as a tearoom cocktail. If I'd gotten paid better, I think I could have made time and a half with her. Anyhow, thinking so made me feel better.

"The Hope diamond, Gilroy?" she asked.

"More likely a stiff," I said.

The little guy showed both front teeth in a smile till he saw my Class B flatfoot scowl. He tore open the bundle and moved aside fast.

"Well, look at that!" whispered Sally. "Some duds!"

"Nice, huh?" I said.

Even I could see they were expensive clothes. Underwear made of black silk trimmed with real lace. Dresses with that $300 simplicity. Shoes made of calf softer than some steaks I've bought.

Those costly rags added up to only one thing. Money. Maid or no maid, Lucille Benson must have had it. And I had my motive, finally. Another nice angle—the store labels and cleaning tags had been cut out of everything. You don't do that when you're trying to get a high price for clothes, unless you don't care to have them traced.

When I went out the door, the little guy was saying, "Believe me, I had to pay plenty for this stuff," and Sally was murmuring, "I can believe it. I wish I could afford 'em."

I took the elevator to the fourteenth floor and hammered on the Hornes' door. Mrs. H opened it a sliver and gave me a cold up and down.

"You're the hotel detective, aren't you?" she asked. "Well, if it's about that package I sent out, it's perfectly all right. I gave the man a note to show the desk."

"I saw it," I said. "That's what I want to talk about."

"There's nothing to discuss," she answered and started closing the door.

I put my hand on it and leaned hard. "You and your husband want to go on a cruise," I told her. "You'd hate to have a police investigation hold you up. Right?"

"Certainly."

"Then maybe you can give me a few answers and there won't be any investigation and you won't miss the boat."

She put on a smile and let me in. I saw then why she'd opened the door only a little way. The smile and a blue satin negligee and a pair of fluffy mules were all she had on. She held the negligee together at the top.

"I'm sure there's nothing to explain, Mr.—uh—?"

"Call me Gilroy," I said. "Everybody does. I guess my kids will, too, if I ever get married and have any."

She sat me down on the couch and stood there letting me look at her.

"You mean a big, handsome man like you can't find a girl anywhere?"

"Not after they find out what this hotel pays me."

"Oh." She drew her lower lip between her teeth and cocked her blonde head at me. Very appealing. "Well, look Mr. Gilroy. This cruise is important to my husband and me. We've been planning it so long, you know, and we have only a certain amount of time. I can't imagine what you've found that would involve us in an investigation, but—well we have money. We'd be willing to tip you handsomely if you helped us make that boat."

I got my eyes up to her face. "I don't have any dope worth dough. Just some questions."

"Such as?"

"Those clothes you sold belonged to Lucille Benson, eh?"

She paused warily. "Of course."

"Pretty expensive things for a maid."

"Some women put every cent they have on their backs."

"That was an awful lot of pennies," I commented. "But it seems to me you should have sent the stuff to her family instead of selling it and keeping the dough."

"Lucille told us she had no family, and we're paying for the funeral. Why shouldn't we defray the expenses?"

"No reason, I guess, if she had no family."

She moved back a little. "Any other questions?"

"Just one," I said. "What happened to the store labels?"

She sat down hard right up against me. "Why, I don't know. Weren't there any?"

"Not a one."

"That's odd," she frowned. "Do you know what I believe, Mr. Gilroy? Lucille planned to commit suicide all along. We didn't suspect, of course, or we would never have hired her. So she took the labels out of her clothing to prevent their being traced. There must have been someone in Sioux Falls she didn't want notified." She put an incandescent smile about six inches from my face. "Isn't that good deduction, Mr. Gilroy?"

"Very sharp," I said. "The only thing wrong is she'd have changed her name. But maybe she didn't think of it."

"I suppose not," the babe agreed. "She wasn't very bright, you know." She stood up and moved over to the bar. "Drink?"

"Scotch if you have it. Anything if you haven't." I got

to my feet and strolled around the room while she mixed the drinks. While I looked here and there, I asked her, "Get your passports and tickets yet?"

"Oh, yes," she said, stripping the cellophane off a bottle neck and keeping her smile on me. "We're leaving on the *Santa Rita* this afternoon. Aren't we lucky?"

"Very." I slid my glance into the wastebasket under the escritoire, I think they call those lacework desks. A little patch of shiny yellow stuff, hidden under the morning paper, hit my eye. "This a kind of second honeymoon?"

"In a way. Except we never had a first. We eloped."

I waited till she poured with a steady, experienced hand. Then I fished fast in the basket. There were several patches under the paper. I put them behind my back until she went to work on the soda bottles, which gave me a chance to slip the things in my side pockets. I didn't see what was on the, but I knew what they were—the missing labels from Lucille Benson's clothes.

She handed me a brimming glass, we clicked and grinned at each other, and her drink went down the hold like a cargo net whose cable suddenly snaps. I sipped mine.

"So you see, Mr. Gilroy," she said, "there really isn't a reason in the world for any investigation. Now is there?"

"Well, now, I'm not so sure," I answered slowly. "The cops would want a look at that stuff of Lucille's, I think."

She stood right up against me. I felt like a guy on an observation tower without a railing—afraid to move, but unable to stop looking.

"Don't you have any romance in your soul, Mr. Gilroy?" she breathed up at me. "Would you stand in the way of love?"

"I kind of thought that was where I was standing," I said shakily. "It takes a lot to make me suppress evidence."

"Well, don't I have a lot? And it's not real evidence. You know the whole truth and so do the police."

I waited for her to continue, or anyhow to do something. She didn't. So I said, "Not to change the subject, you've been putting on weight. You ought to get that bracelet enlarged."

"Don't tell me you like skinny girls!"

"Oh, no. Not me."

A floor board creaked behind me and I whipped around. I'd been expecting something like that, but I wasn't quick enough. A comet came zooming out of space and blew up on my mastoid bone. I didn't even feel the floor tilt against my face.

Wood files were rasping through my brain when I lifted myself on one rubbery elbow. The room kept going out of focus, but what little I saw made me stagger up and to the door.

The shack was naked. The Hornes had packed up and gone on the road. I tried to take off after them like a big-tailed bird, but it was all I could do to lift each foot off the floor.

Brother, I told myself, when it comes to detectiving, forget trying to use your head. Because I'd thought I had the whole deal figured out. I knew Fred Horne was nearby when his wife threw all that rosy-pink merchandise at me—he, not Mrs. H, had signed the release slip the little guy from the swap shop carried, and I hadn't seen him go out through the lobby. So I'd known he was still in the suite. But then, being equipped with a single cylinder brain, I naturally offered him the back of my head to put an egg on.

Some egg it was, too. My kelly, when I picked it up at the switchboard room, sat on top of the lump like a trick hat-tipping gimmick. Sally Fletcher took a look and went all soft and motherly.

"Fred Horne and wife give it to you?" she asked.

"Yeah." I took off my jacket and strapped on the shoulder holster I used to wear on the force. "Fair exchange. One lump for me; the sound of frying meat for them. Their meat."

"Well, don't just stand there!" she beefed. "Go out and get them!"

I got my jacket back on. "Lots of time. I know where they are. First get me Lieutenant Steckel at Homicide, then find out where the *Santa Rita* is docked and when it sails for S.A."

While she checked the ship, I waited for someone at headquarters to locate Steckel. After probably holding out for the winner of the seventh at Hialeah and the day's box scores, the looie finally got on.

"Gilroy at the Blake Hotel," I told him fast. "It's about that Benson dame who went out a window here. She didn't take a 'chute. She was murdered."

"Any evidence?" Steckel demanded.

"Enough to hold the Hornes on a charge. Something you have to check first. Hold on." I felt in my right side pocket. It was empty. My ticker suddenly ran down till I remembered splitting the wad of stuff I'd picked up in the basket and shoving some in each pocket. I took three labels out of my left one and looked at them for the first time. Sally turned red at what I said and Steck wanted to know what was the matter. I told him about the bundle of Lucille's clothes and finished, "Benson had dough, all right, and she wasn't from Sioux Falls."

"No?" he asked. "Where then?"

"Salt Lake City. The same place as the Hornes."

He added to the comment I'd made when I read the labels. Sally, luckily, couldn't hear it. "So they knew her all along," he added. "Give me the names of those shops."

By the time he got them spelled right, Sally had the dope I asked for. "The *Santa Rita* doesn't sail till Friday."

"I kind of thought Mrs. Horne wouldn't give me a free publicity handout. See what ships left or are leaving today. Ask if a couple named Barry is on the passenger list."

"Barry?" she repeated.

"Yeah. I tailed them into the consulates and shipping

offices and found out what name their passports were under. They must have been shopping for a ship and phoned in reservations—they didn't buy tickets while I was dogging them."

I heard Steckel getting action on the labels at the other end as Sally made her calls. When he was finished giving instructions, she had the information. The ship was the *Republic* and it had shoved off thirty minutes before.

Steckel said, "Meet me at Pier Five right away," and the phone went dead.

As I headed for the door, Sally yipped, "I want to go with you, Gilroy!"

"And get docked for time out?" I asked. "This lousy hotel pays little enough as it is."

"I heard that!" said Carlton, coming in. "Where do you think you're going in the middle of the day?"

Maybe Sally thought he'd be tickled when she told him, but he wasn't. He started waving that finger again.

"You step out of the lobby on the Benson case and you can stay out, Gilroy!"

"So long, then, bucket face," I said over my shoulder. "If I'm fired, I'll let the cops know about you suppressing evidence. That Benson dame was murdered and you're not going to stop me from nabbing her killers."

The gasps that came from the lobby squatters gave me a lift you're supposed to get only from a cigarette. Carlton was going to have a headache explaining what I'd yelled. I wished I had time to hang around and listen.

I snagged a cab and highballed down to the pier. Steckel

was there already, trying to keep himself from leaping into a police boat tied up alongside. He shoved me into it, the motor roared, and we streaked out into the harbor.

Quite a ride. At over forty miles or knots an hour, we overtook the *Republic* as she steamed through the Narrows. Steckel got her to stop and we were clambering up the ladder when somebody on the other side yelled, "Man overboard!" The mob that lined the railings heaved to the opposite side of the ship.

I joined the crowd while Steckel explained his mission to the captain. I saw two hats floating in the water, a man's and a woman's. Even before they were picked up by our police boat crew, I had an idea whose they were. The man's sweatband was marked "George Barry" and the woman's had the initials "HB."

"Well," Steckel said, disappointed, "looks like your hunch was right, Gilroy. But they saw us coming first."

"Anybody can toss a couple of hats in the water and yell 'Man overboard,'" I answered. "Everybody was watching us come aboard, so no one saw them jump, if they ever did."

"Don't tell me how to run my business," said Steckel. "I'd search the ship even if there had been witnesses."

He had the captain order everyone aboard to their own quarters, then Steckel and his squad, with me as rear guide, went through the ship room by room.

We went through the hold. They weren't there either. All that was left was the reefer rooms.

A couple of the boys pushed into the cold compartments, poked around the crates of food. The fourth one they tried got them a blast of lead. They socked the deck with their chests and snaked out of there.

I pulled my heater. "I'll get them out."

"We don't need heroes," said Steckel. "Lawrence ought to have a tear gas bomb or two hooked on him. Got 'em with you, Lawrence?"

"Yeah," the dick said and unhooked one.

He flipped it into the ice room where our meat was hunkered down behind a lot of crates. The bomb gave off white streamers as Steck slammed the door.

We waited. Nothing happened; they were trying to take that murderous stuff. Getting close to the floor first, handkerchiefs next over their eyes and mouths. The guy who invents gas-proof hankies will really have something. Meanwhile there aren't any, so the door opened from the inside and the Hornes came out sobbing.

"You looked better in the hotel, chicken," I told her.

She tried to give me a frozen look, but she was shaking and blue from the cold and the tears got in her way. Fred Horne looked still worse and even scareder, but at least he didn't have mascara to run down his face.

They hadn't stopped crying when we got them back to headquarters and Steck put them away. Then the looie pulled a chair right in front of mine so his rough map was only inches away.

"Now what's the pitch, Gilroy?" he demanded. "The Hornes knew Benson had dough, got her to come to New York, then shoved her out the window. Right?"

"Almost," I said.

"But Lucille Benson really came from Sioux Falls; we checked that. And how did they get away with registering a rich dame as a maid? That's the part I don't understand."

I gave him my dirtiest grin. If I wasn't getting any credit out of this, at least I could make him stew.

"Okay, great brain," he snarled. "Let's hear it."

"Lucille Benson came from Sioux Falls, all right, and she didn't mind being registered as a maid."

"Then how come those Salt Lake City labels and what was her angle?"

I stretched my grin a little wider.

"When you get a telegram from Salt Lake City, it'll say those clothes were bought by Mrs. Fred Horne. And as for Lucille Benson's angle, you can find out by asking her."

"Stop horsing around," he snapped. "Stiffs don't talk."

"This one will because she's not a corpse. Here's what happened. Fred Horne signed the register for him, his wife and maid. Then he took the luggage up alone and his wife came over later, saying her maid would be along soon. Only there wasn't any maid. She must have stayed somewhere else for the night, then came over in the morning, helped Horne fling his wife out the window and stayed on as Mrs. Horne."

Steck shoved his chair back hard and glared at me. "Then the dame inside is—"

"Lucille Benson," I said. "That's what I've been trying to tell you."

"How do you know?"

"She made two mistakes. She sold Mrs. Horne's clothes—which wouldn't fit her—instead of destroying them, which gave me a chance to see a maid wouldn't own stuff like that. And she took the woman's bracelet; it was a lot too tight, but it was a razzle-dazzle job and she liked it, so she wore it.

"The whole idea," I continued, "was that Horne wanted to get rid of his wife. She wouldn't let him go. So he and Benson knocked her off, made her the maid—knowing we'd think nobody would want to kill their maid—and were highballing for S.A. Now let's see what the dope is from Salt Lake City."

And that's how it was. The clothes had been bought by Mrs. Fred Horne. Steckel got a full description of Lucille Benson from Sioux Falls, and the babe in the lockup fit it. She and Horne cracked and spilled over before I left headquarters toward evening.

When I got back to the hotel, I strolled into Carlton's office. He was in the middle of telling me just how fast I had to get out, when I heard a cough in the doorway.

It was Sally Fletcher, the telephone operator, and she stood in front of a gang of guys with cards in their hats and pads or cameras in their hands.

"Meet the press, Mr. Carlton," she said sweetly. "I had them come over to hear the country's number one heel fire a detective for uncovering a murder. Will it make good reading, boys?"

"Now wait a minute, fellows!" Carlton howled, running forward. "I'm afraid you got the wrong impression—"

Sally and I left. He was talking like an air drill. The press lads must have given him a rugged time, because I'm still here at the Blake.

Love in the Dark

Being Livy Gilroy wasn't easy. It meant having a face a little too long, a figure a little too plump, brown hair brushed and brushed yet always uncurling at the ends. It meant not being able to make herself more than passably attractive. Worse than that, being Livy Gilroy meant being Mrs. Gilroy, the wife of that smug lump asleep in the other bed.

Gilroy wasn't snoring; he was too neat for that. He was always making even stacks of things, or putting them in alphabetical order on shelves, or straightening rugs and pictures, or breathing neatly in the other bed.

Livy closed the bedroom door with a bang. Gilroy didn't stir; he could fall asleep in one infuriating minute, and wake up eight hours later to the second, in exactly the same unlovely position and disposition. Her high-heeled shoes didn't bother him when she kicked them off, and neither did scraping the chair back against the wall—he hated chair marks on walls—when she sat down to take off her stockings. And Livy Gilroy wanted, venomously, to bother her husband.

Gilroy had married her because he had been made sales manager of the electric battery factory, and he'd had enough of eating in restaurants while he had been a traveling salesman. Besides, it looked better for a man in his position to be married. Livy had accepted him because she was past thirty and nobody else might ask her; besides, she needed someone to support her. So she cooked for him. She cleaned for him. She even tried to keep a budget for him, though that was his idea. He gave her a meager household allowance and nothing else.

Nothing, in this case, must be understood as the complete and humiliating absence of everything. When Livy was particularly incensed about her marriage, which was generally, it was some comfort to know that she could have it easily annulled. And Gilroy couldn't do a thing to stop her. He hadn't, at least, and there was no sign that he intended to, cared to, or even thought of it.

Pulling her slip over her head, Livy wondered about this. She had heard, at least as often as any other girl, that all men were beasts. Gilroy was, of course, a beast in a way—in his special primly exasperating way. But he wasn't a beast in the usual sense. With Livy, anyway. Maybe some woman in a backstreet hovel thought he was. But that wasn't likely; he would have wedded the lady and saved the cost of this apartment.

What was wrong with Gilroy? It wasn't Livy, because she had known her duty and had been grimly prepared for it, though God knew this *tall* and pudgy person inspired nothing at all in her.

"Short and pudgy," she thought, reaching around back for the hooks. "Why doesn't somebody put hooks in front where they belong and where a body can get at them, and make a fortune? Short and pudgy is bad enough, but Gilroy's got to be tall and pudgy, with a stomach that pulls his shoulders down and caves in his chest. And those black-rimmed glasses—some oculist must have been stuck with them for years. That hair of his—thick, oily, wavy and yellow. Like butter starting to melt—"

She looked at him again. What had made her think that marrying him was better than not being married at all? She could have got at least a housekeeper's job somewhere. With the possibility that some man in the household would fall in love with her.

Livy stopped. She crossed her arms over her breasts. It was the oddest sensation.

Somebody was staring at her as she undressed.

Gilroy? It didn't seem possible, but she held her slip in front of her and flipped the switch and looked. He was on his side, one arm under his head, and his back was to her. He never looked at her in the light, so why should he stare at her in the dark?

Livy peered under the window shades. They reached the sills; nobody could see beneath them or around them. She felt like a fool bending to glance under the beds, poking warily among the dresses and suits in the closets, and searching behind the furniture.

The light aroused Gilroy; that was something. He twisted around to face her blurrily.

"What's the matter?" he asked, his thin voice fuzzily peevish.

"Somebody was watching me undress," she said.

"Here?"

She tightened her lips. "I haven't undressed in the street in years," she said. "Of course it was here!"

"You mean somebody's in the room with us?" He reached out for his glasses on the night table. "I don't see anyone."

"I know," she said flatly. "I searched the place. It's empty. Or it might as well be."

He stared at her. He wasn't, of course, looking below her face, though she still had her slip clutched in front of her. He was staring at her face as if she had a smudge on it.

"Do you often have these ideas?" he asked.

"Go on back to sleep," she said. "If you want to act like a psychiatrist, your own case would keep you busy for years."

He was still looking at her face, so she turned off the light. She held the slip until she heard him turn heavily, then grunt as he spread himself in the same position as before.

Livy hung up her slip and began peeling off her girdle. There it was again—hungry eyes peering out of the dark, touching her body with ocular caresses.

It wasn't imagination. It couldn't be. She'd been mentally undressed as often as any other not too attractive girl, and she knew the shrinking, exposed feeling too well to mistake it.

No use turning on the light again. She wouldn't find anyone in the room.

"Let's be reasonable," she thought, fighting an urge to leap into bed and scream. "I'm tired. Pooped, if you want to know. That dreary little Mrs. Hall made a hash out of the bridge game. Why do I always draw town idiots as partners? Is it some curse that was put on my family back in the Middle Ages? That's all I need; it's not enough playing house with this inspecting officer searching for dust under the furniture.

"All right, I'm exhausted and jumpy. I'm normal, or what passes for normal. If anybody mentions Freud to me, I'll start swinging this girdle like a night stick. I'm not losing my mind. I'm not having a wish-fulfillment either, if that's what you're thinking. Livy dear, it's just time I went to bed—and don't go twisting *that* statement around."

Her eyes did ache a bit; all that smoke. Maybe she should cut out cigarettes. Aching eyes could make you see things that weren't there. This wasn't exactly seeing, but maybe it was connected somehow.

Livy closed her eyes experimentally, and the effect was more startling than the skin sensation.

In the dark, with her eyes shut, she could see who was staring at her. It gave her a shock until she realized that she could *imagine* it, rather; she couldn't see unless her eyes were open, could she? She tried it and the image disappeared. She closed them again and there it was.

As long as it was her imagination, she studied the imaginary owner of the imaginary eyes. She stared at him just as intently as she imagined he was staring at her.

"Stunning," was her first verdict, and then, "What a build! I must have been peering unconsciously at those physical culture magazines on the newsstands. That long blue hair and those wide blond eyes and cute little straight nose—I always *did* love a man with a cleft in his chin! Heavens, did you ever see such muscles? And—wait a minute!"

She opened her eyes quickly. A girl had to have some modesty, even if her imagination didn't. And then something jarred her sense of logic.

Long *blue* hair and wide *blond* eyes? It must have been a twist of her subvocal tongue. She meant long blond hair and wide blue eyes. Of course.

She closed her eyes and rechecked. The hair was blue and the eyes were blond, or close enough to it. That wasn't all, either. It wasn't really hair. It was feathers. Long, very fine, like bird-of-paradise plumage; but feathers. As long as they were sort of combed flat, she could never have guessed. But her stunning imaginary man frowned as she stared at him, and the frown lifted his—well, feathers, into an attractive crest. Very attractive, in fact. She liked the effect much better than hair . . .

Peculiar. The dazzling creature was blushing under her stare, and turning his head away shyly. Was it possible to

90

blush a beautiful shocking pink? And to have pointed leprechaun ears much handsomer than the regular male clamshell variety? And since when does a mental image turn bashful?

"Who cares?" thought Livy. "You're a gorgeous thing, and any psychiatrist cures me of this particular delusion over my dead body! Now go away or I won't get a wink of sleep all night."

With her eyes shut, she saw the unearthly vision walk dutifully toward the bedroom door, open it and close it behind him.

"That you, Livy?" asked Gilroy from his bed.

"Is what me?"

"Opening the door."

"I haven't budged from this spot."

She heard him roll over and sit up again. "I'm a practical man with both feet on the ground," he said. "I don't hear things unless there's something to hear. And I heard the door open and close."

Livy pulled on her nightgown over her head—warm, thick flannel because texture and sheerness didn't matter. "All right, you heard the door open and close," she said, falling back luxuriously on her soft mattress and dragging the heavy blankets up. "You can't get me to argue with you this time of night."

"Something's wrong with you," said Gilroy. "We'll find out what it is tomorrow."

As far as she was concerned, there was nothing whatever wrong with her. Why shouldn't an unhappy woman imagine a handsome, thrilling man admiring her? Maybe there was some hidden and sinister significance in the blue plumage and pointed ears, but she didn't care to know about it.

She knew Gilroy wouldn't risk one of her tempers by waking her up to talk, so she firmly pretended to be sleeping while he dressed, made his own breakfast, and drove away. Then she got out of bed and took off the nightgown.

Sure enough, her flesh shrank. She felt as if she were being spied on.

"Look," she said testily to her subconscious, or libido, or whatever the term was, "not the first thing in the morning. Let me at least brush my teeth and have some of that black mud Gilroy calls coffee."

Anyway, it was ridiculous, right in broad daylight. Phantasms are for the dark. Any decent neurosis ought to know that.

Nevertheless, Livy closed her eyes to test her memory. The exciting dreamboat with the blue plumage, blond eyes, and gay ears was exactly the same—staring hungrily at her from somewhere near the vanity. Certainly she saw the vanity; she knew it was there, didn't she? She tried staring back, to see if her imaginary lover boy would blush and turn away again. He didn't, which probably meant that some quirk in her mind had grown bolder, for he grinned becomingly and his blond eyes smiled up and down her body.

"I never would have believed it," she muttered moodily, opening her eyes and proceeding to dress. "Rainy evenings I can understand, but I usually feel so nasty in the morning."

She was washing the dishes after breakfast when she felt the first physical symptoms of her delusion. It was a light, airy kiss on the back of her neck. Goosebumps bloomed, her spine went syrupy, her knees came unhooked.

She swiftly disposed of the thrill by blaming it on a loose end of hair. But she cautiously pinned her thatch all up under a kerchief; another few ethereal kisses there, whether uncurled hair or psychological, and she would climb the wall.

Next time she felt the kiss, it started at her neck and worked down to her shoulder, six distinct and passionate touches of warm, hard lips. Weakly she realized that her hair was still tightly bound and pinned up, and that left only one conclusion to be drawn.

"All right," she said, dizzily happy. "I'm going nutty. Wonder why I never thought of it before."

There were more kisses during the day, enough to keep her glowing. Hallucinations, of course, but wonderful ones, and she resolved to hang grimly onto them. So she left Gilroy his dinner and a note, and then went out to a movie.

In the theater, peculiarly, she felt more alone than she had at home. The picture was nothing to rave about, but she saw it three times to make sure Gilroy would be in bed when she returned.

He was, and breathing. She undressed in no great

hurry, finally accustomed to the peeping sensation. But when she was under the covers, she screamed suddenly and scrambled out. Gilroy was awake by the time she turned on the light.

"Now what?" he grumbled.

She goggled at him in alarm. "It wasn't you?" she asked.

"*What* wasn't me?"

She sat tentatively on the edge of the bed and rubbed her arm. "Somebody—I thought it was you—I could feel his fingers on my arm just as plain—"

"Whom," Gilroy asked, confused, "are you talking about?"

She put her chin out. "Somebody tried to get into bed with me."

"M-mm," Gilroy nodded solemnly, acting not at all astonished. He put his plump, white, flat feet into slippers and wrestled into a bathrobe. He said anxiously, "Now don't get alarmed, Livy. We'll see this thing through."

"Don't bother," she said. "As long as I know it wasn't you, I'm satisfied."

"I am not in the habit of slinking."

"No," she admitted, looking at him appraisingly. "You haven't the physique. Then again, if you did have, you wouldn't have to slink." She gave her head a shake. "I don't know what to think." And she began to cry.

"Now, none of that," he said. "We'll have you all right in a jiffy."

She stood up, ready to run over the beds, if necessary. "Oh, no, not now, you're not."

"I don't know what you mean," he said, and he went to the telephone extension and called Ben Dashman. He agreed with Ben that it was rather late, but added, "It's urgent, Ben, and you're the only one I can turn to. It's Livy nerves. They've—snapped! You'll have to get your clothes on and come right over."

"Ben Dashman," said Livy scornfully. "Here's one consumer whose resistance that business psychologist can't break down. The two of you will just get to your offices all tired out tomorrow, and for what?"

"When there is a crisis, sleep is a secondary consideration," Gilroy said. "Ben and I are men of action. This will not be the first time we've worked through the night."

"But Ben, when he arrived, sat on a chair at one side of her bed, and Gilroy sat on his own bed and explained to Ben, over Livy's indignant body, the little he knew of what he referred to as her case. Though the information didn't amount to much, it made her just as embarrassed as the first peeping incident.

If Gilroy was pompous and oratorical, and he was, Ben Dashman could claim the doubtful credit. Gilroy had modeled himself after that successful expert on business psychology, who had read his way up to the vice presidency in charge of sales. Ben could quote whole chapters of inspirational and analytical studies, whereas Gilroy had mastered no more than brief sentences and paragraphs. The voice had a lot to do with Ben's sensational rise, however. Gilroy had a slightly petulant voice, about Middle C, while Ben had learned to pitch his a full octave below comfort and to propel his words like strung spitballs.

Physically, Ben was even less appetizing than Gilroy. He had a bigger stomach, wider hips, rounder shoulders, white hair split in the center and stuck damply to his pink head, heavy lips that he loved to pucker thoughtfully, and pince-nez. Gilroy would have paid a lot for a pince-nez that would stay on him, but they either stopped his circulation or fell off.

"Well," said Ben when Gilroy was through. Livy won the bet she had made with herself that that would be his first response; it gave him time to think. "Do you have anything to add, Livy?"

"Sure. Go home, or take Gilroy out to a bar. I want to go to sleep."

"I mean about your—strange feeling," Ben persisted.

"I recommend it to all women," she said. "If I knew how, I'd manufacture and sell these dream admirers on the installment plan, and give them free to the needy. It's made me ten years younger. Now go away. I've a date with my delusion."

"Listen," said Gilroy earnestly. "Ben got out of bed and came over here to help you. We both want to help you. Ben has read all there is to know about mental cases."

"I'm not a mental case," Livy said. "I was until now, but I'm not any more. If you both want to help me, you can develop amnesia and wander out of my life. For good. If I'm sick, it's of you."

Gilroy's face went purple, but Ben pacified him hastily:

"Don't answer her, Gilroy. She doesn't know what she's saying. You know how it is with these things."

"The only reason he married me was to save money on a housekeeper," she said in a deliberate tone.

"That's right—" Ben encouraged her, patronizingly.

"Are you agreeing with her?" Gilroy shouted.

"I mean that's right—let her get things off her chest," Ben explained. "It releases tension."

So Livy kept talking and it was wonderful. She said the most insultingly true things about Gilroy and he didn't dare turn them into argument. She didn't know much about psychiatry, but she accused him of all the terms she could remember. It was the first time she had examined out loud the facts of her limitation marriage.

"Come to think of it," she concluded, "I don't know why I stayed here this long. As soon as I can get some money together, or a job, I'll let you know my forwarding address."

Then she went to sleep. Ben assured Gilroy that she seemed to have unburdened her grievances and should have no further disturbances. Her threat to leave he considered mere bravado. He advised rest and a sympathetic attitude.

Taking Ben to the door, Gilroy thanked him abjectly: "I don't know what I would have done without you."

"Forget it," said Ben. "If we didn't all pitch in and help each other when the footing gets rocky, there'd be no cooperation in this world."

"That's right," Gilroy said, brightening. "Wasn't it Emerson who pointed out that cooperation is the foundation of civilization?"

"It's always safe to give Emerson the credit," Ben answered. "Now just don't worry about Livy. If she shows any alarming signs of tension, call me up, day or night, and I'll be glad to do what I can."

It was two months before Livy moved out, actually, and then only because she had no real choice. Finding a job had been harder than she anticipated. She had no experience and the best part of the day to go job-hunting had usually been taken up by cooking, cleaning, shopping, sending out the laundry, and reading. For she had begun consuming psychology books—both normal and abnormal—searching for a parallel to her condition.

She found roughly similar cases, some which were almost identical in unimportant respects. But the really significant symptom, which urged her on in her hunt, she found nowhere.

None of the systematically deluded women had ever had a baby by an imaginary sweetheart. And Livy, her doctor had told her after the usual tests, was indisputably pregnant.

"But that's impossible," she had protested.

"I thought so myself," the doctor, who was Gilroy's physician also, had confessed. "But, you see, the profession is full of surprises."

"That isn't what I mean," Livy said in a panic.

She asked for some aromatic spirits in water. She wanted a chance to rehearse her answer. It sounded absurd even to herself.

She and Gilroy had not changed the basis of her marriage. Gilroy *couldn't* be the father of her child. He wasn't. It was impossible. Under the circumstances, it was absolutely impossible. Yet it was also impossible for her to be pregnant. She had an alibi for every minute of their marriage.

But these days, she realized numbly, when a doctor tells a woman she is going to have a baby, she can start buying a layette.

So she shuffled out of the doctor's office, clutching her list of medical instructions, and that night she told Gilroy.

Gilroy didn't bark or howl; he called Ben Dashman instead. Ben understood the situation instantly.

"Livy's conscience caused those delusions," he said. "She has obviously been having an affair."

"There was nothing obvious about it," Livy said. "It was so unobvious, in fact, that I didn't know about it myself."

This time Ben Dashman's presence didn't stop Gilroy from losing his temper. "Are you denying," he yelled, "that you *have* been having an affair?"

"Certainly," said Livy. "I'd know about it, wouldn't I?"

"Well, that's a point, Gilroy," Ben said ponderously. "In the condition Livy's been in lately, she might not have been responsible."

"*I'm* not going to be responsible, and that's for sure," Gilroy said. "We'll find out who the man is if we have to dig clean through her unconscious and down to her pituitary gland!"

Gilroy threw his glasses, the big black-rimmed ones, on the floor and trampled on them. Livy felt a little proud. She had never seen him so angry before. She had never suspected that she could have such an effect on him, or she might have tried it long ago.

"Livy," Ben said gently, "you do know who the man was, don't you?"

"Sure," she said. "It was my dreamboat, my lover boy—the one who ogled me while I was undressing, the one who tried to get into bed with me. I didn't let him until you convinced me he wasn't real. Then I didn't see any reason to be afraid."

"You mean," said Gilroy, terrible in his self-control, "right here in the same room with me?"

"Why not?" she asked reasonably. "It was just a delusion. Do I go around censoring *your* dreams? Though heaven knows they're probably just about selling campaigns and how to make people battery conscious!"

Ben waved Gilroy to silence. "Then am I to understand," he said, "that your only meetings with your so-called dreamboat have been here in your own bedroom, with your husband asleep in the next bed?"

"That's right," Livy said. "Exactly."

Ben stood up and pointed unpleasantly at Gilroy. "You," he said nastily, "are an ungrateful, inconsiderate, lying scoundrel."

"I am?" Gilroy asked, baffled out of his outrage. "How do you figure that, Ben?"

"Because for some obscure reason you're trying to blacken the name of your wife, when it's perfectly clear that the only man who could be the father is you."

"Oh, no! I can prove it isn't!"

"I'll bet," Livy said, "he could at that. But he doesn't have to, Ben. I'll give him an affidavit that he isn't."

"You see?" Gilroy cried triumphantly.

Ben nodded. "I guess I do. Livy, I respect your gallantry, but it's a mistake to protect the guilty party."

"You don't catch me getting gallant at a time like this," Livy said. "I can't tell you his name, because I don't know it, but I'll be glad to tell you who he is."

She described the phantom who loved her.

"Blue feathers!" yelled Gilroy. "Blond eyes! She isn't crazy, Ben. Oh, no, she thinks *we* are!"

Ben stood up. "Gilroy, I think we need a conference." Gilroy followed him unwillingly and when Livy opened the door carefully, a few moments later, she heard Ben say, "I've read about cases like this. It's a very grave, very deep disturbance—too deep for me to handle, though I'd love to try and I believe I'd do pretty well. But the first thing she needs is protection. From herself and this unscrupulous vandal she imagines has blue plumage and blond eyes."

And Gilroy asked, "Then you think she really believes this nonsense?"

And Ben said, "Of course, poor girl. She's batty. Use your head."

And Gilroy said slowly, "I never thought of that. But why would she claim he's invisible?"

Livy could picture Ben lifting his fat shoulders. "It might take months or years to find out, and the important thing right now is to protect her. That wouldn't hurt you either, Gilroy. Nobody puts any stock in what a patient at a rest home says."

There was more discussion, but Livy didn't stay to hear it. She had climbed out the kitchen window and over the low backyard fence. Finding a taxi took a while, but she got downtown and closed out her savings account.

Now all she had to do was find a place to live. She couldn't go back to Gilroy, of course, and she had some bad moments imagining that her description had been broadcast and that she would be picked up and sent to an asylum. She wasn't worried for herself. But Lover Boy might not find her, and she wouldn't be able to get out and search for him.

Among the classified ads she came across a two-room furnished apartment. It turned out to be across the street from a lumber yard, far enough away from Gilroy to be relatively safe; and the rental was low. She could live on her savings until the baby was born. What would happen after that didn't seem to matter much right now.

When she went to bed, she felt strangely alone. It wasn't Gilroy sleeping in the other bed that she missed. She had felt alone in the same room with him up until she thought up Dreamboat. Where was he? She squeezed her eyes shut and concentrated. No, he wasn't there. Gilroy's house must have been the special habitat of that particular hallucination.

She disliked facing Gilroy again, and perhaps Ben too, but there apparently was no other way to bring back her blue-plumed, stunning mental phantom. She dressed and called a cab.

There was a light in the bedroom, but she saved investigating that for last. She let herself in with her own key and took off her shoes, then slid through all the other rooms with her eyes firmly shut. Establishing no contact, she opened the bedroom door—and there he was.

His lips were grim, his cleft chin jutted, his blond eyes were savage, and he held his fists in uppercut position as he crouched like a boxer over Gilroy's raging face. He seemed to be rapping out some harsh words, but even Livy couldn't hear him.

"You stinker," she heard Gilroy snarl. "You hit me when I wasn't looking."

And Ben protested, "Don't be an idiot. Your unconscious is punishing you for the way you treated that sweet, troubled girl. I can show you cases just like yours—"

And Gilroy said, "Are you telling me I walked into something?"

Ben told him in a calm voice, "Every psychiatrist knows about the unconscious wish for punishment."

Gilroy yelled, "There's nothing unconscious about my wish to sock you on that fat jaw." And he did.

Lover Boy looked past the battle and saw her in the doorway. His angry face brought forth a slow, unearthly smile, and he walked carefully around the fighting fat men and took her hand. It may have been her imagination, but she *felt* the passionately warm, hard flesh.

She had to open her eyes outside the house and on the way back to her apartment. But she held desperately to his hand.

It was after she came home from the hospital that Ben found her. He told her he had heard of mothers radiating, but that this was the first time he had seen it. She could feel the glow in her face as she showed him the empty crib.

"I know you can't see him," she said, "but I can when I close my eyes. He's a beautiful baby. He has his father's features."

"You caused a little stir at the hospital," Ben said. "That's how I found you."

She laughed. "Oh, you mean the doctor? I thought he'd order himself a straightjacket."

"Well, delivering an invisible baby is no joke, especially when you're called away from a stag party," Ben said soberly. "He was finally convinced that it was only the liquor, but he hasn't touched a drop since. They never did discover the baby, did they?"

"I had it in my room all the time. They were afraid I'd sue and give them a lot of bad publicity, but I said it was all right." She turned away from the crib. "I don't suppose Gilroy minded the Reno divorce, did he?"

"He knew he was getting off lucky. These kisslessmarriage annulments can drive a man to changing his name and moving to another state. But tell me, Livy, how did you arrange the second marriage?"

"By telephone," she said. "I guess you've heard the groom's name and birthplace."

Ben hissed on his glasses, wiped them meticulously. "There was some mention in the newspapers."

"Clrkxsdyl 93J16," she said gaily. "I call him Clark for short. And he comes from Alpha Centauri somewhere. I wouldn't have known that, except he learned to use a typewriter—we don't hear the same frequencies, he says."

Ben's eyes slid away from hers and looked around the shabby apartment. "Well, you do seem happy, I must say."

"There's only one thing that bothers me," she said. "Clark could have picked any woman on Earth. I'm about as average as you can get without being a freak. Why did he want me?"

"There's no explaining love," Ben evaded uneasily. He put his pudgy hand in his inside pocket and looked directly at her. "Let's not have any false pride," he said. "You haven't asked Gilroy for a cent, but you have no income and I'd be glad—"

"Oh, we're doing fine," said Livy, shaking her hair, which she had let grow long and straight with no sign of a permanent. "We're getting a raise soon."

"A raise?" Ben was surprised. "From where? For doing what?"

"I'm supposed to be working for Grant's Detective

Agency. But it's really Clark who's the operative—private eye, he calls it now, after reading all those mystery stories—and he types up the reports. All I have to do is correct his English now and then. Imagine, he's even learning slang. Grant can't figure out how we get information that's so hard to uncover, but it's easier than pie for Clark."

"Sure," said Ben, going to the door. "But what are you laughing at?"

"Those blue feathers. They tickle!"

Although Ben could have dropped the situation there, there was one thing you could say for him; he was conscientious. He made one more investigation.

"What do you want to know about her for?" Mr. Grant asked coldly and suspiciously.

"I'm a friend of hers," Ben explained, handing Grant his business card. "I just want to make sure she's earning a good living. She divorced a—well, somebody I used to know, and she wouldn't take any alimony. I offered to help out, but she said she's doing all right working for you."

Grant's professionally slitted eyes developed a glint of smug possession. "Oh, I was afraid you might want to hire her away from me," he said. "That girl is the best operative I ever had. She could shadow a nervous sparrow. Why, she's got methods—"

"Good, huh?"

"Good?" repeated Grant. "You'd think she was invisible!"

A Matter of Form

Gilroy's telephone bell jangled into his slumber. With his eyes grimly shut, the reporter flopped over on his side, ground his ear into the pillow and pulled the cover over his head. But the bell jarred on. When he blinked his eyes open and saw rain streaking the windows, he gritted his teeth against the insistence clangor and yanked off the receiver. He swore into the transmitter—not a trite blasphemy, but a poetic opinion of the sort of man who woke tired reporters at four in the morning.

"Don't blame me," his editor replied after a bitter silence. "It was your idea. You wanted the case. They found another whatsit."

Gilroy instantly snapped awake. "They found another catatonic!"

"Over on York Avenue near Ninety-first Street, about an hour ago. He's down in the observation ward at Memorial." The voice suddenly became low and confiding. "Want to know what I think, Gilroy?"

"What?" Gilroy asked in an expectant whisper.

"I think you're nuts. These catatonics are nothing but tramps. They probably drank themselves into catatonia, whatever that is. After all, be reasonable, Gilroy; they're only worth a four-line clip."

Gilroy was out of bed and getting dressed with one hand. "Not this time, chief," he said confidently. "Sure, they're only tramps, but that's part of the story. Look ... *hey*! You should have been off a couple of hours ago. What's holding you up?"

The editor sounded disgruntled. "Old Man Talbot. He's seventy-six tomorrow. Had to pad out a blurb on his life."

"What! Wasting time whitewashing that murderer, racketeer—"

"Take it easy, Gilroy," the editor cautioned. "He's got a half interest in the paper. He doesn't bother us often."

"Okay. But he's still the city's one-man crime wave. Well, he'll kick off soon. Can you meet me at Memorial when you quit work?"

"In this weather?" The editor considered. "I don't know. Your news instinct is tops, and if you think this is big—oh, hell ... yes!"

Gilroy's triumphant grin soured when he ripped his foot through a sock. He hung up and explored empty drawers for another pair.

The street was cold and miserably deserted. The black

snow was melting to grimy slush. Gilroy hunched into his coat and sloshed in the dirty sludge toward Greenwich Avenue. He was very tall and incredibly thin. With his head down into the driving swirl of rain, his coat flapping around his skinny shanks, his hands deep in his pockets, and his sharp elbows sticking away from his rangy body, he resembled an unhappy stork peering around for a fish.

But he was far from being unhappy. He was happy, in fact, as only a man with a pet theory can be when facts begin to fight on his side.

Splashing through the slush, he shivered when he thought of the catatonic who must have been lying in it for hours, unable to rise, until he was found and carried to the hospital. Poor devil! The first had been mistaken for a drunk, until the cop saw the bandage on his neck.

"Escaped post-brain-operatives," the hospital had reported. It sounded reasonable, except for one thing—catatonics don't walk, crawl, feed themselves, or perform *any* voluntary muscular action. Thus Gilroy had not been particularly surprised when no hospital or private surgeon claimed the escaped post-operatives.

A taxi driver hopefully sighted his agitated figure through the rain. Gilroy restrained an urge to hug the hackie for rescuing him from the bitter wind. He clambered in hastily.

"Nice night for a murder," the driver observed conversationally.

"Are you hinting that business is bad?"

"I mean the weather's lousy."

"Well, damned if it isn't!" Gilroy exclaimed caustically. "Don't let it slow you down, though. I'm in a hurry. Memorial Hospital, quick!"

The driver looked concerned. He whipped the car out into the middle of the street and scooted through a light that was just an instant too slow.

Three catatonics in a month! Gilroy shook his head. It was a real puzzler. They couldn't have escaped. In the first place, if they had, they would have been claimed; and in the second place, it was physically impossible. And how did they acquire those neat surgical wounds on the backs of their necks, closed with two professional stitches and covered with a professional bandage? New wounds, too!

Gilroy attached special significance to the fact that they were very poorly dressed and suffered from slight malnutrition. But what was the significance? He shrugged. It was an instinctive hunch.

The taxi suddenly swerved to the curb and screeched to a stop. He thrust a bill through the window and got out. The night burst abruptly. Rain smashed against him in a roaring tide. He battered upwind to the hospital entrance.

He was soaked, breathless, half-repentant for his whim in attaching importance to three impoverished catatonics. He gingerly put his hand in his clammy coat and brought out a sodden identification card.

The girl at the reception desk glanced at it. "Oh, a newspaperman! Did a big story come in tonight?"

"Nothing much," he said casually. "Some poor tramp found on York and Ninety-first. Is he up in the screwball ward?"

She scanned the register and nodded. "Is he a friend of yours?"

"My grandson." As he moved off, both flinched at the sound of water squishing in his shoes at each step. "I must have stepped in a puddle."

When he turned around in the elevator, she was shaking her head and pursing her lips maternally. Then the ground floor dropped away.

He went through the white corridor unhesitantly. Low, horrible moans came from the main ward. He heard them with academic detachment. Near the examination room, the sound of the rising elevator stopped him. He paused, turning to see who it was.

The editor stepped out, chilled, wet, and disgusted. Gilroy reached down and caught the smaller man's arm, guiding him silently through the door and into the examination room. The editor sighed resignedly.

The resident physician glanced up briefly when they unobtrusively took places in the ring of interns about the bed. Without effort, Gilroy peered over the heads before him, inspecting the catatonic with clinical absorption.

The catatonic had been stripped of his wet clothing, toweled, and rubbed with alcohol. Passive, every muscle absolutely relaxed, his eyes were loosely closed, and his mouth hung open in idiotic slackness. The dark line of removed surgical plaster showed on his neck. Gilroy strained to one side. The hair had been clipped. He saw part of a stitch.

"Catatonia, doc?" he asked quietly.

"Who are you?" the physician snapped.

"Gilroy . . . *Morning Post*."

The doctor gazed back at the man on the bed. "It's catatonia, all right. No trace of alcohol or inhibiting drugs. Slight malnutrition."

Gilroy elbowed politely through the ring of interns. "Insulin shock doesn't work, eh? No reason why it should."

"Why shouldn't it?" the doctor demanded, startled. "It always works in catatonia . . . at least, temporarily."

"But it didn't in this case, did it?" Gilroy insisted brusquely.

The doctor lowered his voice defeatedly. "No."

"What's this all about?" the editor asked in irritation. "What's catatonia, anyhow? Paralysis, or what?"

"It's the last stage of schizophrenia, or what used to be called dementia praecox," the physician said. "The mind revolts against responsibility and searches for a period in its existence when it was not troubled. It goes back to childhood and finds that there are childish cares; goes further and comes up against infantile worries; and finally ends up in a prenatal mental state."

"But it's a gradual degeneration," Gilroy stated. "Long before the complete mental decay, the victim is detected and put in an asylum. He goes through imbecility, idiocy, and after years of slow degeneration, winds up refusing to use his muscles or brain."

The editor looked baffled. "Why should insulin shock pull him out?'

"It shouldn't!" Gilroy rapped out.

"It should!" the physician replied angrily. "Catatonia is negative revolt. Insulin drops the sugar content of the blood to the point of shock. The sudden hunger jolts the catatonic out of his passivity."

"That's right," Gilroy said incisively. "But this isn't catatonia! It's mighty close to it, but you never heard of a catatonic who didn't refuse to carry on voluntary muscular action. There's no salivary retention! My guess is that it's paralysis."

"Caused by what?" the doctor asked bitingly.

"That's for you to say. I'm not a physician. How about the wound at the base of the skull?"

"Nonsense! It doesn't come within a quarter inch of the motor nerve. It's *cerias flexibilitas* . . . waxy flexibility." He raised the victim's arm and let go. It sagged slowly. "If it were general paralysis, it would have affected the brain. He'd have been dead."

Gilroy lifted his bony shoulders and lowered them. "You're on the wrong track, doc," he said quietly. "The wound has a lot to do with his condition, and catatonia can't be duplicated by surgery. Lesions can cause it, but the degeneration would still be gradual. And catatonics can't walk or crawl away. He was deliberately abandoned, same as the others."

"Looks like you're right, Gilroy," the editor conceded. "There's something fishy here. All three of them had the same wounds?"

"In exactly the same place, at the base of the skull and to the left of the spinal column. Did you ever see anything so helpless? Imagine him escaping from a hospital, or even a private surgeon!"

The physician dismissed the interns and gathered up his instruments preparatory to harried flight. "I don't see the motive. All three of them were undernourished, poorly clad; they must have been living in substandard conditions. Who would want to harm them?"

Gilroy bounded in front of the doctor, barring his way. "But it doesn't have to be revenge! It could be experimentation!"

"To prove what?"

Gilroy looked at him quizzically. "You don't know?"

"How should I?"

The reporter clapped his drenched hat on backward and darted to the door. "Come on, chief. We'll ask Moss for a theory."

"You won't find Dr. Moss here," the physician said. "He's off at night, and tomorrow, I think, he's leaving the hospital."

Gilroy stopped abruptly. "Moss . . . leaving the hospital!" he repeated in astonishment. "Did you hear that, chief? He's a dictator, a slave driver and a louse. But he's probably the greatest surgeon in America. Look at that. Stories breaking all around you, and you're whitewashing Old Man Talbot's murderous life!" His coat bellied out in the wash of his swift, gaunt stride. "Three catatonics found lying on the street in a month. That never happened before. They can't walk or crawl, and they have mysterious wounds at the base of their skulls. Now the greatest surgeon in the country gets kicked out of the hospital he built up to first place. And what do you do? You sit in the office and write stories about what a swell guy Talbot is underneath his slimy exterior!"

The resident physician was relieved to hear the last of that relentlessly incisive, logical voice trail down the corridor. But he gazed down at the catatonic before leaving the room.

He felt less certain that it was catatonia. He found himself quoting the editor's remark—there definitely *was* something fishy there!

But what was the motive in operating on three obviously destitute men and abandoning them; and how had the operation caused a state resembling catatonia?

In a sense, he felt sorry that Dr. Moss was going to be discharged. The cold, slave-driving dictator might have given a good theory. That was the physician's scientific conscience speaking. Inside, he really felt that anything was worth getting away from that silkily mocking voice and the delicately sneering mouth.

At Fifty-fifth Street, Wood came to the last Sixth Avenue employment office. With very little hope, he read the crudely chalked signs. It was an industrial employment agency. Wood had never been inside a factory. The only job he could fill was that of apprentice upholsterer, ten dollars a week; but he was thirty-two years old and the agency would require five dollars immediate payment.

He turned away dejectedly, fingering the three dimes in his pocket. Three dimes—the smallest, thinnest American coins . . .

"Anything up there, Mac?"

"Not for me," Wood replied wearily. He scarcely glanced at the man.

He took a last glance at his newspaper before dropping it to the sidewalk. That was the last paper he'd buy, he resolved; with his miserable appearance he couldn't answer advertisements. But his mind clung obstinately to Gilroy's article. Gilroy had described the horror of catatonia. A notion born of defeat made it strangely attractive to Wood. At least, the catatonics were fed and housed. He wondered if catatonia could be simulated . . .

But the other had been scrutinizing Wood. "College man, ain't you?" he asked as Wood trudged away from the employment office.

Wood paused and ran his hand over his stubbled face. Dirty cuffs stood away from his fringing sleeves. He knew that his hair curled long behind his ears. "Does it still show?" he asked bitterly.

"You bet. You can spot a college man a mile away."

Wood's mouth twisted. "Glad to hear that. It must be an inner light shining through the rags."

"You're a sucker coming down here with an education. Down here they want poor slobs who don't know any better . . . guys like me, with big muscles and small brains."

Wood looked up at him sharply. He was too well-dressed and alert to have prowled the agencies for any length of time. He might have just lost his job; perhaps he was looking for company. But Wood had met his kind before. He had the hard eyes of the wolf who preyed on the jobless.

"Listen," Wood said coldly, "I haven't a thing you'd want. I'm down to thirty cents. Excuse me while I sneak my books and toothbrush out of my room before the super snatches them."

The other did not recoil or protest virtuously. "I ain't blind," he said quietly. "I can see you're down and out."

"Then what do you want?" Wood snapped ill-temperedly. "Don't tell me you want a threadbare but filthy college man for company—"

His unwelcome friend made a gesture of annoyance. "Cut out the mad-dog act. I was turned down on a job today because I ain't a college man. Seventy-five a month, room and board doctor's assistant. But I got the air because I ain't a grad."

"You've got my sympathy," Wood said, turning away.

The other caught up with him. "You're a college grad.

Do you want the job? It'll cost you your first week's pay ... my cut, see?"

"I don't know anything about medicine. I was a code expert in a stockbroker's office before people stopped having enough money for investments. Want any codes deciphered? That's the best I can do."

He grew irritated when the stranger stubbornly matched his dejected shuffle.

"You don't have to know anything about medicine. Long as you got a degree, a few muscles and a brain, that's all the doc wants."

Wood stopped short and wheeled.

"Is that on the level?"

"Sure. But I don't want to take a deadhead up there and get turned down. I got to ask you the questions they asked me."

In face of a prospective job, Wood's caution ebbed away. He felt the three dimes in his pocket. They were exceedingly slim and unprotective. They meant two hamburgers and two cups of coffee, or a bed in some filthy hotel dormitory. Two thin meals and sleeping in the wet March air; or shelter for a night and no food ...

"Shoot!" he said deliberately.

"Any relatives?"

"Some fifth cousins in Maine."

"Friends?"

"None who would recognize me now." He searched the stranger's face. "What's this all about? What have my friends or relatives got to do—"

"Nothing," the other said hastily. "Only you'll have to travel a little. The doc wouldn't want a wife dragging along, or have you break up your work by writing letters. See?"

Wood didn't see. It was a singularly lame explanation; but he was concentrating on the seventy-five a month, room and *board*—food.

"Who's the doctor?" he asked.

"I ain't dumb." The other smiled humorlessly. "You'll go there with me and get the doc to hand over my cut."

Wood crossed to Eighth Avenue with the stranger. Sitting in the subway, he kept his eyes from meeting casual, disinterested glances. He pulled his feet out of the aisle, against the base of the seat, to hide the loose, flapping right sole. His hands were cracked and scaly, with tenacious dirt deeply embedded. Bitter, defeated, with the appearance of a mature waif. What a chance there was of being hired! But at least the stranger had risked a nickel on his fare.

Wood followed him out at 103rd Street and Central Park West; they climbed the hill to Manhattan Avenue and headed several blocks downtown. The other ran briskly up the stoop of an old house. Wood climbed the steps more slowly. He checked an urge to run away, but he experienced in advance the sinking feeling of being turned away from a job. If he could only have his hair cut, his suit pressed, his shoes mended! But what was the use of thinking about that? It would cost a couple of dollars. And nothing could be done about his ragged hems.

"Come on!" the stranger called.

Wood tensed his back and stood looking at the house while the other brusquely rang the doorbell. There were three floors and no card above the bell, no doctor's white glass sign in the darkly curtained windows. From the outside it could have been a neglected boardinghouse.

The door opened. A man of his own age, about middle height, but considerably overweight, blocked the entrance. He wore a white laboratory apron. Incongruous in his pale, soft face, his nimble eyes were harsh.

"Back again?" he asked impatiently.

"It's not for me this time," Wood's persistent friend said. "I got a college grad."

Wood drew back in humiliation when the fat man's keen glance passed over his wrinkled, frayed suit and stopped distastefully at the long hair blowing wildly around his hungry, unshaven face. There—he could see it coming: "Can't use him."

But the fat man pushed back a beautiful collie with his leg and held the door wide. Astounded, Wood followed his acquaintance into the narrow hall. To give an impression of friendliness, he stooped and ruffled the dog's ears. The fat man led them into a bare front room.

"What's your name?" he asked indifferently.

Wood's answer stuck in his throat. He coughed to clear it. "Wood," he replied.

"Any relatives?" Wood shook his head.

"Friends?"

"Not anymore."

"What kind of degree?"

"Science, Columbia, 1925."

The fat man's expression did not change. He reached into his left pocket and brought out a wallet. "What arrangement did you make with this man?"

"He's to get my first week's salary." Silently, Wood observed the transfer of several green bills; he looked at them hungrily, pathetically. "May I wash up and shave, doctor?" he asked.

"I'm not the doctor," the fat man answered. "My name is Clarence, without a mister in front of it." He turned swiftly to the sharp stranger. "What are you hanging around for?"

Wood's friend backed to the door. "Well, so long," he said. "Good break for both of us, eh, Wood?"

Wood smiled and nodded happily. The trace of irony in the stranger's hard voice escaped him entirely.

"I'll take you upstairs to your room," Clarence said when Wood's business partner had left. "I think there's a razor there."

They went out into the dark hall, the collie close behind them. An unshaded lightbulb hung on a single wire above a gate-leg table. On the wall behind the table an oval, gilt mirror gave back Wood's hairy, unkempt image. A worn carpet covered the floor to a door cutting off the rear of the house, and narrow stairs climbed in a swift spiral to the next story. It was cheerless and neglected, but Wood's conception of luxury had become less exacting.

"Wait here while I make a telephone call," Clarence said.

He closed the door behind him in a room opposite the stairs. Wood fondled the friendly collie. Through the panel he heard Clarence's voice, natural and unlowered.

"Hello, Moss? . . . Pinero brought back a man. All his answers are all right . . . Columbia, 1925 . . . Not a cent, judging from his appearance . . . Call Talbot? For when? . . . Okay . . . You'll get back as soon as you get through with the board? . . . Okay . . . Well, what's the difference? You got all you wanted from them, anyhow."

Wood heard the receiver's click as it was replaced and taken off again. Moss? That was the head of Memorial Hospital—the great surgeon. But the article about the catatonics hinted something about his removal from the hospital.

"Hello, Talbot?" Clarence was saying. "Come around at noon tomorrow. Moss says everything'll be ready then . . . Okay, don't get excited. This is positively the last one! . . . Don't worry. Nothing can go wrong."

Talbot's name sounded familiar to Wood. It might have been the Talbot that the *Morning Post* had written about—the seventy-six-year-old philanthropist. He probably wanted Moss to operate on him. Well, it was none of his business.

When Clarence joined him in the dark hall, Wood thought only of his seventy-five a month, room and board; but more than that, he had a job! A few weeks of decent food and a chance to get some new clothes, and he would soon get rid of his defeatism.

He even forgot his wonder at the lack of shingles and waiting-room signs that a doctor's house usually had. He could only think of his neat room on the third floor, overlooking a bright backyard. And a shave . . .

Dr. Moss replaced the telephone with calm deliberation. Striding through the white hospital corridor to the elevator, he was conscious of curious stares. His pink, scrupulously shaven, clean-scrubbed face gave no answer to their questioning eyes. In the elevator he stood with his hands thrust casually into his pockets. The operator did not dare to look at him or speak.

Moss gathered his hat and coat. The space around the reception desk seemed more crowded than usual, with men who had the penetrating look of reporters. He walked swiftly past.

A tall, astoundingly thin man, his stare fixed predatorily on Moss, headed the wedge of reporters that swarmed after Moss.

"You can't leave without a statement to the press, doc!" he said.

"I find it very easy to do," Moss taunted without stopping.

He stood on the curb with his back turned coldly on the reporters and unhurriedly flagged a taxi.

"Well, at least you can tell us whether you're still director of the hospital," the tall reporter said.

"Ask the board of trustees."

"Then how about a theory on the catatonics?"

"Ask the catatonics." The cab pulled up opposite Moss. Deliberately he opened the door and stepped in. As he rode away, he heard the thin man exclaim: "What a cold, clammy reptile!"

He did not look back to enjoy their discomfiture. In spite of his calm demeanor, he did not feel too easy himself. The man on the *Morning Post*, Gilroy or whatever his name was, had written a sensational article on the abandoned catatonics, and even went so far as to claim they were not catatonics. He had had all he could do to keep from being involved in the conflicting riot of theory. Talbot owned a large interest in the paper. He must be told to strangle the articles, although by now all the papers were taking up the cry.

It was a clever piece of work, detecting the fact that the victims weren't suffering from catatonia at all. But the *Morning Post* reporter had cut himself a man-size job in trying to understand how three men with general paralysis could be abandoned without a trace of where they had come from, and what connection the incisions had on their condition. Only recently had Moss himself solved it.

The cab crossed to Seventh Avenue and headed uptown.

The trace of his parting smile of mockery vanished. His mobile mouth whitened, tight-lipped and grim. Where was he to get money from now? He had milked the hospital funds to a frightening debt, and it had not been enough. Like a bottomless maw, his research could drain a dozen funds.

If he could convince Talbot, prove to him that his failures had not really been failures, that this time he would not slip up . . .

But Talbot was a tough nut to crack. Not a cent was coming out of his miserly pocket until Moss completely convinced him that he was past the experimental stage. This time there would be no failure!

At Moss's street, the cab stopped and the surgeon sprang out lightly. He ran up the steps confidently, looking neither to the left nor to the right, though it was a fine day with a warm yellow sun, and between the two lines of old houses Central Park could be seen budding greenly.

He opened the door and strode almost impatiently into the narrow, dark hall, ignoring the friendly collie that bounded out to greet him.

"Clarence!" he called out. "Get your new assistant down. I'm not even going to wait for a meal." He threw off his hat, coat, and jacket, hanging them up carelessly on a hook near the mirror.

"Hey, Wood!" Clarence shouted up the stairs. "Are you finished?"

They heard a light, eager step race down from the third floor.

"Clarence, my boy," Moss said in a low, impetuous voice, "I know what the trouble was. We didn't really fail at all. I'll show you . . . we'll follow exactly the same technique!"

"Then why didn't it seem to work before?"

Wood's feet came into view between the rails on the second floor. "You'll understand as soon as it's finished," Moss whispered hastily, and then Wood joined them.

Even the short time that Wood had been employed was enough to transform him. He had lost the defeatist feeling of being useless human flotsam. He was shaved and washed, but that did not account for his kindled eyes.

"Wood . . . Dr. Moss," Clarence said perfunctorily.

Wood choked out an incoherent speech that was meant to inform them that he was happy, though he didn't know anything about medicine.

"You don't have to," Moss replied silkily. "We'll teach you more about medicine than most surgeons learn in a lifetime."

It could have meant anything or nothing. Wood made no attempt to understand the meaning of the words. It was the hint of withdrawn savagery in the low voice that puzzled him. It seemed a very peculiar way of talking to a man who had been hired to move apparatus and do nothing but the most ordinary routine work.

He followed them silently into a shining, tiled operating room. He felt less comfortable than he had in his room; but when he dismissed Moss's tones as a characteristically sarcastic manner of speech, hinting more than it contained in reality, his eagerness returned. While

Moss scrubbed his hands and arms in a deep basin, Wood gazed around.

In the center of the room an operating table stood, with a clean sheet clamped unwrinkled over it. Above the table five shadowless light globes branched. It was a compact room. Even Wood saw how close everything lay to the doctor's hand—trays of tampons, swabs and clamps, and a sterilizing instrument chest that gave off puffs of steam.

"We do a lot of surgical experimenting," Moss said. "Most of your work'll be handling the anesthetic. Show him how to do it, Clarence."

Wood observed intently. It appeared simple—cut-ins and shut-offs for cyclopropane, helium, and oxygen; watch the dials for overrich mixture; keep your eye on the bellows and water filter . . .

Trained anesthetists, he knew, tested their mixture by taking a few sniffs. At Clarence's suggestion he sniffed briefly at the whispering cone. He didn't know cyclopropane—so lightning-fast that experienced anesthetists are sometimes caught by it . . .

Wood lay on the floor with his arms and legs sticking up into the air. When he tried to straighten them, he rolled over on his side. Still they projected stiffly. He was dizzy with the anesthetic. Something that felt like surgical plaster pulled on a sensitive spot on the back of his neck.

The room was dark, its green shades pulled down against the outer day. Somewhere above him and toward the end of the room, he heard painful breathing. Before he could raise himself to investigate, he caught the multiple tread of steps ascending and approaching the door. He drew back defensively.

The door flung open. Light flared up in the room. Wood sprang to his feet—and found he could not stand erect. He dropped back to a crawling position, facing the men who watched him with cold interest.

"He tried to stand up," the old one stated.

"What'd you think I'd do?" Wood snapped. His voice was a confused, snarling growl without words. Baffled and raging, he glared up at them.

"Cover him, Clarence," Moss said. "I'll look at the other one."

Wood turned his head from the threatening muzzle of the gun aimed at him, and saw the doctor lift the man on the bed. Clarence backed to the window and raised the shade. Strong moonlight roused the man. His profile was turned to Wood. His eyes fastened blankly on Moss's scrubbed pink face, never leaving it. Behind his ears curled long, wild hair.

"There you are, Talbot," Moss said to the old man. "He's sound."

"Take him out of bed and let's see him act like you said he would." The old man jittered anxiously on his cane.

Moss pulled the man's legs to the edge of the bed and raised him heavily to his feet. For a short time he stood without aid; then all at once he collapsed to his hands and knees. He stared full at Wood.

It took Wood a minute of startled bewilderment to recognize the face. He had seen it every day of his life, but never so detachedly. The eyes were blank and round, the facial muscles relaxed, idiotic.

But it was his own face . . .

Panic exploded in him. He gaped down at as much of himself as he could see. Two hairy legs stemmed from his shoulders, and a dog's forepaws rested firmly on the floor.

He stumbled uncertainly toward Moss. "What did you do to me?" he shouted. It came out in an animal howl. The doctor motioned the others to the door and backed away warily.

Wood felt his lips draw back tightly over his fangs. Clarence and Talbot were in the hall. Moss stood alertly in the doorway, his hand on the knob. He watched Wood closely, his eyes glacial and unmoved. When Wood sprang, he slammed the door, and Wood's shoulder crashed against it.

"He knows what happened," Moss's voice came through the panel.

It was not entirely true. Wood knew something had happened. But he refused to believe that the face of the crawling man gazing stupidly at him was his own. It was, though. And Wood himself stood on the four legs of a dog, with a surgical plaster covering a burning wound in the back of his neck.

It was crushing, numbing, too fantastic to believe. He thought wildly of hypnosis. But just by turning his head, he could look directly at what had been his own body, braced on hands and knees as if it could not stand erect.

He was outside his own body. He could not deny that. Somehow he had been removed from it; by drugs or hypnosis, Moss had put him in the body of a dog. He had to get back into his own body again.

But how do you get back into your own body?

His mind struck blindly in all directions. He scarcely heard the three men move away from the door and enter the next room. But his mind suddenly froze with fear. His human body was complete and impenetrable, closed hermetically against his now-foreign identity.

Through his congealed terror, his animal ears brought the creak of furniture. Talbot's cane stopped its nervous, insistent tapping.

"That should have convinced even you, Talbot," he heard Moss say. "Their identities are exchanged without the slightest loss of mentality."

Wood started. It meant—no, it was absurd! But it did account for the fact that his body crawled on hands and knees, unable to stand on its feet. It meant that the collie's identity was in Wood's body!

"That's okay," he heard Talbot say. "How about the operation part? Isn't it painful, putting their brains into different skulls?"

"You can't put them into different skulls," Moss answered with a touch of annoyance. "They don't fit. Besides, there's no need to exchange the whole brain. How do you account for the fact that people have retained their identities with parts of their brains removed?"

There was a pause. "I don't know," Talbot said doubtfully.

"Sometimes the parts of the brain that were removed contained nerve centers, and paralysis set in. But the identity was still there. Then what part of the brain contained the identity?"

Wood ignored the old man's questioning murmur. He listened intently, all his fears submerged in the straining of his sharp ears, in the overwhelming need to know what Moss had done to him.

"Figure it out," the surgeon said. "The identity must have been in some part of the brain that wasn't removed, that couldn't be touched without death. That's where it was. At the absolute base of the brain, where a scalpel couldn't get at it without having to cut through the skull, the three medullae, and the entire depth of the brain itself. There's a mysterious little body hidden away safely down there—less than a quarter of an inch in diameter—called the pineal gland. In some way it controls the identity. Once it was a third eye."

"A third eye, and now it controls the identity?" Talbot exclaimed.

"Why not? The gills of our fish ancestors became the Eustachian canal that controls the sense of balance.

"Until I developed a new technique in removing the gland—by excising from beneath the brain instead of through it—nothing at all was known about it. In the first place, trying to get at it would kill the patient; and oral or intravenous injections have no effect. But when I exchanged the pineals of a rabbit and a rat, the rabbit acted like a rat, and the rat like a rabbit—within their limitations, of course. It's empiricism—it works, but I don't know why."

"Then why did the first three act like . . . what's the word?"

"Catatonics. Well, the exchanges were really successful, Talbot; but I repeated the same mistake three times, until I figured it out. And by the way, get that reporter on something a little less dangerous. He's getting pretty warm. Excepting the salivary retention, the victims acted almost like catatonics, and for nearly the same reason. I exchanged the pineals of rats for the men's. Well, you can imagine how a rat would act with the relatively huge body of a man to control. It's beyond him. He simply gives up, goes into a passive revolt. But the difference between a dog's body and a man's isn't so great. The dog is puzzled, but at any rate he makes an attempt to control his new body."

"Is the operation painful?" Talbot asked anxiously.

"There isn't a bit of pain. The incision is very small, and heals in a short time. And as for recovery—you can see for yourself how swift it is. I operated on Wood and the dog last night."

Wood's dog's brain stampeded, refusing to function intelligently. If he had been hypnotized on drugged, there might have been a chance of his eventual return. But his identity had been violently and permanently ripped from his body and forced into that of a dog. He was absolutely helpless, completely dependent on Moss to return him to his body.

"How much do you want?" Talbot was asking craftily.

"Five million!"

The old man cackled in a high, cracked voice. "I'll give you fifty thousand, cash," he offered.

"To exchange your dying body for a young, strong, healthy one?" Moss asked, emphasizing each adjective with special significance. "The price is five million."

"I'll give you seventy-five thousand," Talbot said with finality. "Raising five million is out of the question. It can't be done. All my money is tied up in my . . . uh . . . syndicates. I have to turn most of the income back into merchandise, wages, overhead, and equipment. How do you expect me to have five million in cash?"

"I don't," Moss replied with faint mockery.

Talbot lost his temper. "Then what are you getting at?"

"The interest on five million is exactly half your income. Briefly, to use your business terminology, I'm muscling into your rackets."

Wood heard the old man gasp indignantly. "Not a chance!" he rasped. "I'll give you eighty thousand. That's all the cash I can raise."

"Don't be a fool, Talbot," Moss said with deadly calm. "I don't want money for the sake of feeling it. I need an assured income, and plenty of it; enough to carry on my experiments without having to bleed hospitals dry and still not have enough. If this experiment didn't interest me, I wouldn't do it even for five million, much as I need it."

"Eighty thousand!" Talbot repeated.

"Hang onto your money until you rot! Let's see, with your advanced angina pectoris, that should be about six months from now, shouldn't it?"

Wood heard the old man's cane shudder nervelessly over the floor.

"You win, you cold-blooded blackmailer," the old man surrendered.

Moss laughed. Wood heard the furniture creak as they rose and set off toward the stairs.

"Do you want to see Wood and the dog again, Talbot?"

"No. I'm convinced."

"Get rid of them, Clarence. No more abandoning them in the street for Talbot's clever reporters to theorize over. Put a silencer on your gun. You'll find it downstairs. Then leave them in the acid vat."

Wood's eyes flashed around the room in terror. He and his body had to escape. For him to escape alone would mean the end of returning to his own body. Separation would make the task of forcing Moss to give him back his body impossible.

But they were on the second floor, at the rear of the house. Even if there had been a fire escape, he could not have opened the window. The only way out was through the door.

Somehow he had to turn the knob, chance meeting Clarence or Moss on the stairs or in the narrow hall, and open the heavy front door—guiding and defending himself and his body!

The collie in his body whimpered baffledly. Wood fought off the instinctive fear that froze his dog's brain. He had to be cool.

Below, he heard Clarence's ponderous steps as he went through the rooms looking for a silencer to muffle his gun.

Gilroy closed the door of the telephone booth and fished in his pocket for a coin. Of all of mankind's scientific gadgets, the telephone booth most clearly demonstrates that this is a world of five feet nine. When Gilroy pulled a coin out of his pocket, his elbow banged against the shut door; and as he dialed his number and stooped over the mouthpiece, he was forced to bend himself into the shape of a cane. But he had conditioned his lanky body to adjust itself to things scaled below its need. He did not mind the lack of room.

But he shoved his shapeless felt hat on the back of his head and whistled softly in a discouraged manner.

"Let me talk to the chief," he said. The receiver rasped in his ear. The editor greeted him abstractedly; Gilroy knew he had just come on and was scattering papers over his desk, looking at the latest. "Gilroy, chief," the reporter said.

"What've you got on the catatonics?"

Gilroy's sharply planed face wrinkled in earnest defeat. "Not a thing, chief," he replied hollowly.

"Where were you?'

"I was in Memorial all day, looking at the catatonics and waiting for an idea."

The editor became sympathetic. "How'd you make out?" he asked.

"Not a thing. They're absolutely dumb and motionless, and nobody around here has anything to say worth listening to. How'd you make out on the police and hospital reports?"

"I was looking at them just before you called." There was a pause. Gilroy heard the crackle of papers being shoved around. "Here they are—the fingerprint bureau has no records of them. No police department in any village, town, or city recognizes their pictures."

"How about the hospitals outside New York?" Gilroy asked hopefully.

"No missing patients."

Gilroy sighed and shrugged his thin shoulders eloquently. "Well, all we have is a negative angle. They must have been picked damned carefully. All the papers around the country printed their pictures, and they don't seem to have any friends, relatives, or police records."

"How about a human-interest story," the editor encouraged; "what they eat, how helpless they are, their torn, old clothes? Pad out a story about their probable lives, judging from their features and hands. How's that? Not bad, eh?"

"Aw, chief," Gilroy moaned, "I'm licked. That padding stuff isn't my line. I'm not a sob sister. We haven't a thing to work on. These tramps had absolutely no connection with life. We can't find out who they were, where they came from, or what happened to them."

The editor's voice went sharp and incisive. "Listen to me, Gilroy!" he rapped out. "You stop that whining, do you hear me? I'm running this paper, and as long as you don't see fit to quit, I'll send you out after birth lists if I want to.

"You thought this was a good story and you convinced me that it was. Well, I'm still convinced! I want these catatonics tracked down. I want to know all about them, and how they wound up behind the eight ball. So does the public. I'm not stopping until I *do* know. Get me?

"You get to work on this story and hang onto it. Don't let it throw you! And just to show you how I'm standing behind you . . . I'm giving you a blank expense account and your own discretion. Now track these catatonics down in any way you can figure out!"

Gilroy was stunned for an instant. "Well, gosh," he stammered, confused, "I'll do my best, chief. I didn't know you felt that way."

"The two of us'll crack this story wide open, Gilroy. But just come around to me with another whine about being licked, and you can start in as copy boy for some other sheet. Do you get me? That's final!"

Gilroy pulled his hat down firmly. "I get you, chief," he declared manfully. "You can count on me right up to the hilt."

He slammed the receiver on its hook, yanked the door open, and strode out with a new determination. He felt like the power of the press, and the feeling was not unjustified. The might and cunning of a whole vast metropolitan newspaper was ranged solidly behind him. Few secrets could hide from its searching probe.

All he needed was patience and shrewd observation. Finding the first clue would be hardest; after that the story would unwind by itself. He marched toward the hospital exit.

He heard steps hastening behind him and felt a light, detaining touch on his arm. He wheeled and looked down at the resident physician, dressed in street clothes and coming on duty.

"You're Gilroy, aren't you?" the doctor asked. "Well, I was thinking about the incisions on the catatonics' necks—"

"What about them?" Gilroy demanded alertly, pulling out a pad.

"Quitting again?" the editor asked ten minutes later.

"Not me, chief!" Gilroy propped his stenographic pad on top of the telephone. "I'm hot on the trail. Listen to this. The resident physician over here at Memorial tipped me off to a real clue. He figured out that the incisions on the catatonics' necks aimed at some part of their brains. The incisions penetrate at a tangent a quarter of an inch off the vertebrae, so it couldn't have been to tamper with the spinal cord. You can't reach the posterior part of the brain from that angle, he says, and working from the back of the neck wouldn't bring you to any important part of the neck that can't be reached better from the front or through the mouth.

"If you don't cut the spinal cord with that incision, you can't account for general paralysis; and the cords definitely weren't cut.

"So he thinks the incisions were aimed at some part of the base of the brain that can't be reached from above. He doesn't know what part or how the operation would cause general paralysis.

"Got that? Okay. Well, here's the payoff:

"To reach the exact spot of the brain you want, you ordinarily take off a good chunk of skull, somewhere around the spot. But these incisions were predetermined to the last centimeter. And he doesn't know how. The surgeon worked entirely by measurements—like blind flying. He says only three or four surgeons in the country could've done it."

"Who are they, you cluck? Did you get their names?"

Gilroy became offended. "Of course. Moss in New York; Faber in Chicago; Crowninshield in Portland; maybe Johnson in Detroit."

"Well, what're you waiting for?" the editor shouted. "Get Moss!"

"Can't locate him. He moved from his Riverside Drive apartment and left no forwarding address. He was peeved. The board asked for his resignation and he left with a pretty bad name for mismanagement."

The editor sprang into action. "That leaves us four men to track down. Find Moss. I'll call up the other boys you named. It looks like a good tip."

Gilroy hung up. With half a dozen vast strides, he had covered the distance to the hospital exit, moving with ungainly, predatory swiftness.

Wood was in a mind-freezing panic. He knew it hindered him, prevented him from plotting his escape, but he was powerless to control the fearful darting of his dog's brain.

It would take Clarence only a short time to find the silencer and climb the stairs to kill him and his body. Before Clarence could find the silencer, Wood and his body had to escape.

Wood lifted himself clumsily, unsteadily, to his hind legs and took the doorknob between his paws. They refused to grip. He heard Clarence stop, and the sound of scraping drawers came to his sharp ears.

He was terrified. He bit furiously at the knob. It slipped between his teeth. He bit harder. Pain stabbed his sensitive gums, but the bitter brass dented. Hanging to the knob, he lowered himself to the floor, bending his neck sharply to turn it. The tongue clicked out of the lock. He threw himself to one side, flipping back the door as he fell. It opened a crack. He thrust his snout in the opening and forced it wide.

From below, he heard the ponderous footfalls moving again. Wood stalked noiselessly into the hall and peered down the well of the stairs. Clarence was out of sight.

He drew back into the room and pulled at his body's clothing, backing out into the hall again until the dog crawled voluntarily. It crept after him and down the stairs.

All at once Clarence came out of a room and made for the stairs. Wood crouched, trembling at the sound of metallic clicking that he knew was a silencer being fitted to a gun. He barred his body. It halted, its idiot face hanging down over the step, silent and without protest.

Clarence reached the stairs and climbed confidently. Wood tensed, waiting for Clarence to turn the spiral and come into view.

Clarence sighted them and froze rigid. His mouth opened blankly, startled. The gun trembled impotently at his side, and he stared up at them with his fat, white neck exposed and inviting. Then his chest heaved and his larynx tightened for a yell.

But Wood's long teeth cleared. He lunged high, directly at Clarence, and his fangs snapped together in midair.

Soft flesh ripped in his teeth. He knocked Clarence over; they fell down the stairs and crashed to the floor. Clarence thrashed around, gurgling. Wood smelled a sudden rush of blood that excited an alien lust in him. He flung himself clear and landed on his feet.

His body clumped after him, pausing to sniff at Clarence. He pulled it away and darted to the front door.

From the back of the house he heard Moss running to investigate. He bit savagely at the doorknob, jerking it back awkwardly, terrified that Moss might reach him before the door opened.

But the lock clicked, and he thrust the door wide with his body. His human body flopped after him on hands and knees to the stoop. He hauled it down the steps to the sidewalk and herded it anxiously toward Central Park West, out of Moss's range.

Wood glanced back over his shoulder, saw the doctor glaring at them through the curtain on the door, and, in terror, he dragged his body in a clumsy gallop to the corner where he would be protected by traffic.

He had escaped death, and he and his body were still together; but his panic grew stronger. How could he feed it, shelter it, defend it against Moss and Talbot's gangsters? And how could he force Moss to give him back his body?

But he saw that first he would have to shield his body from observation. It was hungry, and it prowled around on hands and knees, searching for food. The sight of a crawling, sniffing human body attracted disgusted attention; before long they were almost surrounded.

Wood was badly scared. With his teeth, he dragged his body into the street and guided its slow crawl to the other side, where Central Park could hide them with its trees and bushes.

Moss had been more alert. A black car sped through a red light and crowded down on them. From the other side a police car shot in and out of traffic, its siren screaming, and braked dead beside Wood and his body.

The black car checked its headlong rush.

Wood crouched defensively over his body, glowering at the two cops who charged out at them. One shoved Wood away with his foot; the other raised his body by the armpits and tried to stand it erect.

"A nut—he thinks he's a dog," he said interestedly. "The screwball ward for him, eh?"

The other nodded. Wood lost his reason. He attacked, snapping viciously. His body took up the attack, snarling horribly and biting on all sides. It was insane, hopeless; but he had no way of communicating, and he had to do something to prevent being separated from his body. The police kicked him off.

Suddenly he realized that if they had not been burdened with his body, they would have shot him. He darted wildly into traffic before they sat his body in the car.

"Want to get out and plug him before he bites somebody?" he heard.

"This nut'll take a hunk out of you," the other replied. "We'll send out an alarm from the hospital."

It drove off downtown. Wood scrambled after it. His legs pumped furiously; but it pulled away from him, and other cars came between. He lost it after a few blocks.

Then he saw the black car make a reckless turn through traffic and roar after him. It was too intently bearing down on him to have been anything but Talbot's gangsters.

His eyes and muscles coordinated with animal precision. He ran in the swift traffic, avoiding being struck, and at the same time kept watch for a footpath leading into the park.

When he found one, he sprinted into the opposite lane of traffic. Brakes screeched; a man cursed him in a loud voice. But he scurried in front of the car, gained the sidewalk, and dashed along the cement path until he came to a miniature forest of bushes.

Without hesitation, he left the path and ran through the woods. It was not a dense growth, but it covered him from sight. He scampered deep into the park.

His frightened eyes watched the carload of gangsters scour the trees on both sides of the path. Hugging the ground, he inched away from them. They beat the bushes a safe distance away from him.

While he circled behind them, creeping from cover to cover, there was small danger of being caught. But he was appalled by the loss of his body. Being near it had given him a sort of courage, even though he did not know how he was going to force Moss to give it back to him. Now, besides making the doctor operate, he had to find a way of getting near it again.

But his empty stomach was knotted with hunger. Before he could make plans he had to eat.

He crept furtively out of his shelter. The gangsters were

far out of sight. Then, with infinite patience, he sneaked up on a squirrel. The alert little animal was observant and wary. It took an exhaustingly long time before he ambushed it and snapped its spine. The thought of eating an uncooked rodent revolted him.

He dug back into his cache of bushes with his prey. When he tried to plot a line of action, his dog's brain balked. It was terrified and maddened with helplessness.

There was good reason for its fear—Moss had Talbot's gangsters out gunning for him, and by this time the police were probably searching for him as a vicious dog.

In all his nightmares he had never imagined any so horrible. He was utterly impotent to help himself. The forces of law and crime were ranged against them; he had no way of communicating the fact that he was a man to those who could possibly help him; he was completely inarticulate; and besides, *who* could help him, except Moss? Suppose he *did* manage to evade the police, the gangsters, and sneaked past a hospital's vigilant staff, and somehow succeeded in communicating . . .

Even so, only Moss could perform the operation!

He had to rule out doctors and hospitals; they were too routinized to have much imagination. But, more important than that, they could not influence Moss to operate.

He scrambled to his feet and trotted cautiously through the clumps of brush in the direction of Columbus Circle. First, he had to be alert for police and gangsters. He had to find a method of communicating—but to somebody who could understand him and exert tremendous pressure on Moss.

The city's smells came to his sensitive nostrils. Like a vast blanket, covering most of them, was a sweet odor that he identified as gasoline vapor. Above it hovered the scent of vegetation, hot and moist; and below it, the musk of mankind.

To his dog's perspective, it was a different world, with a broad, distant, terrifying horizon. Smells and sounds formed scenes in his animal mind. Yet it was interesting. The pad of his paws against the soft, cushioned ground gave him an instinctive pleasure; all the clothes he needed, he carried on him; and food was not hard to find.

While he shielded himself from the police and Talbot's gangsters, he even enjoyed a sort of freedom—but it was a cowardly freedom that he did not want, that was not worth the price. As a man, he had suffered hunger, cold, lack of shelter and security, indifference. In spite of all that, his dog's body harbored a human intelligence; he belonged on his hind legs, standing erect, living the life, good or bad, of a man.

In some way he must get back to that world, out of the solitary anarchy of animaldom. Moss alone could return him. He must be forced to do it! He must be compelled to return the body he had robbed!

But how could Wood communicate, and who could help him?

Near the end of Central Park, he exposed himself to overwhelming danger.

He was padding along a path that skirted the broad road. A cruising black car accelerated with deadly, predatory swiftness and sped abreast of him. He heard a muffled pop. A bullet hissed an inch over his head.

He ducked low and scurried back into the concealing bushes. He snaked nimbly from tree to tree, keeping obstacles between him and the line of fire.

The gangsters were out of the car. He heard them beating the brush for him. Their progress was slow, while his fleet legs pumped three hundred yards of safety away from them.

He burst out of the park and scampered across Columbus Circle, reckless of traffic. On Broadway he felt more secure, hugging the buildings with dense crowds between him and the street.

When he felt certain that he had lost the gangsters, he turned west through one-way streets, alert for signs of danger.

In coping with physical danger, he discovered that his animal mind reacted instinctively and always more cunningly than a human brain.

Impulsively, he cowered behind stoops, in doorways, behind any sort of shelter, when the traffic moved. When it stopped, packed tightly, for the light, he ran at topnotch speed. Cars skidded across his path, and several times he was almost hit; but he did not slow to a trot until he had zigzagged downtown, going steadily away from the center of the city, and reached West Street, along North River.

He felt reasonably safe from Talbot's gangsters. But a police car approached slowly under the express highway. He crouched behind an overflowing garbage can outside a filthy restaurant. Long after it was gone, he cowered there.

The shrill wind blowing over the river and across the covered docks picked a newspaper off the pile of garbage and flattened it against the restaurant window.

Through his animal mind, frozen into numbing fear, he remembered the afternoon before—standing in front of the employment agency, talking to one of Talbot's gangsters.

A thought had come to him then: that it would be pleasant to be a catatonic instead of having to starve. He knew better now. But . . .

He reared to his hind legs and overturned the garbage can. It fell with a loud crash, rolling down toward the gutter, spilling refuse all over the sidewalk. Before a restaurant worker came out, roaring abuse, he pawed through the mess and seized a twisted newspaper in his mouth. It smelled of sour, rotting food, but he caught it up and ran.

Blocks away from the restaurant, he ran across a wide, torn lot, to cover behind a crumbling building. Sheltered from the river wind, he straightened out the paper and scanned the front page.

It was a day old, the same newspaper that he had

thrown away before the employment agency. On the left column he found the catatonic story. It was signed by a reporter named Gilroy.

Then he took the edge of the street between his teeth and backed away with it until the newspaper opened clumsily, wrinkled, at the next page. He was disgusted by the fetid smell of putrefying food that clung to it; but he swallowed his gorge and kept turning the huge, stiff, unwieldy sheets with his inept teeth. He came to the editorial page and paused there, studying intently the copyright box.

He set off at a fast trot, wary against danger, staying close to walls of buildings, watching for cars that might contain either gangsters or policemen, darting across streets to shelter, trotting on . . .

The air was growing darker, and the express highway cast a long shadow. Before the sun went down, he covered almost three miles along West Street, and stopped not far from the Battery.

He gaped up at the towering *Morning Post* building. It looked impregnable, its heavy doors shut against the wind.

He stood at the main entrance, waiting for somebody to hold a door open long enough for him to lunge through it. Hopefully, he kept his eyes on an old man. When he opened the door, Wood was at his heels. But the old man shoved him back with gentle firmness.

Wood bared his fangs. It was his only answer. The man hastily pulled the door shut.

Wood tried another approach. He attached himself to a tall, gangling man who appeared rather kindly in spite of his intent face. Wood gazed up, wagging his tail awkwardly in friendly greeting. The tall man stooped and scratched Wood's ears, but he refused to take him inside. Before the door closed, Wood launched himself savagely at the thin man and almost knocked him down.

In the lobby, Wood darted through the legs surrounding him. The tall man was close behind, roaring angrily. A frightened stampede of thick-soled shoes threatened to crush Wood; but he twisted in and out between the surging feet and gained the stairs.

He scrambled up them swiftly. The second-floor entrance had plate glass doors. It contained the executive offices.

He turned the corner and climbed up speedily. The stairs narrowed, artificially illuminated. The third and fourth floors were printing-plant rooms; he ran past; clambered by the business offices, classified advertising...

At the editorial department he panted before the heavy fire door, waiting until he regained his breath. Then he gripped the knob between his teeth and pulled it around. The door swung inward.

Thick, bitter smoke clawed his sensitive nostrils; his ears flinched at the clattering, shouting bedlam.

Between rows of littered desks, he inched and gazed around hopefully. He saw abstracted faces, intent on typewriters that rattled out stories; young men racing around to gather batches of papers; men and women swarming in and out of the elevators. Shrewd faces, intelligent and alert . . .

A few had turned for an instant to look at him as he passed, then turned back to their work, almost without having seen him.

He trembled with elation. These were the men who had the power to influence Moss, and the acuteness to understand him! He squatted and put his paw on the leg of a typing reporter, staring up expectantly. The reporter stared, looked down agitatedly, and shoved him away.

"Go on, beat it!" he said angrily. "Go home!"

Wood shrank back. He did not sense danger. Worse than that, he had failed. His mind worked rapidly: suppose he *had* attracted interest, how would he have communicated his story intelligibly? How could he explain in the equivalent of words?

All at once the idea exploded in his mind. He had been a code translator in a stockbroker's office . . .

He sat back on his haunches and barked, loud, broken, long and short yelps. A girl screamed. Reporters jumped up defensively, surged away in a tightening ring. Wood barked out his message in Morse, painful, slow, straining a larynx that was foreign to him. He looked around optimistically for someone who might have understood.

Instead, he met hostile, annoyed stares—and no comprehension.

"That's the hound that attacked me!" the tall, thin man said.

"Not for food, I hope," a reporter answered.

Wood was not entirely defeated. He began to bark his message again; but a man hurried out of the glass-enclosed editor's office.

"What's all the commotion here?' he demanded. He sighted Wood among the ring of withdrawing reporters. "Get that damned dog out of here!"

"Come on—get him out of here!" the thin man shouted.

"He's a nice, friendly dog. Give him the hypnotic eye, Gilroy."

Wood stared pleadingly at Gilroy. He had not been understood, but he had found the reporter who had written the catatonic articles! Gilroy approached cautiously, repeating phrases calculated to soothe a savage dog.

Wood darted away through the rows of desks. He was so near to success—he only needed to find a way of communicating before they caught him and put him out!

He lunged to the top of a desk and crashed a bottle of ink to the floor. It splashed into a dark puddle. Swiftly, quiveringly, he seized a piece of white paper, dipped his paw into the splotch of ink, and made a hasty attempt to write.

His surge of hope died quickly. The wrist of his forepaw was not the universal joint of a human being; it had a single upward articulation! When he brought his paw down on the paper, it flattened uselessly, and his claws worked in a unit. He could not draw back three to write with one. Instead, he made a streaked pad print.

Dejectedly, rather than antagonize Gilroy, Wood permitted himself to be driven back into an elevator. He wagged his tail clumsily. It was a difficult feat, calling into use alien muscles that he employed with intellectual deliberation. He sat down and assumed a grin that would have been friendly on a human face; but, even so, it reassured Gilroy. The tall reporter patted his head. Nevertheless, he put him out firmly.

But Wood had reason to feel encouraged. He had managed to get inside the building and had attracted attention. He knew that a newspaper was the only force powerful enough to influence Moss, but there was still the problem of communication. How could he solve it? His paw was worthless for writing, with its single articulation; and nobody in the office could understand Morse code.

He crouched against the white cement wall, his harried mind darting wildly in all directions for a solution. Without a voice or prehensile fingers, his only method of communication seemed to be barking in code. In all that throng, he was certain there would be one to interpret it.

Glances *did* turn to him. At least, he had no difficulty in arousing interest. But they were uncomprehending looks.

For some moments he lost his reason. He ran in and out of the deep, hurrying crowd, barking his message furiously, jumping up at men who appeared more intelligent than the others, following them short distances until it was overwhelmingly apparent that they did not understand, then turning to other men, raising an ear-shattering din of appeal.

He met nothing but a timid pat or frightened rebuffs. He stopped his deafening yelps and cowered back against the wall, defeated. No one would attempt to interpret the barking of a dog in terms of code. When he was a man, he would probably have responded in the same way. The most intelligible message he could hope to convey by his barking was simply the fact that he was trying to attract interest. Nobody would search for any deeper meaning in a dog's barking.

He joined the traffic hastening toward the subway. He trotted along the curb, watchful for slowing cars, but more intent on the strewing of rubbish in the gutter. He was murderously envious of the human feet around him that walked swiftly and confidently to a known destination; smug, selfish feet, undeviating from their homeward path to help him. Their owners could convey the finest shadings and variations in emotion, commands, abstract thought, by speech, writing, print, through telephone, radio, books, newspapers . . .

But his voice was only a piercing, inarticulate yelp that infuriated human beings; his paws were good for nothing but running; his pointed face transmitted no emotions.

He trotted along the curbs of three blocks in the business district before he found a pencil stump. He picked it up in his teeth and ran to the docks on West Street, though he had only the vague outline of a last experiment in communication.

There was plenty of paper blowing around in the river wind, some of it even clean. To the stevedores, waiting at the dock for the payoff, he appeared to be frisking. A few of them whistled at him. In reality, he chased the flying paper with deadly earnestness.

When he captured a piece, he held it firmly between his forepaws. The stub of pencil was gripped in the even space separating his sharp canine fangs.

He moved the pencil in his mouth over the sheet of paper. It was clumsy and uncertain, but he produced long, wavering block letters. He wrote: "I AM A MAN." The short message covered the whole page, leaving no space for further information.

He dropped the pencil, caught up the paper in his teeth, and ran back to the newspaper building. For the first time since he had escaped from Moss, he felt assured. His attempt at writing was crude and unformed, but the message was unmistakably clear.

He joined a group of tired young legmen coming back from assignments. He stood passively until the door was opened, then lunged confidently through the little procession of cub reporters. They scattered back cautiously, permitting him to enter without a struggle.

Again he raced up the stairs to the editorial department, put the sheet of paper down on the floor, and clutched the doorknob between his powerful teeth.

He hesitated for only an instant, to find the cadaverous reporter. Gilroy was seated at a desk, typing out his article. Carrying his message in his mouth, Wood trotted directly to Gilroy. He put his paw on the reporter's sharp knee.

"What the hell!" Gilroy gasped. He pulled his leg away startledly and shoved Wood away.

But Wood came back insistently, holding his paper stretched out to Gilroy as far as possible. He trembled hopefully until the reporter snatched the message out of his mouth. Then his muscles froze, and he stared up expectantly at the angular face, scanning it for signs of growing comprehension.

Gilroy kept his eyes on the straggling letters. His face darkened angrily.

"Who's being a wise guy here?" he shouted suddenly. Most of the staff ignored him. "Who let this mutt in and gave him a crank note to bring to me? Come on—who's the genius?"

Wood jumped around him, barking hysterically, trying to explain.

"Oh, shut up!" Gilroy rapped out. "Hey, copy! Take this dog down and see that he doesn't get back in! He won't bite you."

Again Wood had failed. But he did not feel defeated. When his hysterical dread of frustration ebbed, leaving his mind clear and analytical, he realized that his failure was only one of degree. Actually, he had communicated, but lack of space had prevented him from detailed clarity. The method was correct. He only needed to augment it.

Before the copy boy cornered him, Wood swooped up at a pencil on an empty desk.

"Should I let him keep the pencil, Mr. Gilroy?" the boy asked.

"I'll lend you mine, unless you want your arm snapped off," Gilroy snorted, turning back to his typewriter.

Wood sat back and waited beside the copy boy for the elevator to pick them up. He clenched the pencil possessively between his teeth. He was impatient to get out of the building and back to the lot on West Street, where he could plan a system of writing a more explicit message. His block letters were unmanageably huge and shaky; but, with the same logical detachment he used to employ when he was a code translator, he attacked the problem fearlessly.

He knew that he could not use the printed or written alphabet. He would have to find a substitute that his clumsy teeth could manage, and that could be compressed into less space.

Gilroy was annoyed by the collie's insistent returning. He crumpled the enigmatic, unintelligible note and tossed it in the wastebasket, but beyond considering it as a practical joke, he gave it no further thought.

His long, large-jointed fingers swiftly tapped out the last page of his story. He ended it with a short line of zeros and dashes, gathered a sheaf of papers, and brought it to the editor.

The editor studied the lead paragraph intently and

skimmed hastily through the rest of the story. He appeared uncomfortable.

"Not bad, eh?" Gilroy exulted.

"Uh—what?" The editor jerked his head up blankly. "Oh. No, it's pretty good. Very good, in fact."

"I've got to hand it to you," Gilroy continued admiringly. "I'd have given up. You know—nothing to work on, just a bunch of fantastic events with no beginning and no end. Now, all of a sudden, the cops pick up a nut who acts like a dog and has an incision like the catatonics. Maybe it isn't any clearer, but at least we've got something actually happening. I don't know—I feel pretty good. We'll get to the bottom—"

The editor listened abstractedly, growing more uneasy from sentence to sentence. "Did you see the latest case?" he interrupted.

"Sure. I'm in soft with the resident physician. If I hadn't been following this story right from the start, I'd have said the one they just hauled in was a genuine screwball. He goes bounding around on the floor, sniffs at things, and makes a pathetic attempt to bark. But he has an incision on the back of his neck. It's just like the others—even has two professional stitches, and it's the same number of millimeters away from the spine. He's a catatonic, or whatever we'll have to call it now—"

"Well, the story's shaping up faster than I thought it would," the editor said, evening the edges of Gilroy's article with ponderous care. "But—" his voice dropped huskily. "Well, I don't know how to tell you this, Gilroy."

The reporter drew his brows together and looked at him obliquely. "What's the hard word this time?" he asked, mystified.

"Oh, the usual thing. You know. I've got to take you off this story. It's too bad, because it was just getting hot. I hated to tell you, Gilroy; but, after all, what the hell. That's part of the game."

"It is, huh?" Gilroy flattened his hands on the desk and leaned over them resentfully. "Whose toes did we step on this time? Nobody's. The hospital has no kick coming. I couldn't mention names because I didn't know any to mention. Well, then, what's the angle?"

The editor shrugged. "I can't argue. It's a front-office order. But I've got a good lead for you to follow tomorrow—"

Savagely, Gilroy strode to the window and glared out at the darkening street. The business department wasn't behind the order, he reasoned angrily; they weren't getting ads from the hospital. And as for the big boss—Talbot never interfered with policy, except when he had to squash a revealing crime story. By eliminating the editors, who yielded an inch when public opinion demanded a mile, the business department, who fought only when advertising was at stake, Gilroy could blame no one but Talbot.

Gilroy rapped his bony knuckles impatiently against the window casement. What was the point of Talbot's order? Perhaps he had a new way of paying off traitors. Gilroy dismissed the idea immediately; he knew Talbot wouldn't go to that expense and risk possible leakage when the old way of sealing a body in a cement block and dumping it in the river was still effective and cheap.

"I give up," Gilroy said without turning around. "I can't figure out Talbot's angle."

"Neither can I," the editor admitted.

At that confession, Gilroy wheeled. "Then you *know* it's Talbot!"

"Of course. Who else could it be? But don't let it throw you, pal." He glanced around cautiously as he spoke. "Let this catatonic yarn take a rest. Tomorrow you can find out what's behind this bulletin that Johnson phoned in from City Hall."

Gilroy absently scanned the scribbled note. His scowl wrinkled into puzzlement.

"What the hell is this? All I can make out of it is the ASPCA and dog lovers are protesting to the mayor against organized murder of brown and white collies."

"That's just what it is."

"And you think Talbot's gang is behind it, naturally." When the editor nodded, Gilroy threw up his hands in despair. "This gang stuff is getting too deep for me, chief. I used to be able to call their shots. I knew why a torpedo was bumped off, or a crime was pulled; but I don't mind telling you that I can't see why a gang boss wants a catatonic yarn hushed up, or sends his mob around plugging innocent collies. I'm going home . . . get drunk—"

He stormed out of the office. Before the editor had time to shrug his shoulders, Gilroy was back again, his deep eyes blazing furiously.

"What a pair of prize dopes we are, chief!" he shouted. "Remember that collie—the one that came in with a hunk of paper in his mouth? We threw him out, remember? Well, *that's the bound Talbot's gang is out gunning for*! *He's trying to carry messages to us*!"

"Hey, you're right!" The editor heaved out of the chair and stood uncertainly. "Where is he?"

Gilroy waved his long arms expressively.

"Then come on! To hell with hats and coats!"

They dashed into the staff room. The skeleton night crew loafed around, reading papers before moping out to follow up undeveloped loads.

"Put those papers down!" the editor shouted. "Come on with me—every one of you."

He herded them, baffled and annoyed, into the elevator. At the entrance to the building, he searched up and down the street.

"He's not around, Gilroy. All right, you deadbeats, divide up and chase around the streets, whistling. When you see a brown and white collie, whistle to him. He'll come to you. Now beat it and do as I say."

They moved off slowly. "Whistle?" one called back anxiously.

"Yes, whistle!" Gilroy declared. "Forget your dignity. Whistle!"

They scattered, whistling piercingly the signals that

are supposed to attract dogs. The few people around the business district that late were highly interested and curious, but Gilroy left the editor whistling at the newspaper building, while he whistled toward West Street. He left the shrill calls blowing away from the river, and searched along the wide highway in the growing dark.

For an hour he pried into dark spaces between the docks, patiently covering his ground. He found nothing but occasional longshoremen unloading trucks and a light uptown traffic. There were only homeless, prowling mongrels and starving drifters: no brown and white collie.

He gave up when he began to feel hungry. He returned to the building hoping the others had more luck, and angry with himself for not having followed the dog when he had the chance.

The editor was still there, whistling more frantically than ever. He had gathered a little band of inquisitive onlookers, who waited hopefully for something to happen. The reporters were also returning.

"Find anything?" the editor paused to ask.

"Nope. He didn't show up here?"

"Not yet. Oh, he'll be back, all right. I'm not afraid of that." And he went back to his persistent whistling, disregarding stares and rude remarks. He was a man with an iron will. He sneered openly at the defeated reporters when they slunk past him into the building.

In the comparative quiet of the city, above the editor's shrills, Gilroy heard swiftly pounding feet. He gazed over the heads of the pack that had gathered around the editor.

A reporter burst into view, running at top speed and doing his best to whistle attractively through dry lips at a dog streaking away from him.

"Here he comes!" Gilroy shouted. He broke through the crowd and his long legs flashed over the distance to the collie. In his excitement, empty, toneless wind blew between his teeth; but the dog shot straight for him just the same. Gilroy snatched a dirty piece of paper out of his mouth. Then the dog was gone, toward the docks; and a black car rode ominously down the street.

Gilroy half started in pursuit, paused, and stared at the slip of paper in his hand. For a moment he blamed the insufficient light, but when the editor came up to him, yelling blasphemy for letting the dog escape, Gilroy handed him the unbelievable note.

"That dog can take care of himself," Gilroy said. "Read this." The editor drew his brows together over the message.

"Well, I'll be damned!" the editor exclaimed.

"Is it a gag?"

"Gag, my eye!"

"Well, I can't make head or tail of it!" the editor protested.

Gilroy looked around undeterminedly, as if for someone to help them. "You're not supposed to. It's a code message." He swung around, stabbing an enormously long, knobbed finger at the editor. "Know anyone who can translate code—cryptograms?"

"Uh—let's see. How about the police, or the G-men—"

Gilroy snorted. "Give it to the bulls before we know what's in it!" He carefully tucked the crudely penciled note into his breast pocket and buttoned his coat. "You stick around outside here, chief. I'll be back with the translation. Keep an eye out for the pooch."

He loped off before the editor could more than open his mouth.

In the index room of the Forty-second Street Library, Gilroy crowded into the telephone booth and dialed a number. His eyes ached and he had a dizzy headache. Close reasoning always scrambled his wits. His mind was intuitive rather than ploddingly analytical.

"Executive office, please," he told the night operator. "There must be somebody there. I don't care if it's the business manager himself. I want to speak to somebody in the executive office. I'll wait." He lolled, bent into a convenient shape, against the wall. "Hello. Who's this? . . . Oh, good. Listen, Rothbart, this is Gilroy. Do me a favor, huh? You're nearest the front entrance. You'll find the chief outside the door. Send him into the telephone, and take his place until he gets through. While you're out there, watch for a brown and white collie. Nab him if he shows up and bring him inside . . . Will you? . . . Thanks!"

Gilroy held the receiver to his ear, defeatedly amusing himself by identifying the sounds coming over the wire. He was no longer in a hurry, and when he had to pay another nickel before the editor finally came to the telephone, he did not mind.

"What's up, Gilroy?" the editor asked hopefully.

"Nothing, chief. That's why I called up. I went through a military code book, some kids' stuff, and a history of cryptography through the ages. I found some good codes, but nobody seems to've thought of this punctuation code. Ever see the Confederate cipher? Boy, it's a real dazzler—wasn't cracked until after the Civil War was over! The old Greeks wound strips of paper around identical sticks. When they were unrolled, the strips were gibberish; around the sticks, the words fell right into order."

"Cut it out," the editor snapped. "Did you find anything useful?"

"Sure. Everybody says the big clue is the table of frequency—the letters used more often than others. But, on the other hand, they say that in short messages, like ours, important clues like the single words 'a' and 'I,' bigrams like 'am,' 'as,' and even trigrams like 'the' or 'but' are often omitted entirely."

"Well, that's fine. What're you going to do now?"

"I don't know. Try the cops after all, I guess."

"Nothing doing," the editor said firmly. "Ask a librarian to help."

Gilroy seized the inspiration. He slammed down the receiver and strode to the reference desk.

"Where can I get hold of somebody who knows cryptograms?" he rasped.

The attendant politely consulted his colleagues. "The guard of the manuscript room is pretty good," he said, returning. "Down the hall—"

Gilroy shouted his thanks and broke into an ungainly run, ignoring the attendant's order to walk. At the manuscript room he clattered the gate until the keeper appeared and let him in.

"Take a look at this," he commanded, flinging the message on a table.

The keeper glanced curiously at it. "Oh, cryptogram, eh?"

"Yeah. Can you make anything out of it?"

"Well, it looks like a good one," the guard replied cautiously, "but I've been crackling them all for the last twenty years." They sat down at the table in the empty room. For some time the guard stared fixedly at the scrawled note. "Five symbols," he said finally. "S colon, period, comma, colon, quotation marks. Thirteen word units, each with an even number of symbols. They must be used in combinations of two."

"I figured that out already," Gilroy rapped out. "What's it say?"

The guard lifted his head, offended. "Give me a chance. Bacon's code wasn't solved for three centuries."

Gilroy groaned. He did not have so much time on his hands.

"There're only thirteen word units here," the guard

went on, undaunted by the Bacon example. "Can't use frequency, bigrams or trigrams."

"I know that already," Gilroy said hoarsely.

"Then why'd you come to me if you're so smart?"

Gilroy hitched his chair away. "Okay, I won't bother you."

"Five symbols to represent twenty-six letters. Can't be. Must be something like the Russian nihilist code. They can represent only twenty-five letters. The missing one is either 'q' or 'j,' most likely, because they're not used much. Well, I'll tell you what I think."

"What's that?' Gilroy demanded, all alert.

"You'll have to reason *a priori*, or whatever it is."

"Any way you want," Gilroy sighed. "Just get on with it."

"The square root of twenty-five is five. Whoever wrote this note must've made a square of letters, five wide and five deep. That sounds right." The guard smiled and nodded cheerfully. "Possible combinations in a square of twenty-five letters is . . . uh . . . 625. The double symbols must identify the lines down and across. Possible combinations, twenty-five. Combinations all told . . . hmmm . . . 15,625. Not so good. If there's a key word, we'll have to search the dictionary until we find it. Possible combinations, 15,625 multiplied by the English vocabulary—that is, if the key word *is* English."

Gilroy raised himself to his feet. "I can't stand it," he moaned. "I'll be back in an hour."

"No, don't go," the guard said. "You've been helping me

a lot. I don't think we'll have to go through more than 625 combinations at the most. That'll take no time at all."

He spoke, of course, in relative terms. Bacon code, three centuries; Confederate code, fifteen years; wartime Russian code, unsolved. Cryptographers must look forward to eternity.

Gilroy seated himself, while the guard plotted a square:

;	"	,	.	:	
a	b	c	d	e	;
f	g	h	i	j	"
k	l	m	n	o	,
p	r	s	t	u	.
v	w	x	y	z	:

The first symbol combination, two semicolons, translated to "a," by reading down the first line, from the top semicolon, and across from the side semicolon. The next, a semicolon and a comma, read "I." He went on in this fashion until he screwed up his face and pushed the half-completed translation to Gilroy. It read:

"akdd kyoiztou kp tbo eztztkprepd"

"Does it make sense to you?" he asked anxiously.

Gilroy strangled, unable to reply.

"It could be Polish," the guard explained, "or Japanese."

The harassed reporter fled.

When he returned an hour later, after having eaten and tramped across town, nervously chewing cigarettes, he found the guard defended from him by a breastwork of heaped papers.

"Does it look any better?" Gilroy asked hoarsely.

The guard was too absorbed to look up or answer. By peering over his shoulder, Gilroy saw that he had plotted another square. The papers on the table were covered with discarded letter keys; at a rough guess, Gilroy estimated that the keeper had made over a hundred of them.

The one he was working with had been formed as the result of methodical elimination. His first square the guard had kept, changing the positions of the punctuation marks. When that had failed, he altered his alphabet square, tried that, and reversed his punctuation marks once more. Patient and plodding the guard had formed this square:

,	.	;	"	:	
z	u	o	j	e	,
y	t	n	i	d	.
x	s	m	h	c	;
w	r	l	g	b	"
v	p	k	f	a	:

Without haste, he counted down under the semicolon and across from the side semicolon, stopping at "m."

Gilroy followed him, nodding at the result. He was faster than the old guard at interpreting the semicolon and comma—"o." The period and semicolon, repeated twice, came to "ss." First word: "moss."

Gilroy straightened up and took a deep breath. He bent over again and counted down and across with the guard, through the whole message, which the old man had lined off between every two symbols. Completed, it read,

;; ;, .; .; ;, .: :, " :: .. :, :. ;, ;. .. "; :, :; :: .. :: .. ;, ;. ", :; .;

m o s s o p e r a t e d o n t h e c a t a t o n i c s

.. :: ; " ;" ;, .. " .; " : " .; :: ;. :; " .; .. "" " ; " .;; .: ." ;, .. :, :; .. ;; :, " : ." ;,

;; .. "; :, ;;

t a l b o t i s f i n a n c i n g h i m p r o t e c t m e f r o m t h e m

"Hmmm," the guard mused. "That makes sense, if I knew what it meant."

But Gilroy had snatched the papers out of his hand. The gate clanged shut after him.

Returning to the office in a taxi, Gilroy was not too joyful. He rapped on the inside window. "Speed it up! I've seen the sights."

He thought, if the dog's been bumped off, good-bye catatonic story! The dog was his only link with the code writer.

Wood slunk along the black, narrow alleys behind the wholesale fruit markets on West Street. Battered cans and crates of rotting fruit made welcome obstacles and shelters if Talbot's gangsters were following him.

He knew that he had to get away from the river section. The gangsters must have definitely recognized him; they would call Talbot's headquarters for greater forces. With their speedy cars they could patrol the borders of the district he was operating in, and close their lines until he was trapped.

More important was the fact that reporters had been sent out to search for him. Whether or not his simple code had been deciphered did not matter very much; the main thing was that Gilroy at last knew he was trying to communicate with him.

Wood's unerring animal sense of direction led him through the maze of densely shadowed alleys to a point nearest the newspaper office. He peered around the corner, up and down the street. The black gang car was out of sight. But he had to make an unprotected dash of a hundred yards, in the full glare of the streetlights, to the building entrance.

His powerful leg muscles gathered. He sped over the hard cement sidewalk. The entrance drew nearer. His legs pumped more furiously, shortening the dangerous space more swiftly than a human being could; and for that he was grateful.

He glimpsed a man standing impatiently at the door. At the last possible moment, Wood checked his rush and flung himself toward the thick glass plate.

"There you are!" the editor cried. "Inside—quick!"

He thrust open the door. They scurried inside and commandeered an elevator, then ran through the newsroom to the editor's office.

"Boy, I hope you weren't seen! It'd be curtains for both of us."

The editor squirmed uneasily behind his desk, from time to time glancing disgruntledly at his watch and cursing Gilroy's long absence. Wood stretched out on the cold floor and panted. He had expected his note to be deciphered by then, and even hoped to be recognized as a human being in a dog's body. But he realized that Gilroy probably was still engaged in decoding it.

At any rate he was secure for a while. Before long, Gilroy would return; then his story would be known. Until then he had patience.

Wood raised his head and listened. He recognized Gilroy's characteristic pace that consumed at least four feet at a step. Then the door slammed open and shut behind the reporter.

"The dog's here, huh? Wait'll you take a look at what I got!"

He threw a square of paper before the editor. Wood scanned the editor's face as he eagerly read it. He ignored the vast hamburger that Gilroy unwrapped for him. He was bewildered by Gilroy's lack of more than ordinary interest in him; but perhaps the editor would understand.

"So that's it! Moss and Talbot, eh? It's getting a lot clearer."

174

"I get Moss's angle," Gilroy said. "He's the only guy around here who could do an operation like that. But Talbot—I don't get his game. And who sent the note—how'd he get the dope—where is he?"

Wood almost went mad with frustration. He could explain; he knew all there was to be known about Talbot's interest in Moss's experiment. The problem of communication had been solved. Moss and Talbot were exposed; but he was as far as ever from regaining his own body.

He had to write another cipher message—longer, this time, and more explicit, answering the questions Gilroy raised. But to do that—he shivered. To do that, he would have to run the gang patrol; and his enciphering square was in the corner of a lot. It would be too dark . . .

"We've got to get him to lead us to the one who wrote the message," Gilroy said determinedly. "That's the only way we can corner Moss and Talbot. Like this, all we have is an accusation and no legal proof."

"He must be around here somewhere."

Gilroy fastened his eyes on Wood. "That's what I think. The dog came here and barked, trying to get us to follow him. When we chased him out, he came back with a scrawled note about a half-hour later. Then he brought the code message within another hour. The writer must be pretty near here. After the dog eats, we'll—" He gulped audibly and raised his bewildered gaze to the editor. Swiftly, he slipped off the edge of the desk and fumbled in the long hair on Wood's neck. "Look at that, chief—a piece of surgical plaster. When the dog bent his head to eat, the hair fell away from it."

"And you think he's a catatonic." The editor smiled pityingly and shook his head. "You're jumpy, Gilroy."

"Maybe I am. But I'd like to see what's under the plaster."

Wood's heart pumped furiously. He knew that his incision was the precise duplicate of the catatonics', and if Gilroy could see it, he would immediately understand. When Gilroy picked at the plaster, he tried to bear the stabbing pain; but he had to squirm away. The wound was raw and new, and the deeply rooted hair was firmly glued to the plaster. He permitted Gilroy to try again. The sensation was far too fierce; he was afraid the incision would rip wide open.

"Stop it," the editor said squeamishly. "He'll bite you."

Gilroy straightened up. "I could take it off with some ether."

"You don't really think he was operated on, do you? Moss doesn't operate on dogs. He probably got into a fight, or one of Talbot's torpedoes creased him with a bullet."

The telephone bell rang insistently. "I'd still like to see what's under it," Gilroy said as the editor removed the receiver. Wood's hopes died suddenly. He felt that he was to blame for resisting Gilroy.

"What's up, Blaine?" the editor asked. He listened absorbedly, his face darkening. "Okay. Stay away if you don't want to take a chance. Phone your story in to the rewrite desk." He replaced the receiver and said to Gilroy: "Trouble, plenty of it. Talbot's gang cars are cruising around this district. Blaine was afraid to run them. I don't know how you're going to get the dog through."

Wood was alarmed. He left his meal unfinished and agitated toward the door, whimpering involuntarily.

Gilroy glanced curiously at him. "I'd swear he understood what you said. Did you see the change that came over him?"

"That's the way they react to voices," the editor said.

"Well, we've got to get him to his master." Gilroy mused, biting the inside of his cheek. "I can do it—if you're in with me."

"Of course I am. How?"

"Follow me." Wood and the editor went through the newsroom on the cadaverous reporter's swift heels. In silence they waited for an elevator, then descended to the lobby. "Wait here beside the door," Gilroy said. "When I give the signal, come running."

"What signal?" the editor cried, but Gilroy had loped into the street and out of sight.

They waited tensely. In a few minutes a taxi drew up to the curb and Gilroy opened the door, sitting alertly inside. He watched the corner behind him. No one moved for a long while; then a black gang car rode slowly and vigilantly past the taxi. An automatic rifle barrel glinted in the yellow light. Gilroy waited until a moment after it turned into West Street. He waved his arms frantically.

"Step on it!" Gilroy ordered harshly. "Up West Street!"

The editor scooped Wood up in his arms, burst open the door, and darted across the sidewalk into the cab.

The taxi accelerated suddenly. Wood crouched on the floor, trembling, in despair. He had exhausted his ingenuity and he was as far as ever from regaining his body. They expected him to lead them to his master; they still did not realize that he had written the message. Where should he lead them—how could he convince them that he was the writer?

"I think this is far enough," Gilroy broke the silence. He tapped on the window. The driver stopped. Gilroy and the editor got out, Wood following indecisively. Gilroy paid and waved the driver away. In the quiet isolation of the broad commercial highway, he bent his great height to Wood's level. "Come on, boy!" he urged. "Home!"

Wood was in a panic of dismay. He could think of only one place to lead them. He set off at a slow trot that did not tax them. Hugging the walls, sprinting across streets, he headed cautiously downtown.

They followed him behind the markets fronting the highway, over a hemmed-in lot. He picked his way around the deep, treacherous foundation of a building that had been torn down, up and across piles of rubbish, to a black-shadowed clearing at the lot's end. He halted passively.

Gilroy and the editor peered around into the blackness. "Come out!" Gilroy called hoarsely. "We're your friends. We want to help you."

When there was no response, they explored the lot, lighting matches to illuminate dark corners of the foundation. Wood watched them with confused emotions. By searching in the garbage heaps and the crumbling walls of the foundation, they were merely wasting time.

As closely as possible in the dark, he located the site of his enciphering square. He stood near it and barked clamorously. Gilroy and the editor hastily left their futile prodding.

"He must've seen something," the editor observed in a whisper.

Gilroy cupped a match in his hand and moved the light back and forth in the triangular corner of the cleared space. He shrugged.

"Not around there," the editor said. "He's pointing at the ground."

Gilroy lowered the match. Before its light struck the ground, he yelped and dropped it, waving his burned fingers in the cool air. The editor murmured sympathy and scratched another match.

"Is this what you're looking for—a lot of letters in a square?"

Wood and Gilroy crowded close. The reporter struck his own match. In its light he narrowly inspected the crudely scratched encoding square.

"Be back in a second," he said. It was too dark to see his face, but Wood heard his voice, harsh and strained. "Getting flashlight."

"What'll I do if the guy comes around?" the editor asked hastily.

"Nothing," Gilroy rasped. "He won't. Don't step on the square."

Gilroy vanished into the night. The editor struck another match and scrutinized the ground with Deerslayer thoroughness.

"What the hell did he see?" he pondered. "That guy—" He shook his head defeatedly and dropped the match.

Never in his life had Wood been so passionately excited. What *had* Gilroy discovered? Was it merely another circumstantial fact, like his realization that Talbot's gangsters were gunning for Wood; or was it a suspicion of Wood's identity? Gilroy had replied that the writer would not reappear, but that could have meant anything or nothing. Wood frantically searched for a way of finally demonstrating who he really was. He found only a negative plan—he would follow Gilroy's lead.

With every minute that passed, the editor grew angrier, shifting his leaning position against the brick wall, pacing around. When Gilroy came back, flashing a bright cone of light before him, the editor lashed out.

"Get it over with, Gilroy. I can't waste the whole night. Even if we do find out what happened, we can't print it—"

Gilroy ignored him. He splashed the brilliant ray of his huge five-celled flashlight over the enciphering square.

"Now look at it," he said. He glanced intently at Wood, who also obeyed his order and stood at the editor's knee, searching the ground. "The guy who made that square was very cautious—he put his back to the wall and faced the lot, so he wouldn't be taken by surprise. The square is upside-down to us. No, wait!" he said sharply as the editor moved to look at the square from its base. "I don't want your footprints on it. Look at the bottom, where the writer must've stood."

The editor stared closely. "What do you see?" he asked puzzledly.

"Well, the ground is moist and fairly soft. There should be footprints. There are. *Only they're not human!*"

Raucously, the editor cleared his throat. "You're kidding."

"*Gestalt*," Gilroy said, almost to himself, "the whole is greater than the sum of its parts. You get a bunch of unconnected facts, all apparently unrelated to each other. Then suddenly one fact pops up—it doesn't seem any more important than the others—but all at once the others click into place, and you get a complete picture."

"What are you mumbling about?" the editor whispered anxiously.

Gilroy stooped his great height and picked up a yellow stump of pencil. He turned it over in his hand before passing it to the editor.

"That's the pencil this dog snatched before we threw him out. You can see his teethmarks on the sides, where he carried it. But there're teethmarks around the unsharpened end. Maybe I'm nuts—" He took the dirty code message out of his inside breast pocket and smoothed it out. "I saw these smudges the minute I looked at the note, but they didn't mean anything to me then. What do you make of them?"

The editor obediently examined the note in the glare of the flash. "They could be palmprints."

"Sure—a baby's," Gilroy said witheringly. "Only they're not. We both know they're pawprints, the same as are at the bottom of the square. You know what I'm thinking. Look't the way the dog is listening."

Without raising his voice, he half turned his head and said quite casually, "Here comes the guy who wrote the note, right behind the dog."

Involuntarily, Wood spun around to face the dark lot. Even his keen animal eyes could detect no one in the gloom. When he lifted his gaze to Gilroy, he stared full into grim, frightened eyes.

"Put that in your pipe," Gilroy said tremulously. "That's his reaction to the pitch of my voice, eh? You can't get out of it, chief. We've got a werewolf on our hands, thanks to Moss and Talbot."

Wood barked and frisked happily around Gilroy's towering legs. He had been understood!

But the editor laughed, a perfectly normal, humorous, unconvinced laugh. "You're wasting your time writing for a newspaper, Gilroy—"

"Okay, smart guy," Gilroy replied savagely. "Stop your cackling and tell me the answer to this—

"The dog comes into the newsroom and starts barking. I thought he was just trying to get us to follow him; but

I never heard a dog bark in long and short yelps before. He ran up the stairs, right past all the other floors— business office, advertising department, and so on—to the newsroom, because that's where he wanted to go. We chased him out. He came back with a scrawled note, saying: 'I am a man.' Those four words took up the whole page. Even a kid learning how to write wouldn't need so much space. But if you hold the pencil in your mouth and try to connect the bars of the letters, you'd have letters something like the ones on the note.

"He needed a smaller system of letters, so he made up a simple code. But he'd lost his pencil. He stole one of ours. Then he came back, watching out for Talbot's gang cars.

"There aren't any footprints at the bottom of this square—only a dog's pawprints. And there's two smudges on the message, where he put his paws to hold down the paper while he wrote on it. All along he's been listening to every word we said. When I said in a conversational tone that the writer was standing behind him, he whirled around. Well?"

The editor was still far from convinced. "Good job of training—"

"For a guy I used to respect, you certainly have the brain of a flea. Here—I don't know your name," he said to Wood. "What would you do if you had Moss here?"

Wood snarled.

"You're going to tell us where to find him. I don't know how, but you were smart enough to figure out a code, so you can figure out another way of communicating. Then you'll tell us what happened."

It was Wood's moment of supreme triumph. True, he didn't have his body yet, but now it was only a matter of time. His joy at Gilroy's words was violent enough to shake even the editor's literal, unimaginative mind.

"You still don't believe it," Gilroy accused.

"How can I?" the editor cried plaintively. "I don't even know why I'm talking to you as if it could be possible."

Gilroy probed in a pile of rubbish until he uncovered a short piece of wood. He quickly drew a single line of small alphabetical symbols. He threw the stick away, stepped back and flashed the light directly at the alphabet. "Now spell out what happened."

Wood sprang back and forth before the alphabet, stopping at the letters he required and indicating them by pointing his snout down.

"T-a-l-b-o-t w-a-n-t-e-d a y-o-u-n-g h-e-a-l-t-h-y b-o-d-y M-o-s-s s-a-i-d h-e c-o-u-l-d g-i-v-e i-t t-o h-i-m."

"Well, I'll be damned!" the editor blurted.

After that exclamation there was silence. Only the almost inaudible padding of Wood's paws on the soft ground, his excited panting, and the hoarse breathing of the men could be heard. But Wood had won!

Gilroy sat at the typewriter in his apartment; Wood stood beside his chair and watched the swiftly leaping keys; but the editor stamped nervously up and down the floor.

"I've wasted half the night," he complained, "and if I

print this story I'll be canned. Why, damn it, Gilroy—how do you think the public'll take it if I can't believe it myself?"

"Hmmm," Gilroy explained.

"You're sacrificing our job. You know that, don't you?"

"It doesn't mean that much to me," Gilroy said without glancing up. "Wood has to get back his body. He can't do it unless we help him."

"Doesn't that sound ridiculous to you? 'He has to get back his body.' Imagine what the other papers'll do to that sentence!"

Gilroy shifted impatiently. "They won't see it," he stated.

"Then why in hell are you writing the story?" the editor asked, astounded. "Why don't you want me to go back to the office?"

"Quiet! I'll be through in a minute." He inserted another sheet of paper and his flying fingers covered it with black, accusing words. Wood's mouth opened in a canine grin when Gilroy smiled down at him and nodded his head confidently. "You're practically walking around on your own feet, pal. Let's go."

He flapped on his coat and carelessly dropped a battered hat on his craggy head. Wood braced himself to dart off. The editor lingered.

"Where're we going?" he asked cautiously.

"To Moss, naturally, unless you can think of a better place."

Wood could not tolerate the thoughts of delay. He tugged at the leg of the editor's pants.

"You bet I can think of a better place. Hey, cut it out, Wood—I'm coming along. But, hell, Gilroy! It's after ten. I haven't done a thing. Have a heart and make it short."

With Gilroy hastening him by the arm and Wood dragging at his leg, the editor had to accompany them, though he continued his protests. At the door, however, he covered Wood while Gilroy hailed a taxi. When Gilroy signaled that the street was clear, he ran across the sidewalk with Wood bundled in his arms.

Gilroy gave the address. At its sound, Wood's mouth opened in a silent snarl. He was only a short distance from Moss, with two eloquent spokesmen to articulate his demands, and, if necessary, to mobilize public opinion for him! What could Moss do against that power?

They rode up Seventh Avenue and along Central Park West. Only the editor felt that they were speeding. Gilroy and Wood fretted irritably at every stop signal.

At Moss's street, Gilroy cautioned the driver to proceed slowly. The surgeon's house was guarded by two loitering black cars.

"Let us out at the corner," Gilroy said.

They scurried into the entrance of a rooming house.

"Now what?" the editor demanded. "We can't fight past them."

"How about the back way, Wood?"

Wood shook his head negatively. There was no entrance through the rear.

"Then the only way is across the roofs," Gilroy determined. He put his head out and scanned the buildings between them and Moss. "This one is six stories, the next two five, the one right next to Moss's is six, and Moss's is three. We'll have to climb up and down fire escapes and get in through Moss's roof. Ready?"

"I suppose so," the editor said fatalistically.

Gilroy tried the door. It was locked. He chose a bell at random and rang it vigorously. There was a brief pause; then the tripper buzzed. He thrust open the door and burst up the stairs, four at a leap.

"Who's there?" a woman shouted down the stairwell.

They galloped past her. "Sorry, lady," Gilroy called back. "We rang your bell by mistake."

She looked disappointed and rather frightened; but Gilroy anticipated her emotion. He smiled and gaily waved his hand as he loped by.

The roof door was locked with a stout hook that had rusted into its eye. Gilroy smashed it open with the heel of his palm. They broke out onto a tarred roof, chill and black in the overcast, threatening night.

Wood and Gilroy discovered the fire escape leading to the next roof. They dashed for it. Gilroy tucked Wood under his left arm and swung himself over the anchored ladder.

"This is insane!" the editor said hoarsely. "I've never

done such a crazy thing in my life. Why can't we be smart and call the cops?"

"Yeah?" Gilroy sneered without stopping. "What's your charge?"

"Against Moss? Why—"

"Think about it on the way."

Gilroy and Wood were on the next roof, waiting impatiently for the editor to descend. He came down quickly, but his thoughts wandered.

"You can charge him with what he did. He made a man into a dog."

"That would sound swell in the indictment. Forget it. Just walk lightly. This damned roof creaks and lets out a noise like a drum."

They advanced over the tarred sheets of metal. Beneath them, they could hear their occasionally heavy tread resound through hollow rooms. Wood's claws tapped a rhythmic tattoo.

They straddled over a low wall dividing the two buildings. Wood sniffed the air for enemies lurking behind chimneys, vents, and doors. At instants of suspicion, Gilroy briefly flashed his light ahead. They climbed up a steel ladder to the six-story building adjoining Moss's.

"How about a kidnap charge?" the editor asked as they stared down over the wall at the roof of Moss's building.

"Please don't annoy me. Wood's body is in the observation ward at the hospital. How're you going to prove that Moss kidnapped him?"

The editor nodded in the gloom and searched for another legal charge. Gilroy splashed his light over Moss's roof. It was unguarded.

"Come on, Wood," he said, inserting the flashlight in his belt. He picked up Wood under his left arm. In order to use his left hand in climbing, he had to squeeze Wood's middle in a stranglehold.

The only thing Wood was thankful for was that he could not look at the roof three stories below. Gilroy held him securely, tightly enough for his breath to struggle in whistling gasps. His throat knotted when Gilroy gashed his hand on a sharp sliver of dry paint scale.

"It's all right," Gilroy hissed reassuringly. "We're almost there."

Above them, he saw the editor clambering heavily down the insecurely bolted ladder. Between the anchoring plates it groaned and swayed away from the unclean brick wall. Rung by rung they descended warily, Gilroy clutching for each hold, Wood suspended in space and helpless—both feeling their hearts drop when the ladder jerked under their weight.

Then Gilroy lowered his foot and found the solid roof beneath it. He grinned impetuously in the dark. Wood writhed out of his hold. The editor cursed his way down to them.

He followed them to the rear fire escape. This time he offered to carry Wood down. Swinging out over the wall, Wood felt the editor's muscles quiver. Wood had nothing but a miserable animal life to lose, and yet even he was not entirely fearless in the face of the hidden dangers they were braving. He could sympathize with the editor, who had everything to lose and did not wholly believe that Wood was not a dog. Discovering a human identity in an apparently normal collie must have been a staggeringly hard fact for him to swallow.

He set Wood down on the iron bars. Gilroy quickly joined them, and yanked fiercely at the top window. It was locked.

"Need a jimmy to pry it open," Gilroy mused. He fingered the edges of the frame. "Got a knife on you?"

The editor fished absentmindedly through his pockets. He brought out a handful of keys, pencil stubs, scraps of paper, matches, and a cheap sheathed nail file. Gilroy snatched the file.

He picked at the putty in the ancient casement with the point. It chipped away easily. He loosened the top and sides.

"Now," he breathed. "Stand back a little and get ready to catch it."

He inserted the file at the top and levered the glass out of the frame. It stuck at the bottom and sides, refusing to fall. He caught the edges and lifted it out, laying it down noiselessly out of the way.

"Let's go." He backed in through the empty casement. "Hand Wood through."

They stood in the dark room, under the same roof with Moss. Wood exultantly sensed the proximity of the one man he hated—the one man who could return his body to him. "Now!" he thought, "Now!"

"Gilroy," the editor urged, "we can charge Moss with vivisection."

"That's right," Gilroy whispered. But they heard the doorknob rattle in his hand and turn cautiously.

"Then where're you going?" the editor rasped in a panic.

"We're here," Gilroy replied coolly. "So let's finish it."

The door swung back; pale weak light entered timidly. They stared down the long, narrow, dismal hall to the stairs at the center of the house. Down those stairs they would find Moss.

Wood's keen animal sense of smell detected Moss's personal odor. The surgeon had been there not long before.

He crouched around the stairhead and cautiously lowered himself from step to step. Gilroy and the editor clung to banister and wall, resting the bulk of their weight on their hands. They turned the narrow spiral where Clarence had fatally encountered the sharpness of Wood's fangs, down to the hall floor where his fat body had sprawled in blood.

Distantly, Wood heard a cane tap nervously, momentarily; then it stopped at a heated, hissed command that scarcely carried even to his ears. He glanced up triumphantly at Gilroy, his deep eyes glittering, his mouth grinning savagely, baring the red tongue lolling in the white, deadly trap of fangs. He had located and identified the sounds. Both Moss and Talbot were in a room at the back of the house.

He hunched his powerful shoulders and advanced slowly, stiff-legged, with the ominous air of all meat hunters stalking prey from ambush. Outside the closed door he crouched, muscles gathered for the lunge, his ears flat back along his pointed head to protect them from injury. But they heard muffled voices inaudible to men's dulled senses.

"Sit down, doc," Talbot said. "The truck'll be here soon."

"I'm not concerned with my personal safety," Moss replied tartly. "It's merely that I dislike inefficiency, especially when you claim—"

"Well, it's not Jake's fault. He's coming back from a job."

Wood could envision the faint sneer on Moss's scrubbed pink face. "You'll collapse any minute within the next six months, but the acquisitive nature is as strong as ever in you, isn't it, Talbot? You couldn't resist the chance of making a profit, and at a time like this!"

"Oh, don't lose your head. The cata-whatever-you-call-it can't talk and the dog is probably robbing garbage cans. What's the lam for?"

"I'm changing my residence purely as a matter of precaution. You underestimate human ingenuity, even limited by a dog's inarticulateness."

Wood grinned up at his comrades. The editor was

192

dough-faced, rigid with apprehension. Gilroy held a gun and his left hand snaked out at the doorknob. The editor began an involuntary motion to stop him. The door slammed inward before he completed it.

Wood and Gilroy stalked in, sinister in their grim silence. Talbot merely glanced at the gun. He had stared into too many black muzzles to be frightened by it. When his gaze traveled to Wood his jaw fell and hung open, trembling senilely. His constantly fighting lungs strangled. He screamed, a high, tortured wail, and tore frantically at his shirt, trying to release his chest from crushing pressure.

"An object lesson for you, Talbot," Moss said without emotion. "Do not underestimate an enemy."

Gilroy lost his frigid attitude. "Don't let him strangle. Help him."

"What can I do?" Moss shrugged. "It's angina pectoris. Either he pulls out of the convulsions by himself—or he doesn't. I can't help. But what did you want?"

No one answered him. Horrified, they were watching Talbot go purple in his death agony, lose the power of shrieking, and tear at his chest. Gilroy's gun hand was limp; yet Moss made no attempt to escape. The air rattled through Talbot's predatory nose. He fell in a contorted heap.

Wood felt sickened. He knew that in self-preservation doctors had to harden themselves, but only a monster of brutal callousness could have disregarded Talbot's frightful death as if it had not been going on.

"Oh, come now, it isn't as bad as all that," Moss said acidly.

Wood raised his shocked stare from the rag-doll body to Moss's hard, unfearful eyes. The surgeon had made no move to defend himself, to call for help from the squad of gangsters at the front of the house. He faced them with inhuman prepossession.

"It upsets your plans," Gilroy spat.

Moss lifted his shoulders, urbanely, delicately disdainful. "What difference should his death make to me? I never cared for his company."

"Maybe not, but his money seemed to smell okay to you. He's out of the picture. He can't keep us from printing this story now." Gilroy pulled a thin folded typescript from his inside breast pocket and shoved it out at Moss.

The surgeon read it interestedly, leaning casually against a wall. He came to the end of the short article and read the lead paragraph over again. Politely, he gave it back to Gilroy.

"It's very clear," he said. "I'm accused of exchanging the identities of a man and a dog. You even describe my alleged technique."

"'Alleged!'" Gilroy roared savagely. "You mean you deny it?"

"Of course. Isn't it fantastic?" Moss smiled. "But that isn't the point. Even if I admitted it, how do you think I could be convicted on such evidence? The only witness seems to be the dog you call Wood. Are dogs allowed to testify in court? I don't remember, but I doubt it."

Wood was stunned. He had not expected Moss to brazen out the charge. An ordinary man would have broken down, confronted by their evidence.

Even the shrinking editor was stung into retorting: "We have proof of criminal vivisection!"

"But no proof that I was the surgeon."

"You're the only one in New York who could've done that operation."

"See how far that kind of evidence will get you."

Wood listened with growing anger. Somehow they had permitted Moss to dominate the situation, and he parried their charges with cool, sarcastic deftness. No wonder he had not tried to escape! He felt himself to be perfectly safe. Wood growled, glowering hatred at Moss. The surgeon looked down contemptuously.

"All right, we can't convict you in court," Gilroy said. He hefted his gun, tightening his finger on the trigger. "That's not what we want, anyhow. This little scientific curiosity can make you operate on Wood and transfer his identity back to his own body."

Moss's expression of disdain did not alter. He watched Gilroy's tensing trigger finger with an astonishing lack of concern.

"Well, speak up," Gilroy rasped, waving the gun ominously.

"You can't force me to operate. All you can do is kill me, and I am as indifferent to my own death as I was to Talbot's." His smile broadened and twisted down at the corners, showing his teeth in a snarl that was the civilized, over-refined counterpart of Wood's. "Your alleged operation interests me, however. I'll operate for my customary fee."

The editor pushed Gilroy inside and hurriedly closed the door. "They're coming," he chattered. "Talbot's gangsters."

In two strides Gilroy put Moss between him and the door. His gun jabbed rudely into Moss's unflinching back. "Get over on the other side, you two, so the door'll hide you when it swings back," he ordered.

Wood and the editor retreated. Wood heard steps along the hall, then a pause, and a harsh voice shouted: "Hey, boss! Truck's here."

"Tell them to go away," Gilroy said in a low, suppressed tone.

Moss called, "I'm in the second room at the rest of the house."

Gilroy viciously stabbed him with the gun muzzle. "You're asking for it. I said tell them to go away!"

"You wouldn't dare to kill me until I've operated."

"If you're not scared, why do you want them? What's the gag?"

The door flung open. A gangster started to enter. He stiffened, his keen, battle-trained eyes flashing from Talbot's twisted body to Moss, and to Gilroy, standing menacingly behind the surgeon. In a swift, smooth motion a gun leaped from his armpit holster.

"What happened to the boss?" he demanded hoarsely. "Who's he?"

"Put your gun away, Pinero. The boss died of a heart attack. That shouldn't surprise you—he was expecting it any day."

"Yeah, I know. But how'd that guy get in?"

Moss stirred impatiently. "He was here all along. Send the truck back. I'm not moving. I'll take care of Talbot."

The gangster looked uncertain, but, in lieu of another commander, he obeyed Moss's order, "Well, okay, if you say so." He closed the door.

When Pinero had gone down the hall, Moss turned to face Gilroy.

"You're not scared—much!" Gilroy said.

Moss ignored his sarcastic outburst. "Where were we?" he asked. "Oh, yes. While you were standing there shivering, I had time to think over my offer. I'll operate for nothing."

"You bet you will!" Gilroy wagged his gun forcefully.

Moss sniffed at it. "That has nothing to do with my decision. I have no fear of death, and I'm not afraid of your evidence. If I do operate, it will be because of my interest in the experiment." Wood intercepted Moss's speculative gaze. It mocked, hardened, glittered sinisterly. "But of course," Moss added smoothly, "I will definitely operate. In fact, I insist on it!"

His hidden threat did not escape Wood. Once he lay

under Moss's knife it would be the end. A slip of the knife—a bit of careful carelessness in the gas mixture—a deliberately caused infection—and Moss would clear himself of the accusation by claiming he could not perform the operation, and therefore was not the vivisectionist. Wood recoiled, shaking his head violently from side to side.

"Wood's right," the editor said. "He knows Moss better. He wouldn't come out of the operation alive."

Gilroy's brow creased in an uneasy frown. The gun in his hand was a futile implement of force; even Moss knew he would not use it—could not, because the surgeon was only valuable to them alive. His purpose had been to make Moss operate. Well, he thought, he had accomplished that purpose. Moss offered to operate. But all four knew that under Moss's knife, Wood was doomed. Moss had cleverly turned the victory to utter rout.

"Then what the hell'll we do?" Gilroy exploded savagely. "What do you say, Wood? Want to take the chance, or keep on in a dog's body?"

Wood snarled, backing away.

"At least, he's still alive," the editor said fatalistically.

Moss smiled, protesting with silken mockery that he would do his best to return Wood's body.

"Barring accidents," Gilroy spat. "No soap, Moss. He'll get along the way he is, and you're going to get yours."

He looked grimly at Wood, jerking his head significantly in Moss's direction.

"Come on, chief," he said, guiding the editor through

the door and closing it. "These old friends want to be alone—lot to talk over."

Instantly, Wood leaped before the door and crouched there menacingly, glaring at Moss with blind, vicious hatred. For the first time, the surgeon dropped his pose of indifference. He inched cautiously around the wall toward the door. He realized suddenly that this was an animal . . .

Wood advanced, cutting off his line of retreat. Mane bristling, head lowered ominously between blocky shoulders, bright gums showing above white curved fangs, Wood stalked over the floor, stiff-jointed, in a low, inexorably steady rhythm of approach.

Moss watched anxiously. He kept looking up at the door in an agony of longing. But Wood was there, closing the gap for the attack. He put up his hands to thrust away . . .

And his nerve broke. He could not talk down mad animal eyes as he could a man holding a gun. He darted to the side and ran for the door.

Wood flung himself at the swiftly pumping legs. They crashed against him, tripped. Moss sprawled face down on the floor. He crossed his arms under his head to protect his throat.

Wood slashed at an ear. It tore, streaming red. Moss screeched and clapped his hands over his face, trying to rise without dropping his guard. But Wood ripped at his fingers.

The surgeon's hands clawed out. He was kneeling,

defenseless, trying to fight off the rapid, aimed lunges and those knifelike teeth . . .

Wood gloated. A minute before, the scrubbed pink face had been aloof, sneering. Now it bobbed frantically at his eye level, contorted with overpowering fear, blood flowing brightly down the once scrupulously clean cheeks.

For an instant, the pale throat gleamed exposed at him. It was soft and helpless. He shot through the air. His teeth struck at an angle and snatched—the white flesh parted easily. But a bony structure snapped between his jaws as he swooped by.

Moss knelt there after Wood had struck. His pain-twisted face gaped imbecilically, hands limp at his sides. His throat poured a red flood. Then his face drained to a ghastly lack of color and he pitched over.

He had lost, but he had also won. Wood was doomed to live out his life in a dog's body. He could not even expect to live his own life span. The average life of a dog is fifteen years. Wood could expect perhaps ten years more.

In his human body, Wood had found it difficult to find a job. He had been a code expert; but code experts, salesmen and apprentice workmen have no place in a world of shrinking markets. The employment agencies are glutted with an oversupply of normal human intelligences housed in strong, willing, expert human bodies.

The same normal human intelligence in a handsome collie's body had a greater market value. It was a rarity, a phenomenon to be gaped at after a ticket had been purchased for the privilege.

"Men've always had a fondness for freaks," Gilroy philosophized on their way to the theater where Wood had an engagement. "Mildly amusing freaks are paid to entertain. The really funny ones are given seats of honor and power. Figure it out, Wood. I can't. Once we get rid of our love of freaks and put them where they belong, we'll have a swell world."

The taxi stopped in a side street, at the stage entrance. Lurid red-and-yellow posters, the size of cathedral murals, plastered the theater walls; and from them smirked prettified likenesses of Wood.

"Gosh!" their driver gasped. "Wait'll my kids hear about this. I drove the Talkin' Dog! Gee, is that an honor, or ain't it?"

On all sides, pedestrians halted in awe, taxis stopped with a respectful screech of brakes; then an admiring swarm bore down on him.

"Isn't he cute?" women shrieked. "So intelligent-looking!"

"Sure," Wood heard their driver boast proudly, "I drove him down here. What's he like?" His voice lowered confidentially. "Well, the guy with him—his manager, I guess—he was talkin' to him just as intelligent as I'm talking' to you. Like he could understand ev'y word."

"Bet he could, too," a listener said definitely.

"G'on," another theorized. "He's just trained, like Rin Tin Tin, on'y better. But he's smart all right. Wish't I owned him."

The theater-district squad broke through the tangle of traffic and formed a lane to the stage door.

"Yawta be ashamed ayehselves," a cop said. "All this over a mutt!"

Wood bared his fangs at the speaker, who retreated defensively.

"Wise guy, huh?" the mob jeered. "Think he can't understand?"

It was a piece of showmanship that Wood and Gilroy had devised. It never failed to find a feeder in the form of an officious policeman and a response from the crowd.

Even in the theater, Wood was not safe from overly enthusiastic admiration. His fellow performers persisted in scratching his unitching back and ears, cooing and burbling in a singularly unintelligent manner.

The thriller that Wood had made in Hollywood was over; and while the opening acts went through their paces, Wood and Gilroy stood as far away from the wings as the theater construction would permit.

"Seven thousand bucks a week, pal," Gilroy mused over and over. "Just for doing something that any mug out in the audience can do twice as easily. Isn't that the payoff?"

In the year that had passed, neither was still able to accustom himself to the mounting figures in their bankbooks. Pictures, personal appearances, endorsements, highly fictionalized articles in magazines—all at astronomical prices . . .

But he could never have enough money to buy back the human body he had starved in.

"Okay, Wood," Gilroy whispered. "We're on."

They were drummed onto the stage with deafening applause. Wood went through his routine perfunctorily. He identified objects that had been named by the theater manager, picking them out of a heap of piled objects.

Ushers went through the aisles, collecting questions the audience had written on slips of paper. They passed them up to Gilroy.

Wood took a long pointer firmly in his mouth and stood before a huge lettered screen. Painfully, he pointed out, letter by letter, the answers to the audience's questions. Most of them asked about the future, market tips, racing information. A few seriously probed his mind.

White light stabbed down at him. Mechanically, he spelled out the simple answers. Most of his bitterness had evaporated; in its place was a dreary defeat, and dull acceptance of his dog's life. His bankbook had six figures to the left of the decimal—more than he had ever conceived of, even as a distant utopian possibility. But no surgeon could return his body to him, or increase his life expectancy of less than ten years.

Sharply, everything was washed out of sight: Gilroy, the vast alphabet screen, the heavy pointer in his mouth, the black space smeared with pale, gaping blobs of faces, even the white light staring down ...

He lay on a cot in a long ward. There was no dreamlike

quality of illusion in the feel of smooth sheets beneath and above him, or in the weight of blankets resting on his outstretched body.

And independently of the rest of his hand, his finger moved in response to his will. Its nail scratched at the sheet, loudly, victoriously.

"You're coming back," the intern said at last.

"I'm coming back," Wood spoke quietly, before the scene vanished and he heard Gilroy repeat a question he had missed.

He knew then that the body-mind was a unit. Moss had been wrong; there was more to identity than that small gland, something beyond the body. The forced division Moss had created was unnatural; the transplanted tissue was being absorbed, remodeled. Somehow, he knew these returns to his natural identity would recur, more and more—till it became permanent—till he became human once more.

The Old Die Rich

"You again, Gilroy," the Medical Examiner said wearily. I nodded pleasantly and looked around the shabby room with a feeling of hopeful eagerness. Maybe *this* time, I thought, I'd get the answer. I had the same sensation I always had in these places—the quavery senile despair at being closed in a room with the single shaky chair, tottering bureau, dim bulb hanging from the ceiling, the flaking metal bed.

There was a woman on the bed, an old woman with white hair thin enough to show the tight-drawn scalp, her face and body so emaciated that the flesh between the bones formed parchment pockets. The ME was going over her as if she were a side of beef that he had to put a federal grade stamp on, grumbling meanwhile about me and Sergeant Lou Pape, who had brought me here.

"When are you going to stop taking Gilroy around to these cases, Sergeant?" the ME demanded in annoyance. "Damned actor and his morbid curiosity!"

For the first time, Lou was stung into defending me. "Mr. Gilroy is a friend of mine—I used to be an actor, too, before I joined the force—and he's a follower of Stanislavsky."

The beat cop who'd reported the DOA whipped around at the door. "A Red?"

I let Lou Pape explain what the Stanislavsky method of acting was, while I sat down on the one chair and tried to apply it. Stanislavsky was the great pre-Revolution Russian stage director whose idea was that actors had to think and feel like the characters they portrayed so they could *be* them. A Stanislavskian works out everything about a character right up to the point where a play starts—where he was born, when, his relationship with his parents, education, childhood, adolescence, maturity, attitudes toward men, women, sex, money, success, including incidents. The play itself is just an extension of the life history created by the actor.

How does that tie in with the old woman who had died? Well, I'd had the cockeyed kind of luck to go bald at twenty-five and I'd been playing old men ever since. I had them down pretty well—it's not just a matter of shuffling around all hunched over and talking in a high cracked voice, which is cornball acting, but learning what old people are like inside—and these cases I talked Lou Pape into taking me on were studies in senility. I wanted to understand them, know what made them do what they did, *feel* the compulsion that drove them to it.

The old woman on the bed, for instance, had $32,000 in five bank accounts . . . and she'd died of starvation.

You've come across such cases in the news, at least a dozen a year, and wondered who they were and why they did it. But you read the items, thought about them for a little while, and then forgot them. My interest was professional; I made my living playing old people and I had to know as much about them as I could.

That's how it started off, at any rate. But the more cases I investigated, the less sense they made to me, until finally they were practically an obsession.

Look, they almost always have around $30,000 pinned to their underwear, hidden in mattresses, or parked in the bank, yet they starve themselves to death. If I could understand them, I could write a play or have one written; I might really make a name for myself, even get a Hollywood contract, maybe, if I could act them as they should be acted.

So I sat there in the lone chair, trying to reconstruct the character of the old woman who had died rather than spend a single cent of her $32,000 for food.

"Malnutrition induced by senile psychosis," the ME said, writing out the death certificate. He turned to me. "There's no mystery to it, Gilroy. They starve because they're less afraid of death than digging into their savings."

I'd been imagining myself growing weak from hunger and trying to decide that I ought to eat even if it cost me something. I came out of it and said, "That's what you keep telling me."

"I keep hoping it'll convince you so you won't come around anymore. What are the chances, Gilroy?"

"Depends. I will when I'm sure you're right. I'm not."

He shrugged disgustedly, ordered the wicker basket from the meat wagon, and had the old woman carried out. He and the beat cop left with the basket team. He could at least have said good-bye. He never did, though.

A fat lot I cared about his attitude or dogmatic medical opinion. Getting inside this character was more important. The setting should have helped; it was depressing, rank with the feel of solitary desperation and needless death.

Lou Pape stood looking out the one dirty window, waiting patiently for me. I let my joints stiffen as if they were thirty years older and more worn out than they were, and empathized myself into a dilemma between getting still weaker from hunger and drawing a little money out of the bank.

I worked at it for half an hour or so with the deep concentration you acquire when you use the Stanislavsky method. Then I gave up.

"The ME is wrong, Lou," I said. "It doesn't feel right."

Lou turned around from the window. He'd stood there all that time without once coughing or scratching or doing anything else that might have distracted me. "He knows his business, Gilroy."

"But he doesn't know old people."

"What is it you don't get?" he prompted, helping me dig my way through a characterization like the trained Stanislavskian he was—and still would have been if he hadn't gotten so sick of the insecurity of acting that he'd become a cop. "Can't money be more important to a psychotic than eating?"

"Sure," I agreed. "Up to a point. Undereating, yes. Actual starvation, no."

"Why not?"

"You and the ME think it's easy to starve to death. It isn't. Not when you can buy day-old bread at the bakeries, soup bones for about a nickel a pound, wilted vegetables that groceries are glad to get rid of. Anybody who's willing to eat that stuff can stay alive on nearly nothing a day. Nearly nothing, Lou, and hunger is a damned potent instinct. I can understand hating to spend even those few cents. I can't see going without food altogether."

He took out a cigarette; he hadn't until then because he didn't want to interrupt my concentration. "Maybe they get too weak to go out after old bread and meat bones and wilted vegetables."

"It still doesn't figure." I got up off the shaky chair, my joints now really stiff from sitting in it. "Do you know how long it takes to die of starvation?"

"That depends on age, health, amount of activity—"

"Nuts!" I said. "It would take weeks!"

"So it takes weeks. Where's the problem—if there is one?"

I lit the pipe I'd learned to smoke instead of cigarettes—old men seem to use pipes more than anything else, though maybe it'll be different in the next generation. More cigarette smokers now, you see, and they'd stick to the habit unless the doctor ordered them to cut it out.

"Did you ever try starving for weeks, Lou?" I asked.

"No. Did you?"

"In a way. All these cases you've been taking me on for the last couple of years—I've tried to be them. But let's say it's possible to die of starvation when you have thousands of dollars put away. Let's say you don't think of scrounging off food stores or working out a way of freeloading or hitting soup lines. Let's say you stay in your room and slowly starve to death."

He slowly picked a fleck of tobacco off his lip and flicked it away, his sharp black eyes poking holes in the situation I'd built up for him. But he wasn't ready to say anything yet.

"There's charity," I went on, "relief—except for those who have their dough in banks, where it can be checked on—old age pension, panhandling, cadging off neighbors."

He said, "We know these cases are hermits. They don't make contact with anybody."

"Even when they're starting to get real hungry?"

"You've got something, Gilroy, but that's the wrong

tack," he said thoughtfully. "The point is that *they* don't have to make contact; other people know them or about them. Somebody would check after a few days or a week—the janitor, the landlord, someone in the house or the neighborhood."

"So they'd be found before they died."

"You'd think so, wouldn't you?" he agreed reluctantly. "They don't generally have friends, and the relatives are usually so distant, they hardly know these old people and whether they're alive or not. Maybe that's what threw us off. But you don't need friends and relatives to start wondering, and investigate when you haven't shown up for a while." He lifted his head and looked at me. "What does that prove, Gilroy?"

"That there's something wrong with these cases. I want to find out what."

I got Lou to take me down to Headquarters, where he let me see the bankbooks the old woman had left.

"She took damned good care of them," I said. "They look almost new."

"Wouldn't you take damned good care of the most important thing in the world to you?" he asked. "You've seen the hoards of money the others leave. Same thing."

I peered closely at the earliest entry: April 23, 1907, $150. My eyes aren't that bad; I was peering at the ink. It was dark, unfaded. I pointed it out to Lou.

"From not being exposed to daylight much," he said. "They don't haul out the bankbooks or money very often, I guess."

"And that adds up for you? I can see them being psychotics all their lives . . . but not *senile* psychotics."

"They hoarded, Gilroy. That adds up for me."

"Funny," I said, watching him maneuver his cigarette as if he loved the feel of it, drawing the smoke down and letting it out in plumes of different shapes, from rings to slender streams. What a living he could make doing cigarette commercials on TV! "I can see you turn into one of these cases, Lou."

He looked startled for a second, but then crushed out the butt carefully so he could watch it instead of me. "Yeah? How so?"

"You've been too scared by poverty to take a chance. You know you could do all right acting, but you don't dare give up this crummy job. Carry that far enough and you try to stop spending money, then cut out eating, and finally wind up dead of starvation in a cheap room."

"Me?" I'd never get that scared of being broke!"

"At the age of seventy or eighty?"

"Especially then! I'd probably tear loose for a while and then buy into a home for the aged."

I wanted to grin, but I didn't. He'd proved my point. He'd also shown that he was as bothered by these old people as I was.

"Tell me, Lou. If somebody kept you from dying, would you give him any dough for it, even if you were a senile psychotic?"

I could see him using the Stanislavsky method to feel

his way to the answer. He shook his head. "Not while I was alive. Will it, maybe, not give it."

"How would that be as a motive?"

He leaned against a metal filing cabinet. "No good. Gilroy. You know what a hell of a time we have tracking down relatives to give the money to, because these people don't leave wills. The few relatives we find are always surprised when they get their inheritance—most of them hardly remember dear old who-ever-it-was that died and left it to them. All the other estates eventually go to the State treasury, unclaimed."

"Well, it was an idea." I opened the oldest bankbook again. "Anybody ever think of testing the ink, Lou?"

"What for? The banks' records always check. These aren't forgeries, if that's what you're thinking."

"I don't know what I'm thinking," I admitted. "But I'd like to turn a chemist loose on this for a little while."

"Look, Gilroy, there's a lot I'm *willing* to do for you, and I think I've done plenty, but there's a limit—"

I let him explain why he couldn't let me borrow the book and then waited while he figured out how it could be done and did it. He was still grumbling when he helped me pick a chemist out of the telephone directory and went along to the lab with me.

"But don't get any wrong notions," he said on the way. "I have to protect State property, that's all, because I signed for it and I'm responsible."

"Sure, sure," I agreed, to humor him. "If you're not curious, why not just wait outside for me?"

He gave me one of those white-tooth grins that he had no right to deprive women audiences of. "I could do that, but I'd rather see you make a sap of yourself."

I turned the bankbook over to the chemist and we waited for the report. When it came, it had to be translated.

The ink was typical of those used fifty years ago. Lou Pape gave me a jab in the ribs at that. But then the chemist said that, according to the amount of oxidation, it seemed fresh enough to be only a few months or years old, and it was Lou's turn to get jabbed. Lou pushed him about the aging, asking if it couldn't be the result of unusually good care. The chemist couldn't say—that depended on the kind of care; an airtight compartment, perhaps, filled with one of the inert gases, or a vacuum. They hadn't been kept that way, of course, so Lou looked as baffled as I felt.

He took the bankbook and we went out to the street.

"See what I mean?" I asked quietly, not wanting to rub it in.

"I see something, but I don't know what. Do you?"

"I wish I could say yes. It doesn't make any more sense than anything else about these cases."

"What do you do next?"

"Damned if I know. There are thousands of old people in the city. Only a few of them take this way out. I have to try to find them before they do."

"If they're loaded, they won't say so, Gilroy, and there's

no way of telling them from those who are down and out."

I rubbed my pipe disgruntledly against the side of my nose to oil it. "Ain't this a beaut of a problem? I wish I liked problems. I hate them."

Lou had to get back on duty. I had nowhere to go and nothing to do except worry my way through this tangle. He headed back to Headquarters and I went over to the park and sat in the sun, warming myself and trying to think like a senile psychotic who would rather die of starvation than spend a few cents for food.

I didn't get anywhere, naturally. There are too many ways of beating starvation, too many chances of being found before it's too late.

And the fresh ink, over half a century old . . .

I took to hanging around banks, hoping I'd see someone come in with an old bankbook that had fresh ink from fifty years before. Lou was some help there he convinced the guards and tellers that I wasn't an old-looking guy casing the place for a gang, and even got the tellers to watch out for particularly dark ink in ancient bankbooks.

I stuck at it for a month, although there were a few stage calls that didn't turn out right and one radio and two TV parts that did and kept me going. I was almost glad the stage parts hadn't been given to me; they'd have interrupted my outside work.

After a month without a thing turning up at the banks, though, I went back to my two rooms in the theatrical hotel one night, tired and discouraged, and I found Lou there. I expected him to give me another talk on dropping the whole thing; he'd been doing that for a couple of weeks now, every time we got together. I felt too low to put up an argument. But Lou was holding back his excitement—acting like a cop, you know, instead of projecting his feelings—and he couldn't haul me out to his car as fast as he probably wanted me to go.

"Been trying to get in touch with you all day, Gilroy. Some old guy was found wandering around, dazed and suffering from malnutrition, with $17,000 in cash inside the lining of his jacket."

"Alive?" I asked, shocked right into eagerness again.

"Just barely. They're trying intravenous feeding to pull him through. I don't think he'll make it."

"For God's sake, let's get there before he conks out!"

Lou raced me to the City Hospital and up to the ward. There was a scrawny old man in a bed, nothing but a papery skin stretched thin over a face like a skull and a body like a Halloween skeleton, shivering as if he was cold. I knew it wasn't the cold. The medics were injecting a heart stimulant into him and he was vibrating like a rattletrap car racing over a gravel road.

"Who are you?" I practically yelled, grabbing his skinny arm. "What happened to you?"

He went on shaking with his eyes closed and his mouth open. "Ah, hell!" I said, disgusted. "He's in a coma."

"He might start talking," Lou told me. "I fixed it up so you can sit here and listen in case he does."

"So I can listen to delirious ravings, you mean."

Lou got me a chair and put it next to the bed. "What are you kicking about? This is the first live one you've seen, isn't it? That ought to be good enough for you." He looked as annoyed as a director. "Besides, you can get biographical data out of delirium that you'd never get if he was conscious."

He was right, of course. Not only data, but attitudes, wishes, resentments that would normally be repressed. I wasn't thinking of acting at the moment, though. Here was somebody who could tell me what I wanted to know . . . only he couldn't talk.

Lou went to the door. "Good luck," he said and went out.

I sat down and stared at the old man, willing him to talk. I don't have to ask if you've ever done that; everybody has. You keep thinking over and over, getting more and more tense, "Talk, damn you, talk!" until you find that every muscle in your body is a fist and your jaws are aching because you've been clenching your teeth so hard. You might just as well not bother, but once in a while a coincidence makes you think you've done it. Like now.

The old man sort of came to. That is, he opened his eyes and looked around without seeing anything, or it was so far away and long ago that nobody else could see what he saw.

I hunched forward on the chair and willed harder than ever. Nothing happened. He stared at the ceiling and through and beyond me. Then he closed his eyes again and I slumped back, defeated and bitter—but that was when he began talking.

There were a couple of women, though they might have been little girls in his childhood, and he had his troubles with them. He was praying for a toy train, a roadster, to pass his tests, to keep from being fired, to be less lonely, and back to toys again. He hated his father, and his mother was too busy with church bazaars and such to pay much attention to him. There was a sister: she died when he was a kid. He was glad she died, hoping maybe now his mother would notice him, but he was also filled with guilt because he was glad. Then somebody, he felt, was trying to shove him out of his job.

The intravenous feeding kept dripping into his vein and he went on rambling. After ten or fifteen minutes of it, he fell asleep. I felt so disappointed that I could have slapped him awake, only it wouldn't have done any good. Smoking would have helped me relax, but it wasn't allowed, and I didn't dare go outside for one, for fear he might revive again and this time come up to the present.

"Broke!" he suddenly shrieked, trying to sit up.

I pushed him down gently, and he went on in frightful terror, "Old and poor, nowhere to go, nobody wants me, can't make a living, read the ads every day, no jobs for old men."

He blurted through weeks, months, years—I don't know—of fear and despair. And finally he came to something that made his face glow like a radium dial.

220

"An ad. No experience needed. Good salary." His face got dark and awful. All he added was "El Greco," or something that sounded like it, and then he went into terminal breathing.

I rang for the nurse and she went for the doctor. I couldn't stand the long moments when the old man's chest stopped moving, the abrupt frantic gulps of air followed by no breath at all. I wanted to get away from it, but I had to wait for whatever more he might say.

It didn't come. His eyes fogged and rolled up and he stopped taking those spasmodic strangling breaths. The nurse came back with the doctor, who felt his pulse and shook his head. She pulled the blanket over the old man's face.

I left, feeling sick. I'd learned things I already knew about hate and love and fear and hope and frustration. There was an ad in it somewhere, but I had no way of telling if it had been years ago or recently. And a name that sounded like "El Greco." That was a Spanish painter of four to five hundred years ago. Had the old guy been remembering a picture he'd seen?

No, he'd come up at least close to the present. The ad seemed to solve his problem about being broke. But what about the $17,000 that had been found in the lining of his jacket? He hadn't mentioned that. *Of course*, being a senile psychotic, he could have considered himself broke even with that amount of money. None coming in, you see.

That didn't add up, either. His was the terror of being

old and jobless. If he'd had money, he would have figured how to make it last, and that would have come through in one way or another.

There was the ad, there was his hope, and there was this El Greco. A Greek restaurant, maybe, where he might have been bumming his meals.

But where did the $17,000 fit in?

Lou Pape was too fed up with the whole thing to discuss it with me. He just gave me the weary eye and said, "You're riding this too hard, Gilroy. The guy was talking from fever. How do I know what figures and what doesn't when I'm dealing with insanity or delirium?"

"But you admit there's plenty about these cases that doesn't figure?"

"Sure. Did you take a look at the condition the world is in lately? Why should these old people be any exception?"

I couldn't blame him. He'd pulled me in on the cases with plenty of trouble to himself, just to do me a favor. Now he was fed up. I guess it wasn't even that he thought I was ruining myself, at least financially and maybe worse, by trying to run down the problem. He said he'd be glad to see me any time and gas about anything or help me with whatever might be bothering me, if he could, but not these cases any more. He told me to lay off them, and then he left me on my own.

I don't know what he could have done, actually. I didn't need him to go through the want ads with me, which I was doing every day, figuring there might be something in the ravings about an ad. I spent more time than I liked checking those slanted at old people, only to find they were supposed to become messengers and such.

One brought me to an old brownstone five-story house in the East Eighties. I got on line with the rest of the applicants—there were men and women, all decrepit, all looking badly in need of money—and waited my turn. My face was lined with collodion wrinkles and I wore an antique shiny suit and rundown shoes. I didn't look more prosperous or any younger than they did.

I finally came up to the woman who was doing the interviewing. She sat behind a plain office desk down in the main floor hall, with a pile of application cards in front of her and a ballpoint pen in one strong, slender hand. She had red hair with gold lights in it and eyes so pale blue that they would have seemed the same color as the whites if she'd been on the stage. Her face would have been beautiful except for her rigid control of expression; she smiled abruptly, shut it off just like that, looked me over with all the impersonality and penetration of an X-ray from the soles to the bald head, exactly as she'd done with the others. But that skin! If it was as perfect as that all over her slim, stiffly erect, proudly shaped body, she had no business off the stage!

"Name, address, previous occupation, social security number?" she asked in a voice with good clarity, resonance, and diction. She wrote it all down while I gave the information to her. Then she asked me for references, and I mentioned Sergeant Lou Pape. "Fine," she said. "We'll get in touch with you if anything comes up. Don't call us—we'll call you."

I hung around to see who'd be picked. There was only one, an old man, two ahead of me in the line, who had no social security number, no references, not even any relatives or friends she could have checked up on him with.

Damn! Of course that was what she wanted! Hadn't all the starvation cases been people without social security, references, either no friends and relatives or those they'd lost track of?

I'd pulled a blooper, but how was I to know until too late?

Well, there was a way of making it right.

When it was good and dark that evening, I stood on the corner and watched the lights in the brownstone house. The ones on the first two floors went out, leaving only those on the third and fourth. Closed for the day ... or open for business?

I got into a building a few doors down by pushing a button and waiting until the buzzer answered, then racing up to the roof while some man yelled down the stairs to find out who was there. I crossed the tops of the two houses between and went down the fire escape.

It wasn't easy, though not as tough as you might imagine. The fact is that I'm a whole year younger than Lou Pape, even if I could play his grandpa professionally. I still have muscles left and I used them to get down the fire escape at the rear of the house.

The fourth-floor room I looked into had some kind of wire mesh cage and some hooded machinery. Nobody there.

The third floor room was the redhead's. She was coming out of the bathroom with a terry cloth bathrobe and a towel turban on when I looked in. She slid the robe off and began dusting herself with powder. That skin *did* cover her.

She turned and moved toward a vanity against the wall that I was on the other side of. The next thing I knew, the window was flung up and she had a gun on me.

"Come right in—Mr. Gilroy, isn't it?" she said in that completely controlled voice of hers. One day her control would crack, I thought irrelevantly, and the pieces would be found from Dallas to North Carolina. "I had an idea you seemed more curious than was justified by a help-wanted ad."

"A man my age doesn't get to see many pretty girls," I told her, making my own voice crack pathetically in a senile whinny.

She motioned me into the room. When I was inside, I saw a light over the window blinking red. It stopped the moment I was in the room. A silent burglar alarm.

She let her pale blue eyes wash insolently over me. "A man your age can see all the pretty girls he wants to. You're not old."

"And you use a rinse," I retorted.

She ignored it. "I specifically advertised for old people. Why did you apply?"

It happened so abruptly that I hadn't had a chance to use the Stanislavsky method to *feel* old in the presence of a beautiful nude woman. I don't even know if it would have worked. Nothing's perfect.

"I needed a job awful bad," I answered sullenly, knowing it sounded like an ad lib.

She smiled with more contempt than humor. "You had a job, Mr. Gilroy. You were very busy trying to find out why senile psychotics starve themselves to death."

"How did you know that?" I asked, startled.

"A little investigation of my own. I also happen to know you didn't tell your friend Sergeant Pape that you were going to be here tonight."

That was a fact, too. I hadn't felt sure enough that I'd found the answer to call him about it. Looking at the gun in her steady hand, I was sorry I hadn't.

"But you did find out I own this building, that my name is May Roberts, and that I'm the daughter of the late Dr. Anthony Roberts, the physicist," she continued. "Is there anything else you want me to tell you about yourself?"

"I know enough already. I'm more interested in you and the starvation cases. If you weren't connected with them, you wouldn't have known I was investigating them."

"That's obvious, isn't it?" She reached for a cigarette on the vanity and used a lighter with her free hand. The big mirror gave me another view of her lovely body, but that was beginning to interest me less than the gun. I thought of making a grab for it. There was too much distance between us, though, and she knew better than to take her eyes off me while she was lighting up. "I'm not afraid of professional detectives, Mr. Gilroy. They deal only with facts and every one of them will draw the same conclusions from a given set of circumstances. I don't like amateurs. They guess too much. They don't stick to reality. The result," her pale eyes chilled and her shapely mouth went hard, "is that they are likely to get too close to the truth."

I wanted to smoke myself, but I wasn't willing to make a move toward the pipe in my jacket. "I may be close to the truth, Miss Roberts, but I don't know what the devil it is. I still don't know how you're tied in with the senile psychotics or why they starve with all that money. You could let me go and I wouldn't have a thing on you."

She glanced down at herself and laughed for real for the first time. "You wouldn't, would you? On the other hand, you know where I'm working from and could nag Sergeant Pape into getting a search warrant. It wouldn't incriminate me, but it would be inconvenient. I don't care to be inconvenienced."

"Which means what?"

"You want to find out my connection with senile psychotics. I intend to show you."

"How?"

She gestured dangerously with the gun. "Turn your face to the wall and stay that way while I get dressed. Make one attempt to turn around before I tell you to and I'll shoot you. You're guilty of housebreaking, you know. It would be a little inconvenient for me to have an investigation . . . but not as inconvenient as for you."

I faced the wall, feeling my stomach braid itself into a tight, painful knot of fear. Of what, I didn't know yet, only that old people who had something to do with her died of starvation. I wasn't old, but that didn't seem very comforting. She was the most frigid, calculating, *deadly* woman I'd ever met. That alone was enough to scare hell out of me. And there was the problem of what she was capable of.

Hearing the sounds of her dressing behind me, I wanted to lunge around and rush her, taking a chance that she might be too busy pulling on girdle or reaching back to fasten a bra to have the gun in her hand. It was a suicidal impulse and I gave it up instantly. Other women might compulsively finish concealing themselves before snatching up the gun. Not her.

"All right," she said at last.

I faced her. She was wearing coveralls that, if anything, emphasized the curves of her figure. She had a sort of babushka that covered her red hair and kept it in place—the kind of thing women workers used to wear in factories during the war. She had looked lethal with nothing on but a gun and a hard expression. She looked like a sentence of execution now.

"Open that door, turn to the right, and go upstairs," she told me, indicating directions with the gun.

I went. It was the longest, most anxious short walk I've ever taken. She ordered me to open a door on the fourth floor, and we were inside the room I'd seen from the fire escape. The mesh cage seemed like a torture chamber to me, the hooded motors designed to shoot an agonizing current through my emaciating body.

"You're going to do to me what you did to the old man you hired today?" I probed, hoping for an answer that would really answer.

She flipped on the switch that started the motors and there was a shrill, menacing whine. The wire mesh of the cage began blurring oddly, as if vibrating like the tines of a tuning fork.

"You've been an unexpected nuisance, Gilroy," she said above the motors. "I never thought you'd get this far. But as long as you have, we might as well both benefit by it."

"Benefit?" I repeated. "*Both* of us?"

She opened the drawer of a work table and pulled out a stack of envelopes held with a rubber band. She put the stack at the other edge of the table.

"Would you rather have all cash or bank accounts or both?"

My heart began to beat. *She was where the money came from*!

"You trying to tell me you're a philanthropist?" I demanded.

"Business is philanthropy, in a way," she answered calmly. "You need money and I need your services. To that extent, we're doing each other a favor. I think you'll find that the favor I'm going to do for you is a pretty considerable one. Would you mind picking up the envelopes on the table?"

I took the stack and stared at the top envelope. "May 15, 1931," I read aloud, and looked suspiciously at her. "What's this for?"

"I don't think it's something that can be explained. At least it's never been possible before and I doubt if it would be now. I'm assuming you want both cash and bank accounts. Is that right?"

"Well, yes. Only—"

"We'll discuss it later." She looked along a row of shelves against one wall, searching the labels on the stacks of bundles there. She drew one out and pushed it toward me. "Please open that and put on the things you'll find inside."

I tore open the bundle. It contained a very plain business suit, black shoes, shirt, tie and a hat with a narrow brim.

"Are these supposed to be my burial clothes?"

"I asked you to put them on," she said. "If you want me to make that a command, I'll do it."

I looked at the gun and I looked at the clothes and then for some shelter I could change behind. There wasn't any.

She smiled. "You didn't seem concerned about my modesty. I don't see why your own should bother you. Get dressed!"

I obeyed, my mind anxiously chasing one possibility after another, all of them ending up with my death. I got into the other things and felt even more uncomfortable. They were all only an approximate fit: the shoes a little too tight and pointed, the collar of the shirt too stiffly starched and too high under my chin, the gray suit too narrow at the shoulder and the ankles. I wished I had a mirror to see myself in. I felt like an ultra-conservative Wall Street broker and I was sure I resembled one.

"All right," she said. "Put the envelopes in your inside pocket. You'll find instructions on each. Follow them carefully."

"I don't get it!" I protested.

"You will. Now step into the mesh cage. Use the envelopes in the order they're arranged in."

"But what's this all about?"

"I can tell you just one thing, Mr. Gilroy—don't try to escape. It can't be done. Your other questions will answer themselves if you follow the instructions on the envelopes."

She had the gun in her hand. I went into the mesh cage, not knowing what to expect and yet too afraid of her to refuse. I didn't want to wind up dead of starvation, no matter how much money she might have given me—but I didn't want to get shot, either.

She closed the mesh gate and pushed the switch as far as it would go. The motors screamed as they picked up speed; the mesh cage vibrated more swiftly. I could see her through it as if there were nothing between us.

And then I couldn't see her at all.

I was outside a bank on a sunny day in spring.

My fear evaporated instantly—I'd escaped somehow!

But then a couple of realizations slapped me from each side. It was day instead of night. I was out on the street and not in her brownstone house.

Even the season had changed!

Dazed, I stared at the people passing by. They looked like characters in a TV movie, the women wearing long dresses and flowerpot hats, their faces made up with petulant rosebud mouths and bright blotches of rouge; the men in hard straw hats, suits with narrow shoulders, plain black or brown shoes—the same kind of clothes I was wearing.

The rumble of traffic in the street caught me next. Cars with square bodies, tubular radiators . . .

For a moment, I let terror soak through me. Then I remembered the mesh cage and the motors. May Roberts could have given me electro-shock, kept me under long enough for the season to change, or taken me south and left me on a street in daylight.

But this was a street in New York. I recognized it, though some of the buildings seemed changed, the people dressed more shabbily.

Shrewd stage setting? Hypnosis?

That was it, of course! She'd hypnotized me . . .

Except that a subject under hypnosis doesn't know he's been hypnotized.

Completely confused, I took out the stack of envelopes I'd put in my pocket. I was supposed to have both cash and a bank account, and I was outside a bank. She obviously wanted me to go in, so I did. I handed the top envelope to the teller.

He hauled $150 out of it and looked at me as if that was enough to buy and sell the bank. He asked me if I had an account there. I didn't. He took me over to an officer of the bank, a fellow with a Hoover collar and a John Gilbert mustache, who signed me up more cordially than I'd been treated in years.

I walked out to the street, gaping at the entry in the bankbook he'd handed me. My pulse was jumping lumpily, my lungs refusing to work right, my head doing a Hopi rain dance.

The date he'd stamped was May 15, 1931.

I didn't know which I was more afraid of—being stranded, middle-aged, in the worst of the depression, or being yanked back to that brownstone house. I had only an instant to realize that I was a kid in high school uptown right at that moment. Then the whole scene vanished as fast as blinking and I was outside another bank somewhere else in the city.

The date on the envelope was May 29th and it was still 1931. I made a $75 deposit there, then $100 in another place a few days later, and so forth, spending only a few minutes each time and going forward anywhere from a couple of days to almost a month.

Every now and then, I had a stamped, addressed envelope to mail at a corner box. They were addressed to different stock brokers and when I got one open before mailing it and took a look inside, it turned out to be an order to buy a few hundred shares of stock in a soft drink company in the name of Dr. Anthony Roberts. I hadn't remembered the price of the shares being that low. The last time I'd seen the quotation, it was more than five times as much as it was then. I was making dough myself, but I was doing even better for May Roberts.

A few times I had to stay around for an hour or so. There was the night I found myself in a flashy speakeasy with two envelopes that I was to bet the contents of, according to the instructions on the outside. It was June 21, 1932, and I had to bet on Jack Sharkey to take the heavyweight title away from Max Schmeling.

The place was serious and quiet—no more than three women, a couple of bartenders, and the rest male customers, including two cops, huddling up close to the radio. An affable character was taking bets. He gave me a wise little smile when I put the money down on Sharkey.

"Well, it's a pleasure to do business with a man who wants an American to win," he said, "and the hell with the smart dough, eh?"

"Yeah," I said, and tried to smile back, but so much of the smart money was going on Schmeling that I wondered if May Roberts hadn't made a mistake. I couldn't remember who had won. "You know what J. P. Morgan said—don't sell America short."

"I'll take a buck for my share," said a sour guy who barely managed to stand. "Lousy grass growing in the lousy streets, nobody working, no future, nothing!"

"We'll come out if it okay," I told him confidently.

He snorted into his gin. "Not in our lifetime, Mac. It'd take a miracle to put this country on its feet again. I don't believe in miracles." He put his scowling face up close to mine and breathed blearily and belligerently at me. "Do you?"

"Shut up, Gus," one of the bartenders said. "The fight's starting."

I had some tough moments and a lot of bad Scotch, listening. It went the whole fifteen rounds, Sharkey won, and I was in almost as bad shape as Gus, who'd passed out halfway through the battle. All I can recall is the affable character handing over a big roll and saying, "Lucky for me more guys don't sell America short," and trying to separate the money into the right amounts and put them into the right envelopes, while stumbling out the door, when everything changed and I was outside a bank again.

I thought, "My God, what a hangover cure!" I was as sober as if I hadn't had a drink, when I made that deposit.

There were more envelopes to mail and more deposits to make and bets to put down on Singing Wood in 1933 at Belmont Park and Max Baer over Primo Carnera, and then Cavalcade at Churchill Downs in 1934, and James Braddock over Baer in 1935, and a big daily double payoff, Wanoah-Arakay at Tropical Park, and so on, skipping through the years like a flat stone over water, touching here and there for a few minutes to an hour at a time. I kept the envelopes for May Roberts and myself in different pockets and the bankbooks in another. The envelopes were beginning to bulge and the deposits and accrued interest were something to watch grow.

The whole thing, in fact, was so exciting that it was early October of 1938—a total of maybe four or five hours subjectively—before I realized what she had me doing. I wasn't thinking much about the fact that I was time traveling or how she did it. I accepted that, though the sensation in some ways was creepy, like raising the dead. My father and mother, for instance, were still alive in 1938. If I could break away from whatever it was that kept pulling me jumpily through time, I could go and see them.

The thought attracted me enough to make me shake badly with intent, yet pumped dread through me. I wanted so damned badly to see them again and I didn't dare. I couldn't . . .

Why couldn't I?

Maybe the machine covered only the area around the various banks, speakeasies, bars, and horse parlors. If I could get out of the area, whatever it might be, I could avoid coming back to whatever May Roberts had lined up for me.

Because, naturally, I knew now what I was doing: I was making deposits and winning sure bets just as the "senile psychotics" had done. The ink on their bankbooks and bills was fresh because it was fresh; it wasn't given a chance to oxidize—at the rate I was going, I'd be back to my own time in another few hours or so, with $15,000 or better in deposits, compound interest, and cash.

If I'd been around seventy, you see, she could have sent me back to the beginning of the century with the same amount of money, which would have accumulated to something like $30,000.

Get it now?

I did.

And I felt sick and frightened.

The old people had died of starvation somehow with all that dough in cash or banks. I didn't give a hang if the time travel was responsible, or something else was. I wasn't going to be found dead in my hotel and have Lou Pape curse my corpse because I'd been borrowing from him when, since 1931, I'd had a little fortune put away. He'd call me a premature senile psychotic and he'd be right, from his point of view, not knowing the truth.

Rather than make the deposit in October, 1938, I grabbed a battered old cab and told the driver to step on it. When I showed him the $10 bill that was in it for him, he squashed down the gas pedal. In 1938, $10 was real money.

We got a mile away from the bank and the driver looked at me in the rearview mirror.

"How far you want to go, mister?"

My teeth were together so hard that I had to unclench them before I could answer, "As far away as we can get."

"Cops after you?"

"No, but somebody is. Don't be surprised at anything that happens, no matter what it is."

"You mean like getting shot at?" he asked worriedly, slowing down.

"You're not in any danger, friend. I am. Relax and step on it again."

I wondered if she could still reach me, this far from the bank, and handed the guy the bill. No justice sticking him for the ride in case she should. He pushed the pedal down even harder than he had been doing before.

We must have been close to three miles away when I blinked and was standing outside the first bank I'd seen in 1931.

I don't know what the cab driver thought when I vanished out of his hack. He probably figured I'd opened the door and jumped while he wasn't looking. Maybe he even went back and searched for a body splashed all over the street.

Well, it would have been a hopeless hunt. I was a week ahead.

I gave up and drearily made my deposit. The one from early October that I'd missed I put in with this one.

There was no way to escape the babe with the beautiful hard face, gorgeous warm body, and plans for me that all seemed to add up to death. I didn't try any more. I went on making deposits, mailing orders to her stock brokers, and putting down bets that couldn't miss because they were all past history.

I don't even remember what the last one was, a fight or

a race. I hung around the bar that had long ago replaced the speakeasy, until the inevitable payoff, got myself a hamburger, and headed out the door. All the envelopes I was supposed to use were gone and I felt shaky, knowing that the next place I'd see was the room with the wire mesh cage and the hooded motors.

It was.

She was on the other side of the cage, and I had five bankbooks and envelopes filled with cash amounting to more than $15,000, but all I could think of was that I was hungry and something had happened to the hamburger while I was traveling through time. I must have fallen and dropped it, because my hand was covered with dust or dirt. I brushed it off and quickly felt my face and pulled up my sleeves to look at my arms.

"Very smart," I said, "but I'm nowhere near emaciation."

"What made you think you would be?" she asked.

"Because the others always were."

She cut the motors to idling speed and the vibrating mesh slowed down. I glared at her through it. God, she was lovely—as lovely as an ice sculpture! The kind of face you'd love to kiss and slap, kiss and slap . . .

"You came here with a preconceived notion, Mr. Gilroy. I'm a businesswoman, not a monster. I like to think there's even a good deal of the altruist in me. I could hire only young people, but the old ones have more trouble finding work. And you've seen for yourself how I provide nest eggs for them they'd otherwise never have."

"And take care of yourself at the same time."

"That's the businesswoman in me. I need money to operate."

"So do old people. Only they die and you don't."

She opened the gate and invited me out. "I make mistakes occasionally. I sometimes pick men and women who prove to be too old to stand the strain. I try not to let it happen, but they need money and work so badly that they don't always tell the truth about their age and state of health."

"You could take those who have social security cards and references."

"But those who don't have any are in worse need!" She paused. "You probably think I want only the money you and they bring back, that it's merely some sort of profit-making scheme. It isn't."

"You mean the idea is not just to build up a fortune for you with a cut for whoever helps you do it?"

"I said I need money to operate, Mr. Gilroy, and this method serves. But there are other purposes, much more important. What you have gone through is basic training, you might say. You know now that it's possible to travel through time, and what it's like. The initial shock, in other words, is gone and you're better equipped to do something for me in another era."

"Something else?" I stared at her puzzledly. "What else could you want?"

"Let's have dinner first. You must be hungry."

I was, and that reminded me: "I bought a hamburger

just before you brought me back. I don't know what happened to it. My hand was dirty and the hamburger was gone, as if I'd fallen somehow and dropped it and got dirt on my hand."

She looked worriedly at the hand, probably afraid I'd cut it and disqualified myself. I could understand that; you never know what kind of diseases can be picked up in different times, because I remember reading somewhere that germs keep changing according to conditions. Right now, for instance, strains of bacteria are becoming resistant to antibiotics. I knew her concern wasn't really for me, but it was pleasant all the same.

"That could be the explanation, I suppose," she said. "The truth is that I've never taken a time voyage—somebody has to operate the controls in the present so I can't say it's possible or impossible to fall. It must be, since you did. Perhaps the wrench back from the past was too violent and you slipped just before you returned."

She led me down to an ornate dining room, where the table had been set for two. The food was waiting on the table, steaming and smelling tasty. Nobody was around to serve us. She pointed out a chair to me and we sat down and began eating. I was a little nervous at first, afraid there might be something in the food, but it tasted fine and nothing happened after I swallowed a little and waited for some effect.

"You did try to escape the time tractor beam, didn't you, Mr. Gilroy?" she asked. I didn't have to answer; she knew. "That's a mistaken notion of how it functions. The control beam doesn't cover area; it covers era. You could have flown to any part of the world and the beam would still have brought you back. Do I make myself clear?"

She did. Too bloody clear. I waited for the rest.

"I assume you've already formed an opinion of me," she went on. "A rather unflattering one, I imagine."

"'Bitch' is the cleanest word I can find. But a clever one. Anybody who can invent a time machine would have to be a genius."

"I didn't invent it. My father did—Dr. Anthony Roberts—using the funds you and others helped me provide him with." Her face grew soft and tender. "My father was a wonderful man, a great man, but he was called a crackpot. He was kept from teaching or working anywhere. It was just as well, I suppose, though he was too hurt to think so; he had more leisure to develop the time machine. He could have used it to extort repayment from mankind for his humiliation, but he didn't. He used it to help mankind."

"Like how?" I goaded.

"It doesn't matter, Mr. Gilroy. You're determined to hate me and consider me a liar. Nothing I tell you can change that."

She was right about the first part—I hadn't dared let myself do anything except hate and fear her—but she was wrong about the second. I remembered thinking how Lou Pape would have felt if I had died of starvation with over $15,000, after borrowing from him all the time between jobs. Not knowing how I got it, he'd have been sore, thinking I'd played him for a patsy. What I'm trying to say is that Lou wouldn't have had enough information to judge me. I didn't have enough information yet, either, to judge her.

"What do you want me to do?" I asked warily.

"Everybody but one person was sent into the past on specific errands—to save art treasures and relics that would otherwise have been lost to humanity."

"Not because the things might be worth a lot of dough?" I said nastily.

"You've already seen that I can get all the money I want. There were upheavals in the past—great fires, wars, revolutions, vandalism—and I had my associates save things that would have been destroyed. Oh, beautiful things, Mr. Gilroy! The world would have been so much poorer without them!"

"El Greco, for instance?" I asked, remembering the raving old man who had been found wandering with $17,000 in his coat lining.

"El Greco, too. Several paintings that had been lost for centuries." She became more brisk and efficient-seeming. "Except for the one man I mentioned, I concentrated on the past—the future is too completely unknown to us. And there's an additional reason why I tentatively explored it only once. But the one person who went there discovered something that would be of immense value to the world."

"What happened to him?"

She looked regretful "He was too old. He survived just

long enough to tell me that the future has something we need. It's a metal box, small enough to carry, that could supply this whole city with power to run its industries and light its homes and streets!"

"Sounds good. Who'd you say benefits if I get it?"

"We share the profits equally, of course. But it must be understood that we sell the power so cheaply that everybody can afford it."

"I'm not arguing. What's the other reason you didn't bother with the future?"

"You can't bring anything from the future to the present that doesn't exist right now. I won't go into the theory, but it should be obvious that nothing can exist before it exists. You can't bring the box I want, only the technical data to build one."

"Technical data? I'm an actor, not a scientist."

"You'll have pens and weatherproof notebooks to copy it down in."

I couldn't make up my mind about her. I've already said she was beautiful, which always prejudices a man in a woman's favor, but I couldn't forget the starvation cases. They hadn't shared anything but malnutrition, useless money, and death. Then again, maybe her explanation was a good one, that she wanted to help those who needed help most and some of them lied about their age and physical condition because they wanted the jobs so badly. All I knew about were those who had died. How did I know there weren't others—a lot more of them than the fatal cases, perhaps—who came through all right and were able to enjoy their little fortunes?

And there was her story about saving the treasures of the past and wanting to provide power at really low cost. She was right about one thing; she didn't need any of that to make money with; her method was plenty good enough, using the actual records of the past to invest in stocks, bet on sports—all sure gambles.

But those starvation cases . . .

"Do I get any guarantees?" I demanded.

She looked annoyed. "I'll need you for the data. You'll need me to turn it into manufacture. Is that enough of a guarantee?"

"No. Do I come out of this alive?"

"Mr. Gilroy, please use some logic. I'm the one who's taking the risk. I've already given you more money than you've ever had at one time in your life. Part of my motive was to pay for services about to be rendered. Mostly, it was to give you experience in traveling through time."

"And to prove to me that I can't run out," I added.

"That happens to be a necessary attribute of the machine. I couldn't very well move you about through time unless it worked that way. If you'd look at my point of view, you'd see that I lose my investment if you don't bring back the data. I can't withdraw your money, you realize."

"I don't know what to think," I said, dissatisfied with myself because I couldn't find out what, if anything, was wrong with the deal. "I'll get you the data for the power box if it's at all possible and then we'll see what happens."

Finished eating, we went upstairs and I got into the cage.

She closed the circuit. The motors screamed. The mesh blurred.

And I was in a world I never knew.

You'd call it a city, I suppose; there were enough buildings to make it one. But no city ever had so much greenery. It wasn't just tree-lined streets, like Unter den Linden in Berlin, or islands covered with shrubbery, like Park Avenue in New York. The grass and trees and shrubs grew around every building, separating them from each other by wide lawns. The buildings were more glass—or what looked like glass—than anything else. A few of the windows were opaque against the sun, but I couldn't see any shades or blinds. Some kind of polarizing glass or plastic?

I felt uneasy being there, but it was a thrill just the same, to be alive in the future when I and everybody who lived in my day were supposed to be dead.

The air smelled like the country. There was no foul gas boiling from the teardrop cars on the glass-level road. They were made of transparent plastic clear around and from top to bottom, and they moved along at a fair clip, but more smoothly than swiftly. If I hadn't seen the airship overhead, I wouldn't have known it was there. It flew silently, a graceful ball without wings, seeming to be borne by the wind from one horizon to the other, except that no wind ever moved that fast.

One car stopped nearby and someone shouted, "Here we are!" Several people leaped out and headed for me.

I didn't think. I ran. I crossed the lawn and ducked into the nearest building and dodged through long, smoothly walled, shadowlessly lit corridors until I found a door that would open. I slammed it shut and locked it. Then, panting, I fell into a soft chair that seemed to form itself around my body, and felt like kicking myself for the bloody idiot I was.

What in hell had I run for? They couldn't have known who I was. If I'd arrived in a time when people wore togas or bathing suits, there would have been some reason for singling me out, but they had all had clothes just like ours—suits and shirts and ties for the men, a dress and high heels for the one woman with them. I felt somewhat disappointed that clothes hadn't changed any, but it worked out to my advantage; I wouldn't be so conspicuous.

Yet why should anyone have yelled "Here we are!" unless . . . No, they must have thought I was somebody else. I didn't figure any other way. I had run because it was my first startled reaction and probably because I knew I was there on what might be considered illegal business; if I succeeded, some poor inventor would be done out of his royalties.

I wished I hadn't run. Besides its making me feel like a scared fool, I was sweaty, out of breath. Playing old men doesn't make climbing down fire escapes much tougher than it should be, but it doesn't exactly make a sprinter out of you—not by several lungfuls.

I sat there, breathing hard and trying to guess what next. I had no more idea of where to go for what I wanted than an ancient Egyptian set down in the middle of Times Square with instructions to sneak a mummy out of the Metropolitan Museum. I didn't even have that much information. I didn't know any part of the city, how it was laid out, or where to get the data that May Roberts had sent me for.

I opened the door quietly and looked both ways before going out. After losing myself in the cross-connecting corridors a few times, I finally came to an outside door. I stopped, tense, trying to get my courage. My inclination was to slip, sneak, or dart out, but I made myself walk away like a decent, innocent citizen. That was one disguise they'd never be able to crack. All I had to do was act as if I belonged to that time and place and who would know the difference?

There were other people walking as if they were in no hurry to get anywhere. I slowed down to their speed, but I wished wistfully that there was a crowd to dive into and get lost.

A man dropped into step and said politely, "I beg your pardon. Are you a stranger in town?"

I almost halted in alarm, but that might have been a giveaway. "What makes you think so?" I asked, forcing myself to keep at the same easy pace.

"I—didn't recognize your face and I thought—"

"It's a big city," I said coldly. "You can't know everyone."

"If there's anything I can do to help—"

I told him there wasn't and left him standing there. It was plain common sense, I had decided quickly while he was talking to me, not to take any risks by admitting anything. I might have been dumped into a police state, or the country could have been at war without my knowing it, or maybe they were suspicious of strangers. For one reason or another, ranging from vagrancy to espionage, I could be pulled in, tortured, executed, God knows what. The place looked peaceful enough, but that didn't prove a thing.

I went on walking, looking for something I couldn't be sure existed, in a city I was completely unfamiliar with, in a time when I had no right to be alive. It wasn't just a matter of getting the information she wanted. I'd have been satisfied to hang around until she pulled me back without the data.

But then what would happen? Maybe the starvation cases were people who had failed her! For that matter, she could shoot me and send the remains anywhere in time to get rid of the evidence.

Damn it, I didn't know if she was better or worse than I'd supposed, but I wasn't going to take any chances. I had to bring her what she wanted.

There was a sign up ahead. It read: TO SHOPPING CENTER. The arrow pointed along the road. When I came to a fork and wondered which way to go, there was another sign, then another pointing to still more farther on.

I followed them to the middle of the city, a big square with a park in the center and shops of all kinds rimming it. The only shop I was interested in said: ELECTRICAL APPLIANCES.

I went in.

A neat young salesman came up and politely asked me if he could do anything for me. I sounded stupid even to myself, but I said, "No, thanks, I'd just like to do a little browsing," and gave a silly nervous laugh. Me, an actor, behaving like a frightened yokel! I felt ashamed of myself.

He tried not to look surprised, but he didn't really succeed. Somebody else came in, though, for which I was grateful, and he left me alone to look around.

I don't know if I can get my feelings across to you. It's a situation that nobody would ever expect to find himself in, so it isn't easy to tell what it's like. But I've got to try.

Let's stick with the ancient Egyptian I mentioned a while back, the one ordered to sneak a mummy out of the Metropolitan Museum. Maybe that'll make it clearer.

The poor guy has no money he can use, naturally, and no idea of what New York's transportation system is like where the museum is, how to get there, what visitors to a museum do and say, the regulations he might unwittingly break, how much an ordinary citizen is supposed to know about which customs and such. Now add the possible danger that he might be slapped into jail or an insane asylum if he makes a mistake and you've got a rough notion of the spot I felt I was in. Being able to speak English doesn't make much difference; not knowing what's regarded as right and wrong, and the unknown consequences, are enough to panic anybody.

That doesn't make it clear enough.

Well, look, take the electrical appliances in that store; that might give you an idea of the situation and the way it affected me.

The appliances must have been as familiar to the people of that time as toasters and TV sets and lamps are to us. But the things didn't make a bit of sense to me . . . any more than our appliances would to an ancient Egyptian. Can you imagine him trying to figure out what those items are for and how they work?

Here are some gadgets you can puzzle over:

There was a light fixture that you put against any part of a wall—no screws, no cement, no wires, even and it held there and lit up, and it stayed lit no matter where you moved it on the wall. Talk about pin-up lamps . . . this was really it!

Then I came across something that looked like an ashtray with a blue electric shimmer obscuring the bottom of the bowl. I lit my pipe—others I'd passed had been smoking, so I knew it was safe to do the same and flicked in the match. It disappeared. I don't mean it was swirled into some hidden compartment. *It vanished.* I emptied the pipe into the ashtray and that went, too. Looking around to make sure nobody was watching, I dredged some coins out of my pocket and let them drop into the tray. They were gone. Not a particle of them was left. A disintegrator? I haven't got the slightest idea.

There were little mirror boxes with three tiny dials on the front of each. I turned the dials on one—it was like using three dial telephones at the same time—and a pretty girl's face popped onto the mirror surface and looked expectantly at me.

"Yes?" she said, and waited for me to answer.

"I—uh—wrong number, I guess," I answered, putting the box down in a hurry and going to the other side of the shop because I didn't have even a dim notion how to turn it off.

The thing I was looking for was on a counter—a tinted metal box no bigger than a suitcase, with a lipped hole on top and small undisguised verniers in front. I didn't know I'd found it, actually, until I twisted a vernier and every light in the store suddenly glared and the salesman came rushing over and politely moved me aside to shut it off.

"We don't want to burn out every appliance in the place, do we?" he asked quietly.

"I just wanted to see if it worked all right," I said, still shaking slightly. It could have blown up or electrocuted me, for all I knew.

"But they always work," he said.

"Ah—always?"

"Of course. The principle is simple and there are no parts to get worn out, so they last indefinitely." He suddenly smiled as if he'd just caught the gist. "Oh, you were joking! Naturally—everybody learns about the Dynapack in primary education. You were interested in acquiring one?"

"No, no. The—the old one is good enough. I was just—well, you know, interested in knowing if the new models are much different or better than the old ones."

"But there haven't been any new models since 2073," he said. "Can you think of a reason why there should be?"

"I—guess not," I stammered. "But you never can tell."

"You can with Dynapacks," he said, and he would have gone on if I hadn't lost my nerve and mumbled my way out of the store as fast as I could.

You want to know why? He'd asked me if I wanted to "acquire" a Dynapack, not *buy* one. I didn't know what "acquire" meant in that society. It could be anything from saving up coupons to winning whatever you wanted at some kind of lottery, or maybe working up the right number of labor units on the job—in which case he'd want to know where I was employed and the equivalent of social security and similar information, which I naturally didn't have—or it could just be fancy sales talk for buying.

I couldn't guess, and I didn't care to expose myself any more than I had already. And my blunder about the

Dynapack working and the new models was nothing to make me feel at all easier.

Lord, the uncertainties and hazards of being in a world you don't know anything about! Daydreaming about visiting another age may be pleasant, but the reality is something else again.

"Wait a minute, friend!" I heard the salesman call out behind me.

I looked back as casually, I hoped, as the pedestrians who heard him. He was walking quickly toward me with a very worried expression on his face. I stepped up my own pace as unobtrusively as possible, trying to keep a lot of people between us, meanwhile praying that they'd think I was just somebody who was late for an appointment. The salesman didn't break into a run or yell for the cops, but I couldn't be sure he wouldn't.

As soon as I came to a corner, I turned it and ran like hell. There was a sort of alley down the block. I jumped into it, found a basement door, and stayed inside, pressed against the wall, quivering with tension and sucking air like a swimmer who'd stayed underwater too long.

Even after I got my wind back, I wasn't anxious to go out. The place could have been cordoned off, with the police, the army, and the navy all cooperating to nab me.

What made me think so? Not a thing except remembering how puzzled our ancient Egyptian would have been if he got arrested in the subway for something somebody did casually and without punishment in his own time—

spitting! I could have done something just as innocent, as far as you and I are concerned, that this era would consider a misdemeanor or a major crime. And in what age was ignorance of the law ever an excuse?

Instead of going back out, I prowled carefully into the building. It was strangely silent and deserted. I couldn't understand why until I came to a lavatory. There were little commodes and wash basins that came up to barely above my knees. The place was a school. Naturally it was deserted—the kids were through for the day.

I could feel the tension dissolve in me like a ramrod of ice melting, no longer keeping my back and neck stiff and taut. There probably wasn't a better place in the city for me to hide.

A primary school!

The salesman had said to me, "Everybody learns about the Dynapack in primary education."

Going through the school was eerie, like visiting a familiar childhood scene that had been distorted by time into something almost totally unrecognizable.

There were no blackboards, teacher's big desk, children's little desks, inkwells, pointers, globes, or books. Yet it was a school. The small fixtures in the lavatory downstairs had told me that, and so did the miniature chairs drawn neatly under the low, vividly painted tables in the various schoolrooms. A large comfortable chair was evidently where the teacher sat when not wandering around among the pupils.

In front of each chair, firmly attached to the table,

was a box with a screen, and both sides of the box held spools of wire on blunt little spindles. The spools had large, clear numbers on them. Near the teacher's chair was a compact case with more spools on spindles, and there was a large screen on the inside wall, opposite the enormous windows.

I went into one of the rooms and sat down in the teacher's chair, wondering how I was going to find out about the Dynapack. I felt like an archeologist guessing at the functions of strange relics he'd found in a dead city.

Sitting in the chair was like sitting on a column of air that let me sit upright or slump as I chose. One of the arms had a row of buttons. I pressed one and waited nervously to find out if I'd done something that would get me into trouble.

Concealed lights in the ceiling and walls began glowing, getting brighter, while the room gradually turned dark. I glanced around bewilderedly to see why, because it was still daylight.

The windows seemed to be sliding slightly, very slowly, and as they slid, the sunlight was damped out. I grinned, thinking of what my ancient Egyptian would make of that. I knew there were two sheets of polarizing glass, probably with a vacuum between to keep out the cold and the heat, and the lights in the room were beautifully synchronized with the polarized sliding glass.

I wasn't doing so badly. The rest of the objects might not be too hard to figure out.

The spools in the case alongside the teacher's chair could be wire recordings. I looked for something to play them with, but there was no sign of a playback machine. I tried to lift a spool off a spindle. It wouldn't come off.

Hah! The wire led down the spindle to the base of the box, holding the spool in place. That meant the spools could be played right in that position. But what started them playing?

I hunted over the box minutely. Every part of it was featureless—no dials, switches or any unfamiliar counterparts. I even tried moving my hands over it, figuring it might be like a terminal, and spoke to it in different shades of command, because it could have been built to respond to vocal orders. Nothing happened.

Remember the Poe story that shows the best place to hide something is right out in the open, which is the last place anyone would look? Well, these things weren't manufactured to baffle people, any more than our devices generally are. But it's only by trying everything that somebody who didn't know what a switch is would start up a vacuum cleaner, say, or light a big chandelier from a wall clear across the room.

I'd pressed every inch of the box, hoping some part of it might act as a switch, and I finally touched one of the spindles. The spool immediately began spinning at a very low speed and the screen on the wall opposite the window glowed into life.

"The history of the exploration of the Solar System," said an announcer's deep voice, "is one of the most adventuresome in mankind's long list of achievements. Beginning with the crude rockets developed during World War II . . ."

There were newsreel shots of V-1 and V-2 being blasted from their takeoff ramps and a montage of later experimental models. I wished I could see how it all turned out, but I was afraid to waste the time watching. At any moment, I might hear the footsteps of a guard or janitor or whoever tended buildings then.

I pushed the spindle again. It checked the spool, which rewound swiftly and silently, and stopped itself when the rewinding was finished. I tried another. A nightmare underwater scene appeared.

"With the aid of energy screens," said another voice, "the oceans of the world were completely charted by the year 2027 . . ."

I turned it off, then another on developments in medicine, one on architecture, one on history, the geography of such places as the interior of South America and Africa that were—or are—unknown today, and I was getting frantic, starting the wonderful wire films that held full-frequency sound and pictures in absolutely faithful color, and shutting them off hastily when I discovered they didn't have what I was looking for.

They were courses for children, but they all contained information that our scientists are still groping for . . . and I couldn't chance watching one all the way through!

I was frustratedly switching off a film on psychology

when a female voice said from the door, "May I help you?"

I snapped around to face her in sudden fright. She was young and slim and slight, but she could scream loud enough to get help. Judging by the way she was looking at me, outwardly polite and yet visibly nervous, that scream would be coming at any second.

"I must have wandered in here by mistake," I said, and pushed past her to the corridor, where I began running back the way I had come.

"But you don't understand!" she cried after me. "I really want to help—"

Yeah, help, I thought, pounding toward the street door. A gag right out of that psychology film, probably—get the patient to hold still, humor him, until you can get somebody to put him where he belongs. That's what one of our teachers would do, provided she wasn't too scared to think straight, if she found an old-looking guy thumbing frenziedly through the textbooks in a grammar school classroom.

When I came to the outside door, I stopped. I had no way of knowing whether she'd given out an alarm, or how she might have done it, but the obvious place to find me would be out on the street, dodging for cover somewhere.

I pushed the door open and let it slam shut, hoping she'd hear it upstairs. Then I found a door, sneaked it open and went silently down the steps.

In the basement, I looked for a furnace or coal bin or

a fuel tank to hide behind, but there weren't any. I don't know how they got their heat in the winter or cooled the building in the summer. Probably some central atomic plant that took care of the whole city, piping in the heat or coolant in underground conduits that were led up through the walls, because there weren't even any pipes visible.

I hunched into the darkest corner I could find and hoped they wouldn't look for me there.

By the time night came, hunger drove me out of the school, but I did it warily, making sure nobody was in sight.

The streets of the shopping center were more or less deserted. There was no sign of a restaurant. I was so empty that I felt dizzy as I hunted for one. But then a shocking realization made me halt on the sidewalk and sweat with horror.

Even if there had been a restaurant, what would I have used for money?

Now I got the whole foul picture. She had sent old people back through time on errands like mine . . . and they'd starved to death because they couldn't buy food!

No, that wasn't right. I remembered what I had told Lou Pape: anybody who gets hungry enough can always find a truck garden or a food store to rob.

Only . . . I hadn't seen a truck garden or food store anywhere in this city.

And . . . I thought about people in the past having their hands cut off for stealing a loaf of bread.

This civilization didn't look as if it went in for such drastic punishments, assuming I could find a loaf of bread to steal. But neither did most of the civilizations that practiced those barbarisms.

I was more tired, hungry, and scared than I'd ever believed a human being could get. Lost, completely lost in a totally alien world, but one in which I could still be killed or starve to death . . . and God knew what was waiting for me in my own time in case I came back without the information she wanted.

Or maybe even if I came back with it!

That suspicion made up my mind for me. Whatever happened to me now couldn't be worse than what she might do. At least I didn't have to starve.

I stopped a man in the street. I let several others go by before picking him deliberately because he was middle-aged, had a kindly face, and was smaller than me, so I could slug him and run if he raised a row.

"Look, friend," I told him, "I'm just passing through town—"

"Ah?" he said pleasantly.

"—and I seem to have mislaid—" No, that was dangerous. I'd been about to say I'd mislaid my wallet, but I still didn't know whether they used money in this era. He waited with a patient, friendly smile while I decided just how to put it. "The fact is that I haven't eaten all day and I wonder if you could help me get a meal."

He said in the most neighborly voice imaginable, "I'll be glad to do anything I can, Mr. Gilroy."

My entire face seemed to drop open. "You—you called me—"

"Mr. Gilroy," he repeated, still looking up at me with that neighborly smile. "Gilroy, isn't it? From the twentieth century?"

I tried to answer, but my throat had tightened up worse than on any opening night I'd ever had to live through. I nodded, wondering terrifiedly what was going on.

"Please relax," he said persuasively. "You're not in any danger whatever. We offer you our utmost hospitality. Our time, you might say, is your time."

"You know who I am," I managed to get out through my constricted glottis. "I've been doing all this running and ducking and hiding for nothing."

He shrugged sympathetically. "Everyone in the city was instructed to help you, but you were so nervous that we were afraid to alarm you with a direct approach. Every time we tried to, as a matter of fact, you vanished into one place or another. We didn't follow for fear of the effect on you. We had to wait until you came voluntarily to us."

My brain was racing again and getting nowhere. Part of it was dizziness from hunger, but only part. The rest was plain frightened confusion.

They knew who I was. They'd been expecting me. They probably even knew what I was after.

And they wanted to help!

"Let's not go into explanations now," he said, "although I'd like to smooth away the bewilderment and fear on your face. But you need to be fed first. Then we'll call in the others and—"

I pulled back. "What others? How do I know you're not setting up something for me that I'll wish I hadn't gotten into?"

"Before you approached me, Mr. Gilroy, you first had to decide that we represented no greater menace than May Roberts. Please believe me, we don't."

So he knew about that, too!

"All right, I'll take my chances," I gave in resignedly. "Where does a guy find a place to eat in this city?"

It was a handsome restaurant with soft light coming from three-dimensional, full-color nature murals that I might mistakenly have walked into if I'd been alone, they looked so much like gardens and forests and plains. It was no wonder I couldn't find a restaurant or food store or truck garden anywhere—food came up through the pneumatic chutes in each building, I'd been told on the way over, grown in hydroponic tanks in cities that specialized in agriculture, and those who wanted to eat "out" could drop into the restaurant each building had. Every city had its own function. This one was for people in the arts. I liked that.

There was a glowing menu on the table with buttons alongside the various selections. I looked starvingly at the items, trying to decide which I wanted most. I picked oysters, onion soup, breast of guinea hen under plexiglas, and was hunting for the tastiest and most recognizable dessert when the pleasant little guy shook his head regretfully and emphatically.

"I'm afraid you can't eat any of those foods, Mr. Gilroy," he said in a sad voice. "We'll explain why in a moment."

A waiter and the manager came over. They obviously didn't want to stare at me, but they couldn't help it. I couldn't blame them. I'd have stared at somebody from George Washington's time, which is about what I must have represented to them.

"Will you please arrange to have the special food for Mr. Gilroy delivered here immediately?" the little guy asked.

Every restaurant has been standing by for this, Mr. Carr," said the manager. "It's on its way. Prepared, of course—it's been ready since he first arrived."

"Fine," said the little guy, Carr. "It can't be too soon. He's very hungry."

I glanced around and noticed for the first time that there was nobody else in the restaurant. It was past the dinner hour, but, even so, there are always late diners. We had the place all to ourselves and it bothered me. They could have ganged up on me . . .

But they didn't. A light gong sounded, and the waiter and manager hurried over to a slot of a door and brought out a couple of trays loaded with covered dishes.

"Your dinner, Mr. Gilroy," the manager said, putting the plates in front of me and removing the lids.

I stared down at the food.

"This," I told them angrily, "is a hell of a trick to play on a starving man!"

They all looked unhappy.

"Mashed dehydrated potatoes, canned meat and canned vegetables," Carr replied. "Not very appetizing, I know, but I'm afraid it's all we can allow you to eat."

I took the cover off the dessert dish.

"Dried fruits!" I said in disgust.

"Rather excessively dried, I'm sorry to say," the manager agreed mournfully.

I sipped the blue stuff in a glass and almost spat it out. "Powdered milk! Are these things what you people have to live on?"

"No, our diet is quite varied," Carr said in embarrassment. "But we unfortunately can't give you any of the foods we normally eat ourselves."

"And why in blazes not?"

"Please eat, Mr. Gilroy," Carr begged with frantic earnestness. "There's so much to explain—this part of it, of course—and it would be best if you heard it on a full stomach."

I was famished enough to get the stuff down, which wasn't easy; uninviting as it looked, it tasted still worse.

When I was through, Carr pushed several buttons on the glowing menu. Dishes came up from an opening in the center of the table and he showed me the luscious foods they contained.

"Given your choice," he said, "you'd have preferred them to what you have eaten. Isn't that so, Mr. Gilroy?"

"You bet I would!" I answered, sore because I hadn't been given that choice.

"And you would have died like the pathetic old people you were investigating," said a voice behind me.

I turned around, startled. Several men and women had come in while I'd been eating, their footsteps as silent as cats on a rug. I looked blankly from them to Carr and back again.

"These are the clothes we ordinarily wear," Carr said. "An eighteenth-century motif, as you can see—updated knee breeches and shirt waists, modified stock for the men, the daring low bodices of that era, the full skirts treated in a modern way by using sheer materials for the women, bright colors and sheens, buckled shoes of spun synthetics. Very gay, very ornamental, very comfortable, and thoroughly suitable to our time."

"But everybody I saw was dressed like me!" protested.

"Only to keep you from feeling more conspicuous and anxious than you already were. It was quite a project, I can tell you—your styles varied so greatly from decade to decade, especially those for women—and the materials were a genuine problem; they'd gone out of existence long ago. We had the textile and tailoring cities working a full six months to clothe the inhabitants of this city, including, of course, the children. Everybody had to be clad as your contemporaries were, because we knew only that you would arrive in this vicinity, not where you might wander through the city."

"There was one small difference you didn't notice," added a handsome mature woman. "You were the only man in a gray suit. We had a full description of what you were wearing, you see, and we made sure nobody else was dressed that way. Naturally, everyone knew who you were, and so we were kept informed of your movements."

"What for?" I demanded in alarm. "What's this all about?"

Pulling up chairs, they sat down, looking to me like a witchcraft jury from some old painting.

"I'm Leo Blundell," said a tall man in plum-and-gold clothes. "As chairman of—of the Gilroy Committee, it's my responsibility to handle this project correctly."

"Project?"

"To make certain that history is fulfilled, I have to tell you as much as you must know."

"I wish *somebody* would!"

"Very well, let me begin by telling you much of what you undoubtedly know already. In a sense, you are more a victim of Dr. Anthony Roberts than his daughter. Roberts was a brilliant physicist, but because of his eccentric behavior, he was ridiculed for his theories and hated for his arrogance. He was an almost perfect example of self-defeat, the way in which a man will hamper his career and wreck his happiness, and then blame the world for his failure and misery. To get back to his connection with you, however, he invented a time machine—unfortunately, its secret has since been lost and never rediscovered—and used it for antisocial purposes. When he died, his daughter May carried on his work. It was she who sent you to this time to learn the principle by which the Dynapack operates. She was a thoroughly ruthless woman."

"Are you sure?" I asked uneasily.

"Quite sure."

"I know a number of old people died after she sent them on errands through time, but she said they'd lied about their age and health."

"One would expect her to say that," a woman put in cuttingly.

Blundell turned to her and shook his head. "Let Mr. Gilroy clarify his feelings about her, Rhoda. They are obviously very mixed."

"They are," I admitted. "She seemed hard, the first time I saw her, when I answered her ad, but she could have been just acting businesslike. I mean she had a lot of people to pick from and she had to be impersonal and make certain she had the right one. The next time I hope you don't know about that—it was really my fault for breaking into her room. I really had a lot of admiration for the way she handled the situation."

"Go on," Carr encouraged me.

"And I can't complain about the deal she gave me. Sure, she came out ahead on the money I bet and invested for her. But I did all right myself—I was richer than I'd ever been in my life—and she gave that money to me before I even did anything to earn it!"

"Besides which," somebody else said," she offered you half of the profits on the Dynapack."

I looked around at the faces for signs of hostility. I saw none. That was surprising. I'd come from the past to steal something from them and they weren't angry. Well, no, it wasn't really stealing. I wouldn't be depriving them of the Dynapack. It just would have been invented before it was supposed to be.

"She did," I said. "Though I wouldn't call that part of it philanthropy. She needed me for the data and I needed her to manufacture the things."

"And she was a very beautiful woman," Blundell added.

I squirmed a bit. "Yes."

"Mr. Gilroy, we know a good deal about her from notes that have come down to us among her private papers. She had a safety deposit box under a false name. I won't tell you the name; it was not discovered until many years later, and we will not voluntarily meddle with the past."

I sat up and listened sharply. "So that's how you knew who I was and what I'd be wearing and what I came for! You even knew when and where I'd arrive!"

"Correct," Blundell said.

"What else do you know?"

"That you suspected her of being responsible for the deaths of many old people by starvation. Your suspicion was justified, except that her father had caused all those that occurred before 1947, when she took over after his own death. All but two people were sent into the past.

Roberts was curious about the future, of course, but he did not want to waste a victim on a trip that would probably be fruitless. In the past, you understand, he knew precisely what he was after. The future was completely unknown territory."

"But she took the chance," I said.

"If you can call deliberate murder taking a chance, yes. One man arrived in 2094, over fifty years ago. The other was yourself. The first one, as you know, died of malnutrition when he was brought back to your era."

"And what happened to me?" I asked, jittering.

"You will not die. We intend to make sure of that. All the other victims—I presume you're interested in their errands?"

"I think I know, but I'd like to find out just the same."

"They were sent to the past to buy or steal treasures of various sorts—art, sculpture, jewelry, fabulously valuable manuscripts and books, anything that had great scarcity value."

"That's not possible," I objected. "She had all the money she wanted. Any time she needed more, all she had to do was send somebody back to put down bets and buy stocks that she knew were winners. She had the records, didn't she? There was no way she or her father could lose!"

He moved his shoulders in a plum-and-gold shrug. "Most of the treasures they accumulated were for acquisition's sake—and for the sake of vengeance for the way they believed Dr. Roberts had been treated. When there were unusual expenses, such as replacing the very costly parts of the time machine, that required more than they could produce in ready cash, both Roberts and his daughter 'discovered' these treasures."

He waited while I digested the miserable meal and the disturbing information he had given me. I thought I'd found a loophole in his explanation: "You said people were sent back to the past to *buy* treasures, besides stealing them."

"I did," he agreed. "They were provided with currency of whatever era they were to visit."

I felt my forehead wrinkle up as my theory fell apart. "Then they could buy food. Why should they have died of malnutrition?"

"Because, as May Roberts herself told you, nothing can exist before it exists. Neither can anything exist after it is out of existence. If you returned with a Dynapack, for example, it would revert to a lump of various metals, because that was what it was in your period. But let me give you a more personal instance. Do you remember coming back from your first trip with dust on your hand?"

"Yes. I must have fallen."

"On one hand? No, Mr. Gilroy. May Roberts was greatly upset by the incident; she was afraid you would realize why the hamburger had turned to dust—and why the old people died of starvation. *All* of them, not just a few."

He paused, giving me a chance to understand what he had just said. I did, with a sick shock.

"If I ate your food," I said shakily, "I'd feel satisfied until I was returned to my own time. *But the food wouldn't go along with me!*"

Blundell nodded gravely. "And so you, too, would die of malnutrition. The foods we have given you existed in your era. We were very careful of that, so careful that many of them probably were stored years before you left your time. We regret that they are not very palatable, but at least we are positive they will go back with you. You will be as healthy when you arrive in the past as when you left.

"Incidentally, she made you change your clothes for the same reason—they had been made in 1930. She had clothing from every era she wanted visited and chose old people who would fit them best. Otherwise, you see, they'd have arrived naked."

I began to shake as if I were as old as I'd pretended to be on the stage. "She's going to pull me back! If I don't bring her the information about the Dynapack, she'll shoot me!"

"That, Mr. Gilroy, is our problem," Blundell said, putting his hand comfortingly on my arm to calm me.

"Your problem? I'm the one who'll get shot, not you!"

"But we know in complete detail what will happen when you are returned to the twentieth century."

I pulled my arm away and grabbed his. "You know that? Tell me!"

"I'm sorry, Mr. Gilroy. If we tell you what you did,

you might think of some alternate action, and there is no knowing what the result would be."

"But I didn't get shot or die of malnutrition?"

"That much we can tell you. Neither."

They all stood up, so bright and attractive in their colorful clothes that I felt like a shirt-sleeved stagehand who'd wandered in on a costume play.

"You will be returned in a month, according to the notes May Roberts left. She gave you plenty of time to get the data, you see. We propose to make that month an enjoyable one for you. The resources of our city and any others you care to visit—are at your disposal. We wish you to take full advantage of them."

"And the Dynapack?"

"Let us worry about that. We want you to have a good time while you are our guest."

I did.

It was the most wonderful month of my life.

The mesh cage blurred around me. I could see May Roberts through it, her hand just leaving the switch. She was as beautiful as ever, but I saw beneath her beauty the vengeful, vicious creature her father's bitterness had turned her into; Blundell and Carr had let me read some of her notes, and I knew. I wished I could have spent the rest of my years in the future, instead of having to come back to this.

She came over and opened the gate, smiling like an angel welcoming a bright new soul. Then her eyes traveled startledly over me and her smile almost dropped off. But she held it firmly in place.

She had to, while she asked, "Do you have the notes I sent you for?"

"Right here," I said.

I reached into my breast pocket and brought out a stubby automatic and shot her through the right arm. Her closed hand opened and a little derringer clanked on the floor. She gaped at me with an expression of horrified surprise that should have been recorded permanently; it would have served as a model for generations of actors and actresses.

"You—brought back a weapon!" she gasped. "You shot me!" She stared vacantly at her bleeding arm and then at my automatic. "But you can't—bring anything back from the future. And you aren't—dying from malnutrition."

She said it all in a voice shocked into toneless wonder.

"The food I ate and this gun are from the present," I said. "The people of the future knew I was coming. They gave me food that wouldn't vanish from my cells when I returned. They also gave me the gun instead of the plans for the Dynapack."

"And you took it?" she screamed at me. "You idiot! I'd have shared the profits honestly with you. You'd have been worth millions!"

"With acute malnutrition," I amended. "I like it better this way, thanks—poor, but alive. Or relatively poor,

I should say, because you've been very generous and I appreciate it."

"By shooting me!"

"I hated to puncture that lovely arm, but it wasn't as painful as starving or getting shot myself. Now if you don't mind—or even if you do—it's your turn to get into the cage, Miss Roberts."

She tried to grab the derringer on the floor with her left hand.

"Don't bother," I said quietly. "You can't reach it before a bullet reaches you."

She straightened up, staring at me for the first time with terror in her eyes.

"What are you going to do to me?" she whispered.

"I could kill you as easily as you could have killed me. Kill you and send your body into some other era. How many dozens of deaths were you responsible for? The law couldn't convict you of them, but I can. And I couldn't be convicted, either."

She put her hand on the wound. Blood seeped through her fingers as she lifted her chin at me.

"I won't beg for my life, Gilroy, if that's what you want. I could offer you a partnership, but I'm not really in a position to offer it, am I?"

She was magnificent, terrifyingly intelligent, brave clear through . . . and deadlier than a plague. I had to remember that.

"Into the cage," I said. "I have some friends in the future who have plans for you. I won't tell you what they are, of course; you didn't tell me what I'd go through, did you? Give my friends my fondest regards. If I can manage it, I'll visit them—and you."

She backed warily into the cage. It would have been pleasant to kiss those wonderful lips good-bye. I'd thought about them for a whole month, wanting them and loathing them at the same time.

It would have been like kissing a coral snake. I knew it and I concentrated on shutting the gate on her.

"You'd like to be rich, wouldn't you, Gilroy?" she asked through the mesh.

"I can be," I said. "I have the machine. I can send people into the past or future and make myself a pile of dough. Only I'd give them food to take along. I wouldn't kill them off to keep the secret to myself. Anything else on your mind?"

"You want me," she stated.

I didn't argue.

"You could have me."

"Just long enough to get my throat slit or brains blown out. I don't want anything that much."

I rammed the switch closed.

The mesh cage blurred and she was gone. Her blood was on the floor, but she was gone into the future I had just come from.

That was when the reaction hit me. I'd escaped starvation and her gun, but I wasn't a hero and the release of tension flipped my stomach over and unhinged my knees.

Shaking badly, I stumbled through the big, empty house until I found a phone.

Lou Pape got there so quickly that I still hadn't gotten over the tremors, in spite of a bottle of brandy I dug out of a credenza, maybe because the date on the label, 1763, gave me a new case of shivers.

I could see the worry on Lou's face vanish when he assured himself that I was all right. It came back again, though, when I told him what had happened. He didn't believe any of it, naturally. I guess I hadn't really expected him to.

"If I didn't know you, Gilroy," he said, shaking his big, dark head unhappily, "I'd send you over to Bellevue for observation. Even knowing you, maybe that's what I ought to do."

"All right, let's see if there's any proof," I suggested tiredly. "From what I was told, there ought to be plenty."

We searched the house clear down to the basement, where he stood with his face slack.

"Christ!" he breathed. "The annex to the Metropolitan Museum!"

The basement ran the length and breadth of the house and was twice as high as an average room, and the whole glittering place was crammed with paintings in rich, heavy frames, statuettes, books, manuscripts, goblets and ewers and jewelry made of gold and huge gems, and tapestries in brilliant colors . . . and everything was as bright and sparkling and new as the day it was made, which was almost true of a lot of it.

"The dame was loaded and she was an art collector, that's all," Lou said. "You can't tell me that screwy story of yours. She was a collector and she knew where to find things."

"She certainly did," I agreed.

"What did you do with her?"

"I told you. I shot her through the arm before she could shoot me and I sent her into the future."

He took me by the front of the jacket. "You killed her, Gilroy. You wanted all this stuff for yourself, so you knocked her off and got rid of her body somehow."

"Why don't you go back to acting, where you belong, Lou, and leave sleuthing to people who know how?" I asked, too worn to pull his hands loose. "Would I kill her and call you up to get right over here? Wouldn't I have sneaked these things out first? Or more likely I'd have sneaked them out, hidden them and nobody—including you—would know I'd ever been here. Come on, use your head."

"That's easy. You lost your nerve."

"I'm not even losing my patience."

He pushed me away savagely. "If you killed her for this stuff or because of that crazy yarn you gave me, I'm a cop and you're no friend. You're just a plain killer I happened to have known once, and I'll make sure you fry."

"You always did have a taste for that kind of dialogue. Go ahead and wrap me up in an airtight case, have them throw the book at me, send me up the river, put me in the hot squat. But you'll have to do the proving, not me."

He headed for the stairs. "I will. And don't try to make a break or I'll plug you as if I never saw you before."

He put in a call at the phone upstairs. I didn't give a particular damn who it was he'd called. I was too relieved that I hadn't killed May Roberts; destroying anything that beautiful, however evil, would have stayed with me the rest of my life. There was another reason for my relief—if I'd killed her and left the evidence for Lou to find, he'd never help me. No, that's not quite so; he'd probably have tried to get me to plead insanity on the basis of my unbelievable explanation.

But most of all, I couldn't get rid of the look on her face when I'd shot her through the arm, the arm that was so wonderful to look at and that had held a murderous little gun to greet me with.

She was in the future now. She wouldn't be executed by them; they regarded crime as an illness, and they'd treat her with their marvelously advanced therapy and she'd become a useful, contented citizen, living out her existence in an era that had given me more happiness than I'd ever had.

I sat and tried to stupefy myself with brandy that should long ago have dried to brick-hardness, while Lou Pape stood at the door with his hand near his holster and glared at me. He didn't take his eyes off me until somebody named Professor Jeremiah Aaronson came in and was introduced briefly and flatly to me. Then Lou took him upstairs.

It was minutes before I realized what they were going to do. I ran up after them.

I was just in time to see Aaronson carefully take the housing off the hooded motors, and leap back suddenly from the fury of lightning sparks.

The whole machine fused while we watched helplessly—motors, switches, panel, and mesh cage. They flashed blindingly and blew apart and melted together in a charred and molten pile.

"Rigged," Aaronson said in the tone of a bitter curse. "Set to short if it was tampered with. I wouldn't be surprised if there were incendiaries placed at strategic spots. Nothing else could have made a mess like this."

He finally glanced down at his hand and saw it was scorched. He hissed with the realization of pain, blew on the burn, shook it in the air to cool it, and pulled a handkerchief out of his back pocket by reaching all the way around the rear for it with his left hand.

Lou looked worriedly at the heap of cooling slag. "Can you make any sense of it, prof?" he asked.

"Can you?" Aaronson retorted. "Melt down a microtome of any other piece of machinery you're unfamiliar with, and see if you can identify it when it looks like this."

He went out, wrapping his hand in the handkerchief.

Lou kicked glumly at a piece of twisted tubing. "Aaronson is a top physicist, Gilroy. I was hoping he'd make enough out of the machine to—ah, hell, I wanted to believe you! I couldn't. I still can't. Now we'll have to dig through the house to find her body."

"You won't find it or the secret of the machine," I answered miserably. "I told you they said the secret would be lost. This is how. Now I'll never be able to visit the future again. I'll never see them or May Roberts. They'll straighten her out, get rid of her hate and vindictiveness, and it won't do me a damned bit of good because the machine is gone and she's generations ahead of me."

He turned to me puzzledly. "You're not afraid to have us dig for her body, Gilroy?"

"Tear the place apart if you want."

"We'll have to," he said. "I'm calling Homicide."

"Call in the Marines. Call in anybody you like."

"You'll have to stay in my custody until we're through."

I shrugged. "As long as you leave me alone while you're doing your digging, I don't give a hand if I'm under arrest for suspicion of murder. I've got to do some straightening out. I wish the people in the future could take on the job—they could do it faster and better than I can—but some nice, peaceful quiet would help."

He didn't touch me or say a word to me as we waited for the squad to arrive. I sat in the chair and shut out first him and then the men with their sounding hammers and crowbars and all the rest.

She'd been ruthless and callous, and she'd murdered old people with no more pity than a wolf among a herd of helpless sheep.

But Blundell and Carr had told me that she was as much a victim as the oldsters who'd died of starvation with the riches she'd given them still untouched, on deposit in the banks or stuffed into hiding places or pinned to their shabby clothes. She needed treatment for the illness her father had inflicted on her. But even he, they'd said, had been suffering from a severe emotional disturbance, and proper care could have made a great and honored scientist out of him.

They'd told me the truth and made me hate her, and they'd told me their viewpoint and made that hatred impossible.

I was here, in the present, without her. The machine was gone. Yearning over something I couldn't change would destroy me. I had no right to destroy myself. Nobody did, they'd told me, and nobody who reconciles himself to the fact that some situations just are impossible to work out ever could.

I'd realized that when the squad packed up and left and Lou Pape came over to where I was sitting.

"You knew we wouldn't find her," he said.

"That's what I kept telling you."

"Where is she?"

"In Port Said, exotic hellhole of the world, where she's dancing in veils for the depraved—"

"Cut out the kidding! Where is she?"

"What's the difference, Lou? She's not here, is she?"

"That doesn't mean she can't be somewhere else, dead."

"She's not dead. You don't have to believe me about anything else, just that."

He hauled me out of the chair and stared hard at my face. "You aren't lying," he said. "I know you well enough to know you're not."

"All right, then."

"But you're a damned fool to think a dish like that would have any part of you. I don't mean you're nothing a woman would go for, but she's more fang than female. You'd have to be richer and better-looking than her, for one thing—"

"Not after my friends get through with her. She'll know a good man when she sees one and I'd be what she wants." I slid my hand over my naked scalp. "With a head of hair, I'd look my real age, which happens to be a year younger than you, if you remember. She'd go for me—they checked our emotional quotients and we'd be a natural together. The only thing was that I was bald. They could have grown hair on my head, which would have taken care of that, and then we'd have gotten together like gin and tonic."

Lou arched his black eyebrows at me. "They really could grow hair on you?"

"Sure. Now you want to know why I didn't let them." I glanced out the window at the smoky city. "That's why. They couldn't tell me if I'd ever get back to the future. I wasn't taking any chances. As long as there was a possibility that I'd be stranded in my own time, I wasn't going to lose my livelihood. Which reminds me, you have anything else to do here?"

"There'll be a guard stationed around the house and all her holdings and art will be taken over until she comes back—"

"She won't."

"—or is declared legally dead."

"And me?" I broke in.

"We can't hold you without proof of murder."

"Good enough. Then let's get out of here."

"I have to go back on duty," he objected.

"Not any more. I've got over $15,000 in cash and deposits—enough to finance you and me."

"Enough to kill her for."

"Enough to finance you and me," I repeated doggedly. "I told you I had the money before she sent me into the future—"

"All right, all right," he interrupted. "Let's not go into that again. We couldn't find a body, so you're free. Now what's this about financing the two of us?"

I put my fingers around his arm and steered him out to the street.

"This city has never had a worse cop than you," I said.

"Why? Because you're an actor, not a cop. You're going back to acting, Lou. This money will keep us both going until we get a break."

He gave me the slit-eyed look he'd picked up in line of duty. "That wouldn't be a bribe, would it?"

"Call it a kind of memorial to a lot of poor, innocent old people and a sick, tormented woman."

We walked along in silence out in the clean sunshine. It was our silence; the sleek cars and burly trucks made their noise and the pedestrians added their gabble, but a good Stanislavsky actor like Lou wouldn't notice that. Neither would I, ordinarily, but I was giving him a chance to work his way through this situation.

"I won't hand you a lie, Gilroy," he said finally. "I never stopped wanting to act. I'll take your deal on two considerations."

"All right, what are they?"

"That whatever I take off you is strictly a loan."

"No argument. What's the other?"

He had an unlit cigarette almost to his lips. He held it there while he said: "That any time you come across a case of an old person who died of starvation with $30,000 stashed away somewhere, you turn fast to the theatrical page and not tell me or even think about it."

"I don't have to agree to that."

He lowered the cigarette, stopped, and turned to me. "You mean it's no deal?"

"Not that," I said. "I mean there won't be any more of those cases. Between knowing that and both of us back acting again, I'm satisfied. You don't have to believe me. Nobody has to."

He lit up and blew out a pretty plume, fine and slow and straight, which would have televised like a million in the bank. Then he grinned. "You wouldn't want to bet on that, would you?"

"Not with a friend. I do all my sure-thing betting with bookies."

"Then make a token bet," he said. "One buck that somebody dies of starvation with a big poke within a year."

I took the bet. I took the dollar a year later.

Perfect Murder

Science Proves That a Man Can Kill Himself Without Committing Suicide!

Gilroy would never have chosen the way he died. He was far too conservative to have deliberately picked such a spectacular death.

Six days a week, for the past seven years, he had left his rooming house at precisely seven-thirty every morning. To say that people set their clocks by him would perhaps be an exaggeration. But it should be a matter of record that when Mr. Feeney, the janitor, saw Gilroy tramping down the stairs from 4M, that industrious gentleman knew the garbage truck would be around in nine minutes.

"Good morning, Mr. Gilroy," he had said 2,093 times. "How's the Sewage Disposal Department today?"

"Splendid, Mr. Feeney," Gilroy had generally replied. "We're installing a new wrinkle in shockproof mains this week."

But one morning Gilroy didn't come down. Feeney realized that nothing short of disaster could be responsible.

His first act, therefore, was to run up the stairs to 4M and tap gently. It was just possible that Mr. Gilroy had overslept. When Feeney got no response, he attacked the door with more vigor, pounding the panel. But he couldn't rouse Mr. Gilroy.

Worried, and even somewhat frightened, Feeney called the police. A few minutes later a radio patrol car rolled up before the house.

Two burly policemen burst through the front door.

"Upstairs," Feeney blurted. "4M."

They bounded up, their guns cautiously ahead of them. When they got to the door of 4M, it took their combined strength to break it down.

A very large living room stood revealed, with a smaller bedroom off to the right. They looked in on overstuffed furniture in the usual green and rust of the more expensive rooming house. Perhaps the only object worthy of attention was the corpse lying near the bile-green armchair.

"It's murder, sure enough," the first policeman said.

"Why couldn't it be suicide?" Feeney asked.

The second policeman pointed at the murder weapon. It was a pretty decrepit revolver, dating back generations. It looked as if it had been oiled with mud and polished with a mailman's sock. It lay almost twenty feet away from the corpse.

"Couldn't he of threw it?" Mr. Feeney asked innocently.

They snorted. After the deduction, the police examined the rooms. As usual, all the windows and doors were locked, and the nearest fire escape was out in the hall, with no convenient ledges that a fiendish acrobat might have been able to use.

They did find a gun permit in one drawer. It belonged to Gilroy, now deceased. The serial number on the gun matched that on the permit.

It was a perfectly ordinary perfect crime. Gilroy had been murdered in a locked room, with a gun that lay twenty feet away, and, as subsequent investigation proved, he hadn't an enemy in the world. Nobody seemed to think him important enough for hatred. All reports agreed that he had been meek and inoffensive.

Gilroy sat in the green easy chair, reading a fascinating book on the great strides London had made in wastage disposal. It was fascinating how an enormous city like London could do away with its sewage and yet keep its water clean.

Gilroy shook his pale, vague head admiringly. Now take their problem of slum congestion—much greater than New York—

Zzzziiirrr. Whoosh!

He leaped out of the green chair, clutching his fascinating book in thin hands that suddenly had gone cold and white. A mechanical whirring had filled the room.

Instantly, air had burst outward, compressing the excessively atmospheric air of the room.

Gilroy dropped his fascinating book. At the other end of the room stood a man, faultlessly dressed.

He was the exact duplicate of Gilroy!

Of course, there were minor details. He looked more muscular, harder, much more fit. And the mustache on his stern upper lip was real black, streaked with interesting gray, instead of Gilroy's dim, wispy, somewhat straining fringe.

Gilroy abandoned his ridiculous notion, pulled at his collar, for comfort a half size too large.

"Why can't you learn to dress properly?" the other demanded.

But Gilroy wasn't listening. For the first time he had noticed a compact, glistening mechanism behind the illusion who stood there disapprovingly. It was compact, yet Gilroy couldn't help imagining that it extended, somehow, somewhere. Nonsense, of course.

"Who—who are you?" he asked uncertainly.

Raising his neat trousers at the knees just the proper bit, the older man sat distastefully on the squat rust couch. Now that Gilroy felt almost calm, he observed the strong chin, the firm hands, the absolute self-possession of the other. He felt vaguely envious.

"I'm Gilroy," the other man said, more pleasantly. "I know this is quite a shock, but I'm you. You see, I've come from the future. Been dabbling around with time machines for several years, just so I could make this visit. It's very important to both of us."

Gilroy the younger smiled weakly. Weak as that smile was, it angered the other Gilroy.

"Don't be such a sap!" he rapped out. He gestured to the end of the room with a manicured thumb. "There's my time machine. It cuts through the time warp. Time, the fourth dimension, can be traveled as well and easily as any other dimension, provided one has the means. I have. With an elevator or airplane, you can rise into the third dimension. With a time machine, you can rise above, or descend below, the main stream of time."

"Oh," the younger Gilroy said puzzledly. "I see."

"You don't. But that doesn't matter."

They sat in silence for quite a while. The younger Gilroy was conscious of his prototype's keen and obviously disapproving scrutiny. When the older man spoke, however, it was in soft, winning tones.

"Gilroy," he said, and then stopped, his dark brows drawn. "I don't know how we should address each other. You'd better call me Mr. Gilroy. Is that all right, Gilroy?"

Gilroy nodded baffledly. It was the only touch of logic so far in an insane situation.

"Well," Mr. Gilroy continued. "What date is this?"

He strode to the tired end table, which seemed barely able to sustain the weight of an evening paper.

"December eleventh, nineteen forty-one. H-m-mm.

Then Marguerite hasn't married that ugly ape yet. You know—Will Hanson."

"Will Hanson?" Gilroy asked. Then the significance of the small word struck him. "What do you mean, she hasn't married him yet? She is supposed to marry me."

Mr. Gilroy leaned forward, his immaculate elbows on his sharply created knees.

"That's why I'm here, Gilroy," he said gently. "You know you haven't been making much progress with her. She's such a lovely thing, even without her fortune, that I know you'd hate to lose her. Well, let me tell you plainly—on January eleventh, next year, she's going to marry Will Hanson."

"Oh, but—" Gilroy protested, in his usual diffident way.

"But nothing! You and your damned sewage disposal. Is that all you can talk about to her and her father?"

Gilroy sat back primly.

"Marguerite and her father are very intelligent. They encourage me in every way. They always prompt me to talk on the subject."

"Sure! Sarcasm always was wasted on you."

Another bitter silence filled the depressing rust and green room. Now that Gilroy thought back, he could detect signs of irony in their leading questions. But his enthusiasm for his job had been so keen, he would have spoken to a gorilla with the same boring, extensive detail.

"Anyhow," Mr. Gilroy said, "she's under pressure from

her pa. Why she should love an object like you, I don't know, but she does. In January, though, what with high pressure from pa and Willie, and your general lack of everything, she going to take the leap.

"I've just come from sixteen years in the future. Let me tell you, Gilroy—Marguerite, then, is even more beautiful and rich than she is now. If you don't let me—"

Problem in Murder

Gilroy spread the office copy of the *Morning Post* over the editor's desk and stared glumly at the black streamer. The editor was picking at his inky cuticles without looking at them; he watched Gilroy's face.

"Twelfth ax victim found in Bronx," Gilroy muttered to himself. "Twelve—in two weeks, and not a single clue."

The editor started. He drew in his breath with a pained hiss and yanked out a handkerchief to dab at a bleeding finger. Gilroy raised his enormously long, gaunt head, annoyed.

"Why don't you get a manicure, chief? That nail-picking of yours is getting me too used to the sight of blood."

The editor ignored him. He wrapped the handkerchief around his finger and said: "I'm taking you off the torso story, Gilroy. What's the difference who goes down to headquarters and gets the police handout? You gotta admit it yourself—outside of the padding, your stories are exactly the same as any of the other papers'. So why should I keep an expensive man on the job when any cub can do as well, and there're other stories waiting for you to tackle them?"

Gilroy sighed resignedly and sat down. He sighed again and stood up, going behind the editor's desk to the window that looked over the dark river to the lights in Jersey. His incredibly ugly, sharply hewn face twisted thoughtfully.

"I get the point, chief. Sure; so far you're right. But, hell!" He wheeled swiftly. "Why can't we do anything by ourselves? Do we *have* to get our handouts from the cops? How about *us* doing some work! Aw, chief—will you leave that finger alone before I have a stroke?"

The editor looked up hastily, although his thumb continued to caress the bleeding cuticle. "How you gonna do your own detecting?" he demanded. "You—and no other reporter either—ever got near enough to the victims to give an eyewitness description of what they looked like. The cops won't even let you take a peek. They find an arm or a leg, all wrapped up in brown grocery bags; but did you ever see them? All night long they got radio cars riding up and down the Bronx, but pretty nearly every morning they find arms or legs. Well, Sherlock, what're you gonna do by your little self when the cops can't stop the murders?"

"Yeah. Getting a look at the chopped-off limbs is the main thing," Gilroy said, shuffling around slowly to the front of the desk, his hands in his pockets, his head down, and his wide mouth pursed. He was amazingly thin, even for a reporter, and within inches of qualifying as a circus giant. In his stooping position he resembled a furled umbrella. "Why don't the flatties give us a squint? There'd be more chance of identification. Maybe not much more, but more, anyhow."

The editor shrugged and went back to his cuticles.

Suddenly Gilroy raised his head. He stared piercingly at the editor. "If we use our heads, we *can* see one of those limbs!"

"Yeah?" the editor asked, mildly skeptical. "How?"

"Well, the bulldog edition's just hitting the stands. The final hasn't been put to bed yet. Suppose we insert a reward for finding one of the legs, arms, or whatever the next one'll be, and bringing it here. Tell me *that* wouldn't get results!"

The editor stuffed a sheet of paper into his typewriter. "How much should I make it for—two hundred and fifty? The board'll have time to clear it after they see the results."

"*Two fifty!*" Gilroy strangled. "I can think of ten people I'd cut to pieces for less. Make it, say, about fifty bucks—a hundred tops. But they got to bring it here and let us take care of the cops."

The editor nodded and typed hurriedly. "Compromise—seventy-five," he said. "And I got a swell spot for it. I'm dropping the subhead on the ax yarn, and this goes there in a black border. How's that?"

"Swell!" Gilroy grinned and rubbed his huge bony hands together. "Now, if the interns'll only stay out of this, maybe we can grab off an exclusive. Anyhow, I'm going up to the Bronx and look around myself."

The editor leaped out of his chair and grabbed Gilroy's lapel. "The hell you are! I've kept my men out of there so far, and they're staying out until the reign of terror is over. Don't talk like an ass. How'd you like to find yourself hacked to pieces, and all the cops are able to find is an arm or a leg? You're not going, Gilroy. That's that!"

"Okay, chief." Gilroy assumed a mournful expression. "Me no go."

"And I'm not kidding either. I'm no coward—you know that; but that's the one place I wouldn't mess around in. The cops up there're scared witless. If the maniac doesn't get you, they will, with a couple of wild shots. Don't go up there. I mean it!"

Gilroy got off the subway at 174th Street on the Grand Concourse, and walked south along the wide, bright highway. Traffic sped north, south, and east, but none of it turned west into the terror district. He met no pedestrians. The police had been taken off their beats along the Concourse to patrol the dark side streets.

Riding up to the eastern boundary of the danger area, Gilroy had reasoned approximately where he would stay during the night. Dismembered limbs had been found as far north as Tremont Avenue, as far south as 170th Street, west to just short of University Avenue, and east almost to the Concourse. The geographical center of the area would be a few blocks west of the elevated station at 176th Street and Jerome Avenue, but Gilroy knew it was too well patrolled for the murder.

He entered an apartment house. The Concourse at that point is about forty feet above the surrounding streets. He took the automatic elevator down five stories to the street level and walked boldly toward Jerome Avenue. His hands were out of his pockets, ready to shoot over his head if a policeman challenged him. But if anyone in civilian clothes were to approach, his astoundingly long, lean legs were tensed to sprint an erratic course, to dodge bullets.

Several times he crouched in shallow doorways or behind boulders in lots when he caught sight of policemen, who always traveled in pairs. He realized how helpless they were against the crafty murderer, and why, in spite of their vigil, murders had been committed at the rate of one a night, excepting Sundays, for the past two weeks. He, a reporter, not particularly adroit in skulking, found very little difficulty in getting through the police cordon to Jerome Avenue and 174th Street.

He looked carefully before crossing under the elevated; when he saw that the road was completely deserted, he raced from post to post, across to a used-car lot. While he was still on the run, he chose a car slightly to the front of the first row, flung open the door, and crouched down on the floor. From that position, with his eyes just above the dashboard, he had a relatively clear view of the avenue for blocks each way.

He made himself comfortable by resting against the panel. From time to time he cautiously smoked a cigarette, blowing the smoke through the hood ventilator. He was not impatient or in a hurry. The odds were that spending the night in the car would be fruitless; only by an off chance would the murderer happen to pass. But even so, it was better than merely waiting for official police bulletins, and there was always the hope that perhaps the maniac *might* slink by him.

Gilroy relaxed. His eyes did not. Automatically, they peered back and forth along the empty, shadowy avenue.

He wondered whether the murderer got his victims. All through the terror area, only policemen traveled in pairs. House doors were locked. Stores were closed. People getting off from work after dark stayed at hotels rather than go home through the night with horror on their heels. After the first murders, taxi drivers could be bribed to enter the area; now they refused fantastic tips, grimly without regret. Elevated trains roared overhead. They carried few passengers, none getting off here.

Even Gilroy could sense the cloyed atmosphere, the oppression of lurking, ambushed horror. Through those streets, where terror hid and struck, paired policemen walked slowly and fearfully, afraid of somehow being separated—hundreds of police, every available man— watchful as only deathly frightened men can be.

Yet in the morning another victim would be found somewhere within the borders of the danger area—only a limb or part of a limb; the rest of the body would never be found nor identified.

That was another angle that Gilroy found particularly puzzling. Obviously the murderer had some superperfect method of disposing of the bodies. Then why did he casually leave a limb where it could easily be found after each murder? Was it bravado? It must have been, for those dismembered limbs could have been disposed of even more easily than the rest of the bodies. But by destroying them, the murderer could have committed his crimes for an indefinite length of time, without detection.

It was long after midnight. Gilroy fished a cigarette out of an open pack in his pocket. For only an instant he bent under the dash to hide the match's flare. When he straightened up—

A man was walking north along the avenue! A man in a topcoat too large for him, a hat that shadowed his face, a small package in his left hand.

He halted. Gilroy could have sworn that the halt was indecisive. He raised the package and looked at it as if he had just remembered it. Then he dropped it at the curb, near a box of rubbish. He walked on.

Gilroy clutched the door handle. Cursing, he stopped turning it before it opened. A white-roofed police car cruised slowly northward; Gilroy knew that the passenger cop rode with his gun resting alertly on the open window panel.

For a moment he calculated his chance of dashing swiftly across the avenue, scooping up the bundle, and following the murderer before he escaped. But Gilroy sat tensely, biting furiously and impotently at his lip. It would be like running out of a bank at noon.

The elevated pillars hid his view of the corner toward which the murderer had strolled. But when he did not cross into Gilroy's line of vision, the reporter knew that he had turned up that street.

At that point the police car drew abreast, and Gilroy saw the men inside scrutinize every doorway, every shadow behind the posts, the dark lot he was hiding in.

And then they rode past without seeing him. When they reached the corner, Gilroy's hand tightened convulsively on the door handle. They did not accelerate suddenly up the street. Gilroy relaxed and opened the door stealthily. The murderer must have vanished.

Gilroy crouched and scuttled to the nearest pillar, like a soldier running under gunfire. He stood there until he was certain that no one had seen him. Then he darted from post to post, to one that stood opposite the abandoned parcel.

Only an instant he stopped. In the next second he had snatched it up, on the run, and huddled against a wall, hugging the bundle under his arm. He edged swiftly along the building to the corner where the maniac had disappeared.

Nobody was there, of course. But he broke into a long-limbed sprint, stuffing the bundle into his belt under the loose jacket where it could not be seen. At the corner he slowed to an unsuspicious walk.

It was lucky that he did so. Two policemen in the middle of the northwest block shouted for him to halt, came running with drawn guns.

He stopped and waited, his hands ostentatiously above his head. When they reached him, they covered him from both sides.

"Who the hell're you?" one barked nervously. "Why're you out?"

"Gilroy, reporter on the *Morning Post*. You'll find a wallet with my identification papers in my inside breast pocket. I'm unarmed."

Brutally, to cover his intense fear, the cop at his left tore the wallet out and held the papers to the street light. He passed them to his comrade.

"All right," the second growled in unabashed relief, "you can put 'em down, you damned, lousy half-wit. Come snoopin' around up here and scare the living hell out of us!"

"Next time," the other swore, "so help me, I'm gonna plug anything that moves. I don't care if it's the mayor himself. I'll find out who it is later. Anybody who's crazy enough to come up here where he don't belong don't deserve no better!"

"We got all we can do to keep from shootin' each

other when we pass another beat. Why don't you stinkin' reporters have a heart?"

Gilroy grinned. "Now, now, boys. It's only your nerves. All you have to worry about is an ordinary maniac. But I need a story!"

The first policeman ripped out a blast of curses. "Cut it out, Joe," the other said, as quietly as possible. "We'll boot this lug onto the el and report his paper to the commissioner. That'll fix him."

They expected Gilroy to cringe before that threat. It would mean being denied official police bulletins. But as they strode silently toward the elevated station, Gilroy's forearm pressed reassuringly against the brown paper bundle, inside the top of his pants. Bulletins—*huh*!

At five after nine the next morning, Gilroy and his close collaborator, the night editor, were roused from their respective beds and ordered to see the police commissioner immediately. They met outside his office.

"What's up?" Gilroy asked cheerily.

"*You* should ask," the editor grumbled. "Your idea backfired."

"Come on, you two," a police clerk called. "Get inside."

"Here it comes," the editor said resignedly, opening the door that led to the Jehovahesque presence of Police Commissioner Major Green.

The city had revolted against a reform administration, because of the high taxes needed for vital slum clearance; then against a businessmen's administration, because the high taxes remained without social projects being completed; and in desperation had elected a ticket of retired reserve army officers who had an extremely vague idea of civil rights.

Major Green pushed back from his desk and stabbed them with a hostile glare. "You're from the *Morning Post*, eh?" he barked in clipped military tones. "I'm being easy with you. Your paper campaigned for my election. Take that reward offer out and put in a complete retraction. I won't press for suspension of publication."

The editor opened his mouth to speak. But Gilroy cut in sharply: "That sounds like censorship." He fished out a cigarette and lit it.

"Damn right it does," Major Green snapped. "That's just what it is, and the censorship is going to stay clamped on tight just as long as that maniac in the Bronx keeps our citizens terrified. And put out that cigarette before you get thrown out."

"We don't want to fight you, commish," Gilroy said speaking with deadly deliberation around the cigarette that dangled uncharacteristically from the corner of his mouth. "If we have to, of course, we're in a much better position to fight than you are. Our newspapers'll take on only self-imposed censorship—when they think it's to the public's advantage."

Green's cold eyes bulged out of his stern face. Rage flushed every burly inch. Independent of his tense arms, his fingers clawed the desk.

"Why don't you shut up, Gilroy?" the editor hissed viciously.

"Gilroy, eh? That's the rat who sneaked inside the cordon—"

"Why should I shut up?" Gilroy broke in, ignoring the commissioner. "Ask him what he's done these last two weeks. Don't. I'll tell you.

"He's the only one in the police department who's allowed to make statements to the press. Reporters can't interview cops or captains; they can't even get inside the danger area at night—unless they try. He forces retractions on papers that step out of line.

"Well, what good has it done? He hasn't identified a single victim. He can't find the rest of the bodies. He doesn't know who the murderer is, or where he is, or what he looks like. And the murders're still going on, every night except Sunday!"

"Don't pay any attention to him, sir," the editor begged.

"I expect an arrest in twenty-four hours," Green said hoarsely.

"Sure," Gilroy's clear baritone drowned out his chief's frightened plea. "For the last two weeks you've been expecting arrests every twenty-four hours. How about giving us one? And I don't mean some poor vag picked up on suspicion.

"I'll give you a better proposition. You've been feeding us that line of goo because you don't have anything else to say. Most of the papers didn't even bother printing it after the first week.

"First of all, let us say anything we want to. We're not going to tip off the maniac. We do our own censoring, and we do it pretty well. Then, let us inside the danger zone with official recognition. We get inside anyhow, one way or another; but there's always the danger of being plugged by your hysterical cops. Finally, let us see the dismembered limbs and photograph them if we want to. Isn't that simple? And you'll get a lot further than you are so far."

Trembling, Major Green stood up, his craggy face shrunken into angles and creases of fury. He pushed his chair away blindly. It toppled and crashed, but he did not hear its clatter.

He caught up the telephone. "I'm—" He strangled and paused to clear his clogged throat. "I'm handling this my own way. I live up in the terror area with my wife and three kids. I'll tell you frankly—every night I'm afraid I'll go home and find one of them missing, I'm scared stiff! Not for myself. For them. You'd be, too, in my place.

"Here's my answer, damn you!" The telephone clicked and they heard a shrill metallic voice. "Get me Albany— the governor!"

Gilroy avoided the editor's worried eyes. He was too concerned with Major Green's reason for calling Albany.

"This is Major Green, sir, police commissioner of New

York City. I respectfully urge you to declare martial law in the Bronx danger district. The situation is getting out of hand. With the mayor's permission, I request the national guard for patrol duty. The confirmatory telegram will be sent immediately . . . Thank you, sir. I appreciate your sympathy—"

He clapped down the receiver and turned to them grimly "Now see if you can squeeze past the militia sentries on every corner in the territory. There'll be a sundown curfew—everyone indoors for the rest of the night.

"Martial law—that's the only answer to a maniac! I should have had it declared long ago. Now we'll see how soon the murders'll stop!

"And," he stated menacingly, "I still want that retraction, or I'll get out an injunction. Fall out!"

In utter gloom, the editor went through the outer office.

"Pretty bad, chief," Gilroy said grudgingly. "We could slip past the police cordon. Napoleon couldn't patrol every street before, but the militia can put a sentry on every corner. It doesn't matter, anyhow, so I guess you'd better print a retraction."

The editor glared. "Really think so?" he asked with curt sarcasm.

Gilroy did not reply. In silence they walked out of the office.

"Well, let's not take it so hard," the editor said finally.

"He was going to declare martial law anyhow. He was just looking for an excuse. It wasn't our fault. But, just the same, that nipplehead—"

"Lousy nipplehead is the term, chief," Gilroy amended.

When they reached the elevator, the switchboard operator called out: "You from the *Morning Post*? They want you down there right away."

They stepped into the elevator. The editor hunched himself into his topcoat collar. "The louse must have called up the board," he said hollowly. "Here's where we get hell from the other side."

Defeated, he hailed a taxi, though he was not in a hurry. Gilroy gave his Greenwich Village address. The editor looked up in surprise.

"Aren't you coming with me?" he asked anxiously.

"Sure, chief. I want to get something first."

At the apartment house, the editor waited in the taxi. Gilroy went upstairs. He took the brown grocery bag out of the refrigerator and made a telephone call.

"Willis, please." He held the wire until he was connected. "Hello. Gilroy speaking. Anything yet, Willis? . . . No? . . . Okay. I'll call later."

He went down with the package in his pocket. As they rode downtown to the newspaper building, Gilroy said, for the first time with concern on his face:

"If declaring martial law'd help, I wouldn't mind, even though it means giving that stiff-necked ape credit for brains. But this ax murderer'll only be scared off the streets; and when martial law'll be lifted, he'll go right back to work again. Green won't get him that way. He's got to be outfoxed. And he's plenty sly."

The editor remained silent. From his set, dazed expression, Gilroy knew he was thinking of a terse note in his pay envelope. Gilroy did not have to worry about his job; he might have to take less than he was getting at the moment, but he could always manage to get on a paper. The editor, though, would have to start again as a legman, and that would completely demoralize him.

"Aw, don't let it get you down, chief," Gilroy said as they stepped out of the taxi at the *Morning Post*'s building. "If I have to, I'll take the whole rap. I'll say I forged your initials to the print order. Anyhow, they're only going to warn us. You know—'A newspaper can't afford to antagonize its sources of information. Make an immediate retraction and don't let it happen again.'"

The editor nodded, unconvinced. Under board orders. Major Green had been the *Morning Post*'s pet candidate in the election campaign.

The day shift in the newsroom greeted them much too heartily. Gilroy recognized the ominous symptom. He had often discovered himself being overcordial to reporters about to be fired.

They entered the city editor's office. When he saw them, the city editor shook his head pityingly.

"You boys certainly started something. The board's sore as hell. They're holding a special meeting right now—"

The night editor stuffed his hands into his pockets and turned away.

"Sit down, boys. It might take some time before they cool off enough to be able to speak distinctly."

"Cut out the funeral march, boss," Gilroy said sharply. "You and the chief can soothe them. And even if Green cuts us off the official bulletin, we still can get along. Take a look at this!"

He had taken the parcel out of his pocket and put it on the desk. He ripped off the brown grocery bag.

"It's a foot!" the city editor cried.

"A *woman's* foot!" the night editor added, horrified. "Cut off at the ankle. *Ugh!*"

The City Editor yanked the telephone toward him. Gilroy held down the receiver grimly. "I'm not calling the cops," the editor explained. "I'm sending for a photog."

"Not yet," Gilroy stated flatly. "It's not as simple as that. Take a look at the foot first." He picked it up callously and showed them its sole. "See what I see? The skin is perfectly even—unthickened even at the pressure points. Not a corn or callus, toe joints straight—"

"So what?" the city editor demanded. "She could've worn made-to-order shoes. Maybe she was perfectly fitted all her life."

"Shoes aren't made that way," Gilroy retorted. "They've got to prevent the foot from spreading somewhat or else they won't stay on, so there are always points of contact that cause callus. Even if she'd walked barefoot on rugs all her life, there'd still be a tiny thickening."

The city editor pursed his mouth and stared. He had not imagined so much trouble from a simple ax murder. The night editor looked fascinatedly at the foot, picking blindly at his cuticles.

"Suppose she was a cripple or a paralytic," the city editor said.

"The muscles aren't atrophied. But for some reason or other, this foot never walked."

He removed the telephone from the city editor's unconscious grasp and called Willis again. When he had finished speaking, his face was grave. He picked up the foot again and pointed to an incision.

"I cut out a piece of muscle in the heel with a safety razor," he said, "and brought it to the chemist at Memorial Hospital. I made the incision because I knew she wasn't a paralytic. Muscles contain glycogen and glucose, which turns to lactic acid. Even if she'd been a complete paralytic—hadn't moved in years—there'd still've been a minute quantity of lactic acid."

"What'd he find?" the night editor asked.

"Not a trace of lactic acid! Chief—get Green on the telephone and find out what time the national guard'll be at their posts."

The night editor was accustomed to Gilroy's unexplained hunches. He quickly got an outside wire. "Major Green? . . . *Morning Post*. What time will the militia

be in the Bronx? . . . Five o'clock? . . . Quick work . . .
Thanks."

"Wow!" Gilroy shouted. "Stay here, chief. I've got to
find him before Green clamps down his martial law, or
he'll be shot or arrested!"

In half the number of strides it would take a normal
man in a normal state of mind, he was at the elevator,
ringing furiously.

The city editor could not keep up with Gilroy's mental
pace. "What the hell was he talking about? Who'll be
shot or arrested—the maniac?"

"I guess so," the night editor replied, unworried, absolutely confident in Gilroy. "Who else could he mean?
I guess he's going up to the Bronx to find him."

But Gilroy did not go to the Bronx. His first stop was at
the Forty-second Street Library. Rapidly, yet carefully,
he flipped through the index files on every subject that
might be a clue. He eliminated hundreds of titles; even
so, he had to write out dozens of slips.

The man at the pneumatic tube was not astonished
by the bundle of slips shoved viciously at him. "Another
case, Mr. Gilroy?" he asked.

"Yeah," the tall reporter growled. "A pip."

In the south hall he appropriated an entire table on
which he spread his books as quickly as they came up
from the stacks. He scanned the contents pages, occasionally going through a chapter for more detailed information; wherever necessary, he looked through the indices

of books that seemed to hold the key. A long sheet of foolscap swiftly became crowded with names.

He groaned at the clock. It was almost noon when he requested the city directory and a map of the Bronx. It was not very recent, but he was certain that the man he sought had lived in the same house for some time. With his ponderous equipment, he would have to, Gilroy reasoned.

He went through the enormous Bronx directory, eliminating every one of his references who did not live in the danger area. When he had finished, it was twenty to one, and there was not a single name left for him to investigate. He had eliminated all of them; not one lived in the district where terror reigned.

And he had only four hours and twenty minutes before that area would be under martial law—when it would be too late!

The two editors listened sympathetically, but they had no plan to offer. Gilroy scarcely heard them tell how they had soothed the board of directors. He was too frantically engaged in thinking.

How do you track down one man out of a city of nearly eight million? You don't know his name, what he looks like, where he came from, what he did before, who knew him. You only know that he lives in a mile-square territory, containing perhaps a hundred thousand people.

Gilroy did not have to ignore the city editor's persistent questioning. The night editor had quieted him to a glowering sulk by telling him that Gilroy would explain when there was no danger of being made a fool by a wild intuition.

"If we had block spies, like they have in Europe," Gilroy muttered, "we'd have had him long ago. But then he'd have been executed for doing something he didn't do. Well, three and a half hours to save the poor lug. How do I go about finding him?"

If he could interview every person in that mile-square district, he could easily find the man. Gilroy dismissed the idea. It was fantastic. But suddenly his eyes sparkled and he grinned at the night editor.

"Chief, I've got to make a canvass of the danger area. Will you back me? I've never let you down so far. Where do we get the dough to hire Peck, the ad distributors?"

The night editor writhed in his chair. He picked at his cuticles and his foot tapped nervously. "Special requisition," he said dully.

"Oh, no!" the city editor stated flatly. "I'm not writing it!"

"You don't have to. I'll do it."

Gilroy and the city editor realized the anguish that the night editor had gone through in making his resolution to back Gilroy. The business staff looked cockeyed at every expenditure, even routine ones; and this requisition, based on an unexplained hunch, they could not justify, even to themselves.

"Okay," Gilroy said in a low, respectful voice. "I'll call Peck and ask for their rates." Reverently, in a manner befitting the night editor's gallant sacrifice possibly of his job—Gilroy made a ritual of dialing. "Peck? . . . *Morning Post*. Can you interview everyone in the territory between the Grand Concourse and University Avenue, from 170th Street to Tremont Avenue, in an hour and a half? . . . Good. How much will it cost? . . . Cheap enough. I'll be right down with a check and a questionnaire."

He waited until the night editor wrote out the requisition, watching sympathetically the whitened, trembling fingers as they scrawled out the numerals. At each figure Gilroy knew that those fingers were trying to rebel against their violation of conditioning.

Gilroy squirmed impatiently in the squad captain's car. It was too much for him to sit by and merely watch the men going in and out of buildings. All over the danger area Peck investigators were ringing doorbells and calming down the terrified inhabitants enough to open their doors.

"I can't sit here," Gilroy protested. He opened the door. "I'm going to cover a few streets myself."

The squad captain restrained him politely. "Please, Mr. Gilroy. The whole territory has been mapped out. Each man's beat dovetails with the next one's. You'll throw them off their stride."

Gilroy subsided, grumbling furiously. He knew that the men were working with maximum efficiency, yet he could not help feeling that his own efforts would speed them up, perhaps inspire them.

Each investigator had a hard-cover notebook in which to write the answers he received. The books were divided into sections—four fifths for "ignorance," one tenth for "no," and the other tenth for "yes."

Gilroy's facile imagination could picture the astonishment his men's questions could cause: "I don't know what you're talkin' about, mister." "Sorry. We don't want any." "*Hah?*"

For a short while he amused himself with various fancied interviews; then he went back to cursing the men's slowness. In spite of his pessimism, the job was finished in the specified hour and a half, and the crew met at the squad captain's car, parked in the center of the district.

Gilroy eagerly collected the filled notebooks. "Send them home now," he said to the squad captain. "But there's ten bucks in it for you if you drive me around to these addresses."

He had been amazed to find so many affirmative answers. With the captain's help he organized the addresses into a route. As they rode to the first, Gilroy saw evidence of the terror that part of the Bronx lived in. Normally, children played noisily in the street, women sat on folding chairs on the sidewalks, delivery men made their rounds. But all was silent, deserted; frightened faces peered through drawn curtains.

At the first he rang cheerfully. A young man cautiously opened the door, which was held by a newly installed chain.

"An investigator was here a short while ago," Gilroy

said, speaking through the narrow crack. "You answered his question affirmatively."

The youth suddenly brightened. "That's right. I've been interested in the problem ever since I began reading science fiction. I think—"

It was a matter of some minutes before Gilroy could escape and go to the next address. There he had less trouble escaping; but after several stops he lost his temper.

"These damned science-fiction fans!" he snarled at the startled squad captain. "The place swarms with them. They've got to explain everything they know about the subject and ask what you think and why you're going around getting opinions. I've got about a hundred fifty addresses to investigate, all in less than an hour—and probably a hundred and forty-nine of them are science-fiction readers!"

At the seventeenth name he stopped abruptly. "This isn't getting me anywhere. Lay out the rest of these addresses in a spiral, starting from the middle of this territory."

The squad captain reorganized the route. They sped to the center of the danger area; and once again Gilroy began ringing doorbells, this time with a growing lack of cheerfulness as he eliminated one science-fiction fan after another. They were all scared to death of opening their doors; they made him wait until they did; and then he couldn't get away.

He came to a street of private houses. Immediately his enthusiasm returned. Inventors and experimenters are more likely to live in their own homes than in apartment houses. Landlords are not very hospitable to the idea of explosions, which, in their minds, are invariably connected with laboratory equipment. Then again, apartment houses hold room space at a premium, and scientists need elbow room.

He had only one address to investigate in this entire street of ultrarespectable, faintly smug one-family houses, each identical with the one next door, each nursing its few pitiful square yards of lawn.

But Gilroy felt exceedingly hopeful when he stopped at the proper house and look up at the dingy curtains, unwashed windows, and the tiny lawn, absolutely untouched in all the years it had been there. Only a scientist, he felt, could be so utterly neglectful. Gilroy was so certain he had come to the end of the trail that, before he left the car, he paid the squad captain and waited until he drove off.

Almost jauntily, then, he rang the bell. When there was no answer, he rapped and waited. He rang a trifle more insistently.

Suddenly children, no longer white-faced and terrified, came dashing happily out of houses for blocks around. Gilroy wheeled in alarm. They were screaming: "Sojers! A parade—*yay!*"

In panic, Gilroy glanced at his watch. It was a quarter to five, and from Jerome Avenue detachments of militia marched along the street, pausing at street corners to post armed guards. When they fell into step and approached Gilroy, the street crossing had four bayoneted sentries.

Gilroy stopped his polite ringing and tapping. His left thumb jabbed at the bell and stayed there; his right fist battered away at the door. And the militia marched closer, more swiftly than Gilroy had ever suspected heavily armed men could walk. The officer stared directly at him.

Just then the door opened and a small, wrinkled, old face peered up at him. The watery eyes behind their thick glasses gazed into his with infinite patience and lack of suspicion.

"Professor Leeds?" Gilroy snapped out. The old man nodded, the webs around his weak eyes wrinkling expectantly, utterly trustful. Gilroy did not look back over his shoulder. He could hear that the guard was nearly abreast now. "May I come in?" he demanded abruptly.

His tall form blocked the soldiers from Professor Leeds' view. The old man said, "Of course," and held the door wide. Gilroy hastily barged into a small dark space between the outer and inner doors. Leeds was saying apologetically: "I'm sorry I was so late answering the door; my servant is ill and I had to come up from my laboratory in the cellar."

"An investigator was here today," Gilroy broke in. "He asked you a question. You answered in the affirmative."

For the first time the old man's eyes clouded, in bewilderment, not suspicion. "That's true. I wanted to discuss the problem with him, but he merely wrote something in a notebook and went away. I thought it was very odd. How do you suppose he knew?"

Without answering or waiting for an invitation, Gilroy strode through the hall to the front room, with the professor pattering behind.

Another old man, considerably more ancient than Leeds, sat at the window in a wheel chair. He turned at their approach. Gilroy suddenly felt uncomfortable under his keen, distrustful scrutiny.

But Leeds still asked, gently persistent; "How do you suppose he knew that I was experimenting with synthetic life?"

"Shut up, perfessor!" the old man in the wheel chair shrieked. "Don't you go blabbin' everythin' you know to no international spy like him. That's what he is, asnoopin' and a-pryin' into your affairs!"

"Nonsense, Abner." Leeds faced Gilroy. "Don't pay any attention to him. You're not a spy, are you, Mr. ...uh—"

"Gilroy. No. I came here—"

"He brought me up from a child. I know he doesn't like to hear this, but his mind isn't what it used to be. He's a nasty-minded old crank."

Abner drew in his creased lips with a hiss of pain. Then he rasped: "No spy, huh? Why's he bustin' in with them sojers on his heels?"

"That's the point, boys," Gilroy said. He shoved his battered hat off his angular brow and sat on a plush sofa that was red only in isolated spots. Most of the nap had come off on countless pants, dust had turned it to a hideous purple, and a number of its springs coiled uselessly into the air. "Sit down, please, professor."

Leeds sat in the depths of a huge Morris chair and folded his hands.

"You *are* trying to synthesize life, aren't you?"

The professor nodded eagerly. "And I almost have, Mr. Gilroy!"

Gilroy leaned forward with his elbows on his high knees. "Do you read newspapers, professor?... I mean lately?"

"I have so much to do," Leeds stammered, his lined, transparent skin flushing. "Abner neglected his diabetic diet—gangrene set in—and his leg had to be amputated. I have to do all the cleaning, cooking, shopping, buy my material and equipment, take care of him—"

"I know," Gilroy interrupted. "I figured you didn't read the—"

He stopped in amazement. The professor had creaked to his feet and rushed to Abner's side, where he stood patting the old servant on the shoulder. Tears wee squeezing out of Abner's eyes.

"Ain't it bad enough I can't do nothin'," the old man wailed, "and I gotta let you take care of me? You're plumb mean, talkin' 'bout it!"

"I'm sorry, Abner. You know I don't mind taking care of you. It's only right that I should. Wouldn't you do it for me?"

Abner wiped his nose on his sleeve and grinned up

326

brokenly. "That's so," he admitted. "Reckon I must be gettin' into my second childhood."

Leeds returned to his seat, confident that Abner was pacified, and looked expectantly at Gilroy. "You were saying—"

"I don't want to scare you, professor. I'm here to help you."

"Fine," Leeds smiled, with absolute trust.

"You watch that there slicker," Abner whispered hoarsely.

"You made several limbs and at least one foot, didn't you?" Gilroy asked. "You weren't satisfied with them, so you threw them away."

"Oh, they were no good at all, complete failures," Leeds confided.

"Let's leave that until later. No doubt you had good reasons for discarding the limbs. But you just threw them away in the street, and people found them. Now the people up here're afraid of being murdered and hacked to pieces. They think those limbs were chopped off corpses!"

"Really?" Leeds smiled tolerantly. "Isn't that silly? A few simple tests would prove that they never lived."

"I made a couple of those tests," Gilroy said. "That's how I found out that they were synthetic limbs. But you won't convince the cops and these people up here that they were. So now there's martial law in this part of the Bronx, with soldiers posted on every corner."

Leeds stood up; he shuffled back and forth, his hands twisting anxiously behind his back. "Oh, dear," he gasped. "My goodness! I had no idea I would cause so much trouble. You understand, don't you, Mr. Gilroy? I was experimenting with limbs, studying them, before I felt I was ready to construct an entire synthetic human being. The limbs were highly imperfect. I had to dispose of them somehow. So, when I went out for walks at night, I wrapped them up and threw them away. They seemed so imperfect to me. They scarcely looked human, I thought—"

Abner's mouth had dropped open in astonishment. He compressed it grimly and said: "You gotta clear yourself, perfessor. You're the first Leeds that anybody ever called a murderer! Go out and tell them!"

"Precisely." Leeds walked purposefully toward his top-coat, draped over a sagging grand piano. "Dear me—I had no idea! I know just how the people feel. They must think I'm just a common Jack the Ripper. Please help me with my coat, Mr. Gilroy. I'll go right down and explain to the authorities that it was all a terrible mistake; and I'll bring a synthetic limb with me as proof. That will clear everything up."

Abner bounced excitedly in his chair. "Atta boy, perfessor!"

"Wait a minute," Gilroy said sharply, before the situation could get out of hand. He snatched the coat and held it tightly under his arm. "You'll be stopped by the sentries. They'll search you. Most of them're green kids out on what they think is a dangerous job—getting a bloodthirsty maniac. If they find a synthetic limb on you, bullets're liable to start flying—plain nervousness, you know, but in the line of duty."

"Heavens!" Leeds cried. "They wouldn't actually *shoot* me!"

"They might. But suppose they let you through. You'd come up against a police commissioner who hates to have anyone prove he's a fool. He's drawn hundreds of cops off their regular beats to patrol this section. Luckily he didn't catch you. So he had to have martial law declared. The papers've been giving him hell, demanding the maniac's arrest. He's jittery. His reputation's at stake.

"Then you come in telling him that the limbs were synthetic, that there weren't any murders. Why, he'd perjure himself and line up hundreds of witnesses to prove that you were the murderer. He'd take your own confession and twist it to prove that you were cutting people up to study them. Don't you see? . . . He's got to solve these murders, but he's got to solve them the right way: with someone in the electric chair!"

Leeds dropped into a chair. His watery eyes clung to Gilroy's, frankly terrified. "What shall I do?" he begged in scared bewilderment.

The reporter had to escape that pleading, frightened stare. He gazed down at the charred fireplace. "Damned if I know. Anything but explaining to Major Green. *Anything* but that!"

"He's right, perfessor," Abner chattered, fearful for his

master's life. "I know them durned coppers. Don't care who they send to the chair, long's they got somebody to send there so's they get the credit."

At that point Leeds broke down. Babbling in horror, he shuffled swiftly out of the room. Gilroy leaped after him, along the hall and down to the cellar.

He heard sobbing in the basement laboratory. He clattered down the steps. He was surrounded by shelves of canned and bottled chemicals that clung to the raw cement walls and had been gathering dust for the good part of a century. A broad bench was constructed in two parts, one on each side of a twin, broad-bellied sink that had originally been meant for laundry. A furnace squatted stolidly in the midst of the apparatus.

Then he saw Leeds, half concealed by the furnace, crouching protectively over a deep zinc tank like a bathtub.

"When will they come to arrest me?" he moaned. "I'd hoped to finish my experiment—I'm so close to the solution!"

Gilroy was touched. "They're not coming to arrest you," he said gently. "So far the cops don't know who did it."

"They don't?" Leeds brightened. "But you found out."

"The cops never know anything. Only—" He hesitated, then blurted his single fear: "There's the chance that Major Green might become panicky that his maniac's slipping out of his fingers. He might have the militia search the houses!"

The old man trembled with redoubled fear. "If they did that—"

"This's what they'd find," Gilroy said, looking into the clear bath that filled the high, sharply square tank. In his career he had seen disgusting sights, but the human skeleton at the bottom of the chemical bath, with shreds of muscle, wisps of fatty nerves and an embryonic tracery of veins and arteries adhering to the almost exposed bones, made his hobnailed heart shrink. It took an effort to realize that the tattered remains were not remains but beginnings. The naked skull bore only the revolting fundamentals of what would eventually become features. "They'd think you were dissolving a body in acid!"

Leeds stared at the corpse in fascinated horror. "It *does* look like a dissolving body, doesn't it?" he quavered. "But it won't when it's complete—"

"When'll that be?" Gilroy demanded hopefully.

"In about twenty-four hours." The old man looked up at Gilroy's abstracted face. "Do you think that will be enough time?"

"God knows. I certainly don't."

The situation definitely held a concrete danger. Gilroy knew that high positions often twisted the morality of men who had them. Most men in Major Green's place would unscrupulously sacrifice a single life for the good will of eight million, and perhaps a national reputation. Major Green, in particular, had been conditioned to think very little of individuals. If the militia searched the house, Leeds was almost in the chair.

They climbed up to the front room. Abner still sat at the window; he seemed to be fascinated by the militiamen standing at ease on the four street corners within his vision.

"Huh—young whippersnappers!" he hissed at the boys standing guard. "If I had my leg back, I'd get past them fast enough, you betcha!"

Leeds' characteristic optimism had ebbed away, sapped by the knowledge of the chaos his lifework had caused. He sat huddled in a chair as far away from the window as the wall would permit, his terrified mind absolutely useless to Gilroy.

The tall reporter saw only one hope. He felt his analysis of Green had been correct, but—he did not have to convince the commissioner! He had only to convince the public. Green would be washed up as a public figure; on the other hand, Leeds would be saved from being railroaded to the electric chair, and the chief's expense account would be cleared by a scoop! For any single item, he would gladly sacrifice Major Green.

He gripped the professor's thin arm in a hand like a tree root. "I'll get you out of this," he promised.

"Can you really?" Leeds asked breathlessly. "You don't know how I—"

"Don't step out of the house until I come back. In a couple of minutes it'll be curfew. Chances are I won't be back before morning—"

Leeds followed him to the door in a panic. "But please don't leave me, Mr. Gilroy! Please—"

"You'll be all right. Abner's here with you."

"Sure," Abner croaked from the front room. "You got nothin' to fret about with me here. But ain't it time for my mush and milk, perfessor?"

"I'll get it for you immediately," Leeds quavered; then Gilroy was out in the darkening street, wondering how he was going to get past the alert sentries, who had already turned to watch his long body glooming up uncertainly toward them.

On the other side of the Concourse, out of the martial-law district, Gilroy crowded himself into an inadequate telephone booth and dialed the office. Getting past the sentries had been ridiculously easy; he had only had to show them his guild card and explain that he worked on the night shift, and they had let him pass.

The night editor answered, rather tiredly.

"Gilroy, chief. Listen carefully. I found the guy. That thing I showed you today wasn't real. It was synthetic. The others were, too. I've got to clear him. He's working on a whole one—you know what I mean. If it's found, he's cooked."

"What do you want me to do?"

Gilroy put his mouth against the transmitter and said in a low tone: "I can clear him and grab off a scoop. That'd fix up that special-requisition business for you. He's got an entire one that's about half done. Send me down a photog with plenty of film. We'll take pix of the thing developing, slap it on the front page, and Nappie can go fly a kite!"

"Nothing doing, Gilroy," the editor said decisively. "This'd fix my job more than the special req. The board has big plans for Nappie. They're making eyes at Albany'n after that it's only a step to the White House. Nope. This'd knife him. It'd mean my job for sure."

"Wouldn't it be worth it?"

"Look Gilroy—I'm taking enough of a chance as it is, backing you. I can't go sticking my chin out at the board any more than that. Just be a good boy and figure out some other way of saving your pal. You can do it. I'll back you all you want. But get a beat if you can."

"Okay, chief," Gilroy said fatalistically. "I'll go home and grab some sleep. Leave me a blank signed req. I'll dope something out."

Long before dawn, Gilroy's mind came awake. He did not open his eyes, for, through his shut lids, he could see that the sun had not yet risen. He lay quietly, thinking. His blanket, which, of course, was too short when spread the usual way, covered him in a diamond shape, one end caught tightly beneath his feet and the other high on his bony neck. His knees were drawn up, soles pressed against the baseboard. Ever since attaining full growth, he had been forced to sleep that way; but his adaptive nature did not rebel against conforming to beds that were too small, telephones in booths that reached his solar plexus unless he shoehorned himself down, or bus seats that scraped his sensitive knees.

In some way, he was thinking, he had to stop the reign of terror in the Bronx; prevent suspicion from being focused on Professor Leeds; and, at the same time, cover the night editor's expense account—which meant getting a beat that would not smash Major Green's reputation.

But, to keep the police commissioner's record clean, he needed a victim. Gilroy knew enough about public pressure to realize that a sacrifice was absolutely vital. Left to himself, Green would find himself one anybody it could be pinned on. The public would be satisfied, and the strutting martinet would again be a hero.

Gilroy's duty was plain; he would have to find a victim for Green.

At that point Gilroy's eyes almost snapped open. By sheer will power he kept them shut, and contented himself with grinning into the dark. What a cinch! he exulted. He'd get a victim, and a good one! All at one shot—end the terror, clear the professor, get a scoop, and save the chief's job! Incidentally, he would also give Napoleon a lush boost, but that was only because it worked out that way.

Gilroy pulled his knees higher, kicking the blanket smooth without even thinking about it, and turned over to go back to sleep. There were a few trifling details, but they would be settled in the morning.

The city editor had scarcely glanced at the memos left on his desk when Gilroy strode in.

"Morning, boss," the reporter greeted cheerily. "Did the chief leave a requisition?"

"Yeah, a blank one, signed. Fill in the amount. I don't know—he must be going soft, leaving himself wide open like that." Gilroy waved his hand confidently. "He's got nothing to worry about. Tonight we'll have an exclusive that'll burn up the other rags.

"But, first of all, do you know a good, reliable *undertaker* and how much he'll charge?"

"Oh, go to hell," the editor growled, puttering about among the papers on his desk. Then his mouth fell open. "An undertaker?"

Instead of answering, Gilroy had dialed a number. "Gilroy . . . How's he coming along? . . . No, not Abner; the other one . . . Good . . . Is there any way of speeding it up? . . . Well, even a few hours'll help. I'll be up as soon as I fix everything down here . . . Oh, you don't have to get panicky. Just stick in the house until I get there."

"Who was that?" the editor demanded. "And why the undertaker?"

"Never mind; I'll take care of it myself. I want your gun. I'll get a hammer and cold chisel off the super. Write a req for the gun—the paper'll take care of it. Let's see, anything else? Oh, yeah—"

Gravely, he took the gun from the astounded city editor. As he sat down at the typewriter and began tapping at the keys, he was completely aware of the city editor's stare. But he went on typing.

Within a few minutes he yanked the paper out of the

machine and disappeared into the elevator. In the basement he borrowed the hammer and cold chisel from the apathetic superintendent. For nearly an hour he pounded, hidden away behind the vast heating system. When he put the gun into his back pocket, the serial numbers had been crudely chiseled off.

Then he took a taxi and made a tour of undertaking establishments. Curiously, he seemed less interested in prices, caskets, and the luxuriousness of the hearses than he was in the condition of the owner's businesses and the character of the drivers.

He found the midtown funeral parlors too flourishing for his satisfaction. he drove to a Tenth Avenue framehouse establishment.

"Rotten," the owner grumbled in reply to Gilroy's question. "The city's taking over these here tenements. Nobody lives here, so how can they be kicking off? I'll have to get out soon, myself."

Gilroy approved of the driver, who had evidently seen plenty of shady funerals. He offered the owner a flat sum for a full day's rental of the hearse and chauffeur. He was extremely pleased to see the gloating light in the owner's sad eyes. There would be no questions asked and no answers given here, he thought shrewdly.

Finally he called the city editor and told him bluntly to have two photographers waiting for his call, ready to meet him anywhere in the city. He slammed down the receiver before the editor began cursing.

It was merely another experience in a reporter's life to

be driving uptown in a hearse. At 125th Street he suddenly remembered something very important. He had the driver stop, walked two blocks toward the Third Avenue el. When he returned twenty minutes later, he carried a bundle, which he threw into the long wicker basket inside the hearse.

He had not anticipated any difficulty in passing the militiamen. He knew that mailmen, street cleaners, telegraph boys, doctors, and hearses would be able to move around freely within the martial-law area.

They rode, unchallenged, directly to Professor Leeds' door. There he and the driver slid the basket out and carried it into the house. The sentries were scarcely aware of their actions.

"I'm so happy to see you again, Mr. Gilroy!" the professor cried. Then he gaped at the basket. "What is our plan?" he asked anxiously.

From the front room came Abner's querulous voice: "They ain't here for me, are they, professor?"

"No, Abner," Gilroy called out assuringly. "Stay here, driver."

He led the professor down to the basement laboratory. Gilroy nodded in a satisfied way at the body in the tank.

"Another two hours and it will be finished." Leeds said.

The epidermis was almost completely formed. Only in isolated spots could the glaring red muscle be seen where the skin had not quite joined. Its fingers and toes had no nails; and, excepting the lack of hair, eyebrows and lashes, its features were distinctly human and complete.

"I'm just waiting for the hair to grow. That's the final stage. The skin will be whole in a few minutes. Then the nails—"

Gilroy heard wheels rumbling over the ceiling. The cellar door flung open and Abner shouted down, in terror: "Perfessor! Hey—them durn sojers're goin' through all the houses on this here street!"

Gilroy leaped up the stairs and dashed through the hall to the front windows. At each end of the block he saw eight soldiers; four stood in the gutter, facing opposite sides of the street with leveled guns. The other four paired off and entered houses with fixed bayonets.

"They can't do that 'thout a warrant," Abner protested.

"Can't they?" Gilroy snorted. "They can, and they're doing it. Sit here by the window, Abner, and warn us when they're getting close. They still have half a block to go before they reach us. Come on, prof—"

He removed the bundle from the long wicker basket and raced down to the cellar. While he ripped off the paper, he ordered the professor to take the body out of the chemical bath and dry it.

Leeds cried out: "He isn't complete yet!" But he removed the body, in spite of his complaints, dragged it to the floor and dried it. "It isn't alive!" he suddenly wailed, his hand shaking against its chest. "It should be—it's perfect!"

Gilroy shook out an entire outfit of clothing, a pair of old shoes and a filthy hat that closely resembled his own. "If he isn't alive, all the better," he said. "Anyhow, I always thought it was too much to expect him to live. Take fish, for instance. Put them in the same kind of water they always lived in—temperature just right, plenty of oxygen, plenty of food—and what do they do? They die. You make a body that's identical to a living one, all the necessary organs, all the chemical ingredients for life—and it just doesn't live. Otherwise, it's perfect.

"Here, lift up his legs so I can slip these pants on him."

"You're on the wrong track, prof, when it comes to making synthetic human beings. You can give them everything but the life force. But there *is* one thing you can do. You can grow limbs on people who don't have 'em. Give Abner a leg. His life force can vitalize the synthetic leg."

They pulled a shirt on the body and tucked it inside the trousers. Gilroy spent a mad few minutes trying to knot a tie in reverse, until he knelt and tied it from behind. While he forced its arms into a vest and jacket, Leeds squeezed its flabby, yielding feet into shoes.

Then Abner croaked: "They're only two houses away, professor!"

Leeds grew too jittery to tie the laces, Gilroy did it,

crammed the battered hat into the body's coat pocket, and roared for the hearse driver to bring down the basket. It was the work of a moment to load the corpse into it and strap on the cover. Almost at a run, he and the driver carried it up the cellar stairs to the front door. They dropped it while Gilroy made a hurried telephone call:

"Boss? Gilroy. Send the two photogs to 138th and Triboro Bridge. Right before the entrance. I'll pick them up in a hearse. Be there with the chief if you can get him to wake up."

He paused a moment to pat Abner on the back encouragingly. He said: "You're all clear, prof. Look in the *Morning Post* tonight. Drain the tank. If they ask about it, say you used to bathe a dog in it. So long!"

They carried the wicker basket to the hearse at a slow, fitting pace, just as the militiamen were leaving the next house. At the same funereal rate of speed they cruised through the martial-law area, which was being thoroughly searched, until they came to the Grand Concourse.

"Open it up!" Gilroy rapped out suddenly.

They streaked through traffic, turned east. At the bridge they had to wait fifteen minutes before the photographers arrived in taxis.

Gilroy dismissed the cabs, paid off his hearse driver, and ordered the photographers to help him with the basket. A scant three minutes later another taxi drew up at the hearse and the city and night editors scrambled out excitedly. They sent their cabs away.

"What the hell is this?" the city editor demanded. "Robbing graves?"

"Just give us a hand and keep quiet," Gilroy said calmly.

They carted the heavy basket to a deserted dumping ground behind two vacant furniture warehouses that had been condemned by the city for the new bridge approach. He removed the basket cover and ordered the photographers to help him take the body out and hold it erect.

"Now watch this," he grinned.

While the editors and photographers watched in horrified amazement, Gilroy backed off ten feet and fired the gun at the corpse's heart. He quietly wiped his fingerprints off the butt, removed the body from the photographers' inert hands, and laid it gently on its back, crooking its right hand around the gun. He placed the cap on the ground beside the naked, hairless head. Then he crumpled a sheet of paper in his hand and just as deliberately smoothed it.

"Snap the body from a few angles. Wind up with a shot of this note."

The two editors snatched at the note in a single wild grab. They read it swiftly.

"Holy smoke!" the night editor shouted. "'I am the torso murderer. I realize that I have been insane for some time, and, during my lapse from sanity, I kidnapped and hacked to death a number of people. But the cordon of soldiers hounded me from one place to another, until I am finally driven to suicide in order to prevent my being captured. My name I shall take to the grave with me, that my former friends be spared the horror of knowing that once they loved this murderous maniac. God save my soul!'"

The four men grinned admiringly at Gilroy. But the towering reporter dismissed their admiration with a modest wave of his astoundingly long, incredibly bony arm.

"The only thing I regret is that this's a gorgeous build-up for Major Green—the lousy nipplehead!" he said mournfully. "The autopsy'll show a thousand proofs that his thing never lived, but a fat lot Nappie'll care. And to think that I'll probably be the cause of making him governor!"

He insisted on holding the creased suicide note for the photographers to aim at, claiming that it required a certain artistic touch.

In the Bison Frontiers of Imagination series

The Disappearance
By Philip Wylie
Introduced by Robert Silverberg

Gladiator
By Philip Wylie
Introduced by Janny Wurts

When Worlds Collide
By Philip Wylie and
Edwin Balmer
Introduced by John Varley

To order or obtain more information on these or other University of Nebraska Press titles, visit www.nebraskapress.unl.edu.